"Get ready to pull an all-nighter because 'Nothus' will pull you in slowly and keep you reading until your eyes melt."

~PAN's Book Reviews

"Just like with Sentinel, the author whisks the reader away on an incredible journey. Nothus is filled with scenic and breathtaking visuals, characters you won't forget, and a storyline that grips you from the start. Be ready for an emotional rollercoaster!"

~Indie Book Addict (Diana Richie)

"These books are, without a second thought, modern classics in the making. He (Starling) uses language like music throughout and eloquently constructs the notion of fear like it's a gift the reader is receiving."

~Caleb Ryan Jones (@the_bookeyman)

"Nothus is a fast-paced read that will pull you into a small town quicker than you thought possible. And Starling uses all the right ways to keep you there, feverishly turning the pages to see what happens next!"

~Alex Pearson (@FindingMontauk1)

"With his second novel, Nothus, Starling returns to the town of Bensalem, and hits the ground running with prose that sings. The scares, the chills, and the building tension are established early in, demonstrating Starling's extraordinary talent at penning a horror tale worth staying up late for just one more chapter."

~Holley Cornetto Author of We Haunt These Woods

NOTHUS

BOOK 2 OF THE BENSALEM FILES
BY DREW STARLING

NOTHUS

Paperback ISBN: 978-1-990245-72-5
Hardcover ISBN: 978-1-990245-73-2
Digital ISBN: 978-1-990245-71-8

Edited by Lyndsey Smith - Horror Smith Publishing
Cover design Francois Vaillancourt
Book Formatting by Michelle River

"But hear me now, and I will tell you what I know. You shall understand that there is not under the heavens so chaste a nation as this of Bensalem; nor so free from all pollution or foulness. It is the virgin of the world."

~ from <u>New Atlantis, A Work Unfinished</u> by Francis Bacon, 1692

For Cara.

DAY 1

Winter came early that year. It started where it always did, in the mountains, when an old, gray wind turned veils of rain into sleet during the waning hours of a day no one would remember. Those mountains, mapped and measured by men who thought they knew them, stood ceremonial over the Bensalem valley, like veterans of an ancient war. Ruffles of stratus clouds rolled in from the west, smothering the dull rind of a moon and casting the craggy face of Old Rag in shadow.

The winter wind, testing its strength after a long summer's nap, whipped down the ridgeline through a palisade of trees. It bristled branches that quartered cardinals and tanagers in the summer but had since been surrendered to little, black cawing things and other mongrels of the sky. Clumps of leaves, fat with rain, washed out the mountain trails and suffocated the cold, hard ground. But never needing a trail to guide it, the wind rolled downhill and spread itself through a rookery of sickly and weather-beaten houses in the valley.

One could look at those houses during the day and confuse

an economy of effort with the crippling, collective depression that tightened its death grip on the town year after year, tragedy after tragedy, secret after secret. One could study the ruddy faces of its slumbering residents and discern upon them traces of Bensalem's original sin, a sin passed down through generations, a sin even further compromising their existence in an Appalachian wasteland.

Like the knock of some angry, dead-handed reaper, the wind clattered the shutters of a narrow, three-story Victorian, once white but now green with age. It seeped in through the bedroom window, fluttered past musty sashes, and hardened the skin of the house's sole occupant. Sheriff Duke Quinlan, once tightly bolted together, sat now as a mere filament of a man on the side of his deathbed.

In the night, Duke's subconscious had once again unshackled itself from its host and traversed down a mountain of its own. Only this mountain was not some slab jutting up into an earthly sky, rather the slope of the old man's soul. That id of his, the zealot for impenetrable truth, would in dreams climb down the mountain and wade around in the muck of his heart.

Deep down in that muck, a seed of shame had been planted four decades ago when he turned a blind eye to the sadistic transformation of a boy—now known as the Sentinel—who was sentenced to face the evil alone for as long as his mutated body could hold out. Duke buried the truth about the boy, upholding the conspiracy the Order demanded of him.

It was easy at first, patching together an affable life of military service, community leadership, and familial joy. But the years, like the rain, washed the varnish off the old man and crept into the seams of his mental scaffolds. His strength failed, his time passed, and the seed grew into a thick and wild growth until it suffocated his mind and his body from the inside. Because through it all, the boy was still out there.

Duke studied the chrome barrel of the shotgun in his hand and exhaled.

He dared not look upon the figure cloaked in shadow in the back corner of the bedroom. It stood wheezing and dripping, emitting sounds of suffering, while Duke whimpered and kept his eyes on the gun.

Hank Teakle's apparition had become a regular fixture in recent months. He would be there one second, gone the next, but always in a particular corner and only ever in the dead of night. Even though Duke never saw Hank's body after the Nothus Noctis tore it open last summer, he knew it was his old friend who had come back to haunt him. The posture gave it away—shoulders broad, back straight, signature overalls torn to strings and tassels.

Duke tried not to look, tried not to gaze into the gaping hole in the middle of Hank's chest—a perfect rectangle of meat and bone cut out with near-surgical precision—tried not to notice drops of blood and chunks of intestine plopping on the hardwood floor. He averted his eyes from Hank's elongated fingers, like spiders, long mangled things scraping the floor and casting spindly shadows on the wall.

And then, for a fraction of a second, the room and the world went dead, and Hank appeared at the foot of the bed. The shock of his sudden teleportation sent a current of ice water surging past the valves of Duke's limping heart.

Hank had no face as he stood inches over Duke. His head was just a smooth and hairless orb of flesh glowing blue from fragmented moonlight. Despite his lack of facial features, he somehow fired whispery missives at the broken old man in the bed.

"Coward," "Shame," and tonight, simply, "Kill yourself."

Duke's trembling hands kept a poor grip on the gun. They shook so badly it took three attempts to snatch the sealed envelope beside him and place it on the nightstand, out of the blast radius.

His hand gripped the handle backwards, and the barrel of the shotgun chattered against his teeth. He wrapped his lips around the chrome and clenched his eyes closed, spilling the remaining tears in them down his sunken cheeks. Before he pulled the trigger, he let out a scream as a second figure appeared, this one only in his mind and showing its face clearly. It was something in the neighborhood of a man. Maybe an entity that had been one long ago, or a thing poorly attempting to mask a more sinister nature. Its face was all black, its eyes all white. Above equally black horns, small like bulbs, a ring of light levitated over a shimmering black head.

He squeezed the trigger. A bang rifled through the house and spilled into the valley, and the contents of his cranium spray-painted the wallpaper in a bubbling maroon stew. Two drops of blood landed on the envelope—one in the top left corner, and one in the crook of the "C" of the only word written on its front:

MAC

· · ·

Skylar McNamara's blue eyes burst open when the shot rang out.

"Ram?" she whispered.

Shadows of snowflakes streaming through the window pulled her gaze away from the blankness of the ceiling and out into the stone-cold night. She blinked twice, rolled her head across the pillow to regard a still-snoring Ramsey Matopher, and slipped her legs out from under clouds of comforter. As she approached one of the windows of the third-floor apartment Ram shared with his parents, the chill of the tile pricked the bottoms of her bare feet, and she shivered as the young winter air lashed itself around her forearms.

Outside, all existed as it should. Peaceful, calm, dead. White. Her car, along with everything else in sight across the valley, had accumulated a delicate layer of snow. Maple trees in the New Colonial Heights courtyard, once beaming as lush green beacons in summer and golden-brown treasures in autumn, now stood as twiggy mirages, half blanked out by snow, half exposed in the nakedness of their dormancy. Tattered white rags covered the faces and tops of the looming Blue Ridge Mountains.

As if somehow compelled, Skylar steered her eyes up to the blue floor of the night, where millions of flakes poured out of a moonless sky. The wintry scene outside morphed into a fog as Skylar's exhales piled up on the glass. She shivered again and slipped back into bed.

"You okay?" Ram whispered, rolling over to face her. He pawed away strands of his long, black hair.

"Yeah."

His glassy brown eyes met hers. He pulled a warm hand, a great mitt of a thing, from under the comforter and placed it on the back of her neck.

"You're freezing," he said.

"Did you hear that sound just now?"

"No. What sound?"

"I don't know. It was a loud bang."

"Just felt you get up."

Skylar sighed and wrapped both hands around his forearm.

"Sheesh, Sky, you're freezing."

"It's cold, dumbass."

Ram smiled. "Which one do you have tomorrow? AP Chem?"

"Lit."

"That'll be fun."

"It's snowing," she whispered.

"I know."

Skylar closed her eyes, and only after the temperature of Ram's forearm and her hands reached equilibrium did she open them again. Ram was still gazing at her, still smiling.

"I should go. My mom's gonna kill me."

. . .

Ellen Dreyer stared in silence out her bedroom window as the night sank into its deepest state of darkness, of cold. Snow poured through her sight line and blanketed a patch of grass in the meadow her eyes had been fixed upon, a patch that had turned permanently brown in the wake of her killing of Jane Harcourt. Staring at it conjured thoughts from that early morning in July.

The crude disposal of her son, Caleb, at Jane's hands.

The burlap sack they found him in.

The twine around his wrists and ankles.

The flutter of his eyelids.

The faint pulse. The joy!

The fear in Aaron's eyes when he saw Jane waiting for them.

The white-hot urge to pull the trigger.

The boom of the shot.

The ropes of blood spewing from the stump of Jane's neck.

The chilling finality of it all, and the unequivocal conviction that there was no other solution.

Caleb Dreyer got his mother back that day, but Mark Harcourt—the Sentinel—lost his.

She touched a soft hand to her chest.

A creak in the hardwood snapped her eyes to the opposite side of the bedroom. Caleb stood in the doorway with a thumb in his mouth. Wind hissed through the house.

"Come here, baby," she whispered, beckoning him with an outstretched hand. "He'll be out soon."

. . .

The Elders called it the Black Door. The Black Door of the Bastard.

The wind curled through the outer reaches of the forest, where animals denned and birds nested, where life lived, and onward through an empty glade, where an old folding chair had frozen to the dirt and an overturned camping lantern sat dead. No sound whatsoever manifested in the glade. Even the branches stayed silent as they scraped against each other in the wind.

Snow fell thicker and faster by the time the wind reached the heart of the forest, where the pines seemed somehow darker than those on the perimeter. Their blackness could have been due to the lack of light and life since sunlight struggled to penetrate the canopy of branches overhead, and no creature dared enter this ground. Or perhaps it was the cold, as the heart of the forest was always inexplicably colder than the climate might suggest, even in the heat of the summer. Or maybe, if certain elements of the natural order could be suspended, the pines in the heart of Bensalem had turned black from bearing witness to things no man, no animal, no insect, even no tree, ever should. Maybe their light had bled out over the course of centuries as they stood like silent prisoners shackled to a patch of earth mercilessly desecrated by both man and cosmic beast.

The trees here were so black on such a night, it would have been nearly impossible to ascertain the contours of an odd structure set conspicuously among them. But there, on a muddy patch of terrain under their boughs, stood a sprawling, tent-like articulation constructed from thousands of branches and sticks and twigs, all jutting up from the ground and leaning against each other at the top to form a kind of thatched and gnarled alcove. And if there were a shade of black so dark it sucked the very light out of even this dimmest of places, that unimaginable blackness formed the rough shape of an entrance—to somewhere, to something—in the middle of the structure.

Deep within that door, under layers of bedrock, a subterranean dimension existed beneath the forest. So secluded and unknown was this dimension, no mortal woman or man had navigated its passageways, explored its earthen rooms, or ever directly colluded with the things that lived there.

The Elders had known only vaguely of its inhabitants and their activities. They knew it was where the Nothus Noctis—the Night Bastard—lay in wait during the day and emerged from during the night. They knew the Sentinel, the unwilling martyr of their cause and protector of Bensalem, dwelt on the opposite side, hiding from the Nothus at day and emerging from the Earth itself at night to engage the Nothus when it sought to feed. But while the Elders had done well to wield tools of alchemy and occultism to understand this realm, there was much they did not know. They did not know of one such room, an innermost sanctum, where the Nothus at this very moment stood.

Its eyes, burning with a crimson fire, peered out over a bony and animalistic snout at the mess of its spindly fingers wrapped around what appeared to be a human body laid upon an altar. Those fingers, long enough to stretch twice across the chest cavity they had hollowed out four months ago, had penetrated a viscous membrane encasing the body.

The Nothus stood this way for hours, with one set of fingers clutched around some human remnant, earthly or otherwise, while its other set twitched in a manic pattern that, through the power of its dark divination, channeled the image of Hank Teakle into Duke Quinlan's bedroom.

And in the back corner of the room, behind dozens of these podded bodies and membranes and altars, another thing crouched in the darkness. Its ghostly white eyes watched the Nothus with a penetrating clarity.

DAY 2

The snow tapered off as an auburn dawn saturated the eastern sky, and the residents of Bensalem prepared to confront another day. A scourge of incandescent light, refracted and amplified off the ivory earth, poured over the open hands of Cheryl McNamara as she sat on the edge of her bed. Her steel-gray eyes traced the cracks in her palms before the alarm clock moaned in rhythmic agony.

"You gonna get that?" her husband, Rick, said, his voice muffled by the pillow over his face.

Cheryl rose, turned off the alarm clock, and shuffled over to the window facing the street. The houses and cars on Masons Street looked like dunes bulging from a rocky, white beach. On any other day, Cheryl would have been struck by their ugliness, their rust, their browns and yellows, their staleness. But today, their roofs glistened in a spotless white sheen. All except one.

"Goddammit," Cheryl said, as her gaze locked onto Skylar's naked blue hatchback in the driveway and the trail of snow-less tire marks behind it.

Rick snaked his hands around her slight waist and rested his chin on her shoulder. "The vanguard of winter."

"What?"

"The first snow."

Cheryl planted her palms on the windowsill, pulling them both closer. "Look at that."

"I see it. Very beautiful."

Cheryl whipped her neck around to face him, bringing the tip of her nose to within an inch of her husband's chin. "Rick. What's wrong with that picture?"

"Ah," Rick said. "Maybe she ran out to buy some flowers."

Cheryl nudged an elbow into Rick's pot belly. "Be more than you give me."

"Want me to talk to her?"

"Lord knows, she won't listen to me. She's your daughter too." Cheryl yawned as she walked back to the nightstand, grabbed her flip phone, and sat back down on the bed. "I don't mind the dating. I mind the sleepovers."

"Ram's a good boy."

"He's a great boy. But he's got a pecker, and Skylar's... Skylar."

"Heard he just got promoted at WLC." Rick ran a comb through his head of salt and pepper hair. "Helluva good job for an eighteen-year-old. Most grown men in this town can't keep a job for two weeks, and here he is, managing most of 'em. You know, they got a second crew goin' now?" His belt buckle jingled in the vapid silence of the bedroom, as if enthusiastically answering Rick's question in Cheryl's stead. He turned around with only one pant leg on. "Bug?"

Cheryl sat in a trance on the bed, her eyes glued to the wall and her flip phone glued to her ear. He watched her as he struggled with the other pant leg.

"Bug, you okay?"

"Something's wrong."

He finished dressing while she remained nearly catatonic, moving only to press the necessary buttons on her phone to replay the message. After four cycles of listening and replaying, Cheryl dialed the last person to call her.

"Mornin', Sheriff," she said into the phone. "I got your message. I'll swing by before I head to the station. I'll let Brady know. Gimme a holler if you get this."

"What's up?"

"Something's wrong with Duke. He left me a voicemail in the middle of the night, and he sounded... distressed."

She threw on her brown and khaki Bensalem Sheriff's Department uniform and pecked him on the cheek on her way downstairs of the bedroom, but the curiosity of Skylar's closed door halted her haste. She leaned her ear to the door and slowly twisted the knob. A tuft of neon-green hair sprouting from a mountain of blankets and pillows served as the evidence she needed to prove her daughter's presence. Cheryl sighed, careful not to do so audibly, and closed the door behind her.

Snow crunching under her patrol car's tires served as welcome harmony to the strained chug of the motor. She waved dryly to the several parka-clad neighbors already out shoveling their driveways, and she placed a call to Derek Brady to let him know she'd be late in relieving him. For a moment, she let her mind drift from the stress of Duke's message and even smiled upon gazing at the snow-covered Christmas decorations perched on the patios of the stores still in business on Main Street. She made certain to look away when passing M&J Fine Gifts.

She pressed the accelerator as she approached the snowy grade leading up to Duke's street. His Victorian stood among several of the town's oldest homes, embedded in overgrowth thriving beneath a latticework of oak branches scraping the sky.

Cheryl parked some distance from the house. It loomed in a solemn repose before her, like some wood-paneled ziggurat that belonged in neither the time nor place in which it existed. The air's chill stung her face as she stepped out, and she yanked the zipper of her leather jacket as high as it could go.

She laid a hand on the butt of her service weapon as she scanned the property. Skiffs of snow half covered two green shutters lying in the front yard, and shards of ice winked in the sunlight around them. His patrol car and his SUV sat snow-covered in a driveway area beside the house. She didn't move her feet, but she took a long glare over each shoulder before calling Duke again, and again receiving no answer. She unclipped the radio from her belt.

"611 to dispatch," she said.

"Mornin', deputy," Brady said.

"I'm up here at Duke's. Little bit of a mess outside. No signs of forced entry. Both cars are here, and neither one of 'em moved since last night. He call in? Over."

"No, ma'am."

"Nothin'?"

"Nothin'. Quiet as a church mouse here. Over."

She glanced over her shoulders again, and then squinted at the broken shutter hinges on either side of Duke's bedroom window. Standing on the porch, she called Duke for the last time and flipped her phone down when she got voicemail. Three times she knocked and called his name. No one, and no thing, answered. She grasped the glass doorknob in its rusted-out casing, and her gloved hand nearly slipped off from the ease at which it twisted open.

The musk of old wood and mildew flooded her nostrils. She scanned the foyer, the living room, the dining room. Every object in view had a sort of white varnish, and she couldn't tell if it was glare from the snow outside or a layer of dust that had been accumulating for years. Furniture, bookshelves, shoes in the foyer—it all seemed to be trending toward the same shade of off-white, calcifying into one giant, collective fossil.

"Duke? You here?" Her voice echoed through the halls.

The floorboards wretched under her boots, their agony amplified by the house's silence. As she ascended the stairs, the smell of age was altogether replaced by the coppery stench of blood.

"Duke, can you hear me? It's Mac," she said while unholstering her service weapon. At the top of the stairs, an ambiguous brown blotch on the hardwood floor pulled her attention to the closed door on the right side of the hallway.

"Duke?" she whispered, somehow sensing it would be the last time she'd call out to him.

Cheryl opened the door and gasped at the half-shorn-off head of her boss and mentor. Now, former.

He sat on the edge of the bed. Feet on the ground, hands by his sides, head against the wall, jaw gone completely and replaced by a waterfall of blood spilling all the way into his lap like a long, red beard. His lifeless eyes—staring dead ahead, staring right at Deputy Cheryl McNamara—and his tongue hanging loose from a jawless skull had turned his face into something resembling an odd grin. "What's so funny?" it seemed to ask.

With one hand now holding a handkerchief over her nose and mouth, she darted her service weapon through the corners of the room, and she yanked open the closet door to clear it. She holstered her weapon and drew the radio.

"611 to dispatch. We're gonna need EMT and crime tech."

"Uh oh," Brady said. "At Duke's?"

"At Duke's."

"He okay?"

"No, he's dead. Send 'em now. I'll call you later. Over."

"Ten four."

Cheryl stared at the halo of blood on the wallpaper behind his head. She looked at his hands, old and dead, looked at the shotgun, still by his side, still somehow pointing at him. Then, she saw the note on the nightstand.

. . .

Skylar left the chem lab, messenger bag slung sloppily over her shoulder and three-ring binder under crossed arms, and paced down the locker-lined corridor of West Hamilton High. The hallway teemed with adolescent life. Girls gaggled in doorways, packs of boys howled and guffawed, and couples held hands in proclamation of their nascent relationships. Skylar's only company was the squelch of her Dr. Martens and the daydream of another evening with Ram. She was the only one of her small handful of friends—who also dressed in all black and smoked pot and listened to hardcore punk—who took AP Chem right before AP Lit, so she walked alone between them.

The squelch slowly faded against a rising tide of voices in a crowded corner. Skylar opened her binder to ignore them, but not a second after she began sifting through its contents did it get smacked from her hands.

"Hey, piglet," a boy's voice said from close range.

A few kids in the corner stared at her as loose paper from the binder bloomed around her feet.

A stone faced boy peered down at her, bloodshot eyes behind

an overly pronounced brow. He put his hands on her shoulders. She jerked one free, but he grabbed the sleeve of her black hoodie.

"The fuck are you doing?" she said.

"Fucking pig."

"Get the fuck off of me, Justin. You're fucked up."

He grabbed her shoulders again, tighter. "Fuck you and your pig ass brother."

"What? What did Lenny do?"

"Your mom gave me a fucking DUI on Friday. I wasn't even drunk. I'm probably gonna do time for that shit."

"You're fucking drunk right now. I can smell it."

"Fuck your mom and fuck your family. You're a pig, just like your mom. You little piglet ass sh—"

Skylar slammed the binder into his chest hard enough to break free. She spun around and escaped through a handful of gawkers.

"God fucking dammit," she whispered under her breath.

Her heart rate didn't slow down until twenty minutes into the AP Lit mid-term.

. . .

"Upstairs!"

Cheryl directed two EMTs as they wheeled a stretcher past her and through Duke's front door. The boot treads they left in the snow were already pooling with the water, and a cue ball of a sun hung high in the cloud-speckled sky. She rose from her seated position on the porch steps after melted snow had saturated her bottoms enough to annoy her. The emotionless sounds of the corpse cleanup process—*clips, zips, thunks*—wafted down through the drafty old windowpanes while a woodpecker tapped diligently some nameless distance away.

She called Brady.

"Hey, what's up?" he said, his eagerness palatable.

"Shotgun blast to the mouth."

"Mother of God. No way. Self-inflicted?"

"Yeah."

"Jesus, Mary, and Joseph."

Cheryl paused and pulled her gaze toward the general direction of the woodpecker, its tapping closer than a moment ago.

"You know, we both saw it, didn't we?" Brady said. "Somethin' wasn't right with him. Ever since that shit went down last summer."

"You're tellin' me."

"He took it hard. I don't know if it was cause it all happened while he was gone, or... I dunno, maybe it was all too personal for him. Hell, maybe just too old for it. Somethin'. He just wasn't the same after that, was he?"

"And I don't think it helped that we never quite saw eye to eye on how it was handled either. We never really got past it, hate to say."

The muffled racket of a toddler filled the empty space of Brady's pause. "Well," he said and paused again, "I'm... I'm sorry, Deputy."

"Heck. Don't be pityin' me. This is gonna hit all of us. In fact, can you do me a favor and tell the rest of the squad? And can you call Sperryville and Martinsville? Just a courtesy, nothin' formal. Just rather they hear it from one of us."

"Of course. You got it, Sheriff."

"Hey now. None of that."

"You're in charge until someone tells me you ain't."

She sighed. "We'll just have to see."

"I'll make those calls. You headin' to the station? Monica's there."

"I am. Boy. Helluva thing to come back to fresh off maternity leave, huh?"

"I don't doubt it."

"Guess I'll tell her when I get there, so cross her off your list."

"You got it."

"Thanks, Derek. Out here."

The thuds of heavy footsteps on stairs caused her to postpone her second phone call. Both EMTs—one male, one female, both much younger and taller than she—nodded curtly as they wheeled the stretcher past her. Duke's obsidian body bag shone in the mid-morning light. It looked like the deflated chrysalis of some giant and terrible stillborn moth, now being ceremoniously ushered off to an unhallowed ground where such things lie.

"All good up there?" Cheryl said to the EMTs.

"Yeah, all good," the young woman said.

"Kinda nasty," added the young man.

Cheryl shook her head.

She waited until the EMTs were well past earshot before calling her husband.

"Well, hey there, bug," Rick said.

"Hey. So, I'm still at Duke's."

"Oh?"

"He's dead, Rick."

"What?"

"Yeah. I, uh…"

"Oh boy. You okay?"

"I… yeah. I just came in, and the door was unlocked, and I just found him in his room."

"What?"

"He shot himself with that old shotgun."

"Oh, dear Lord! Really?"

"His..." Cheryl winced and sat back down on the porch. She grasped her temples with her other hand. "His jaw was... his jaw was—"

"Hey, let me come get you. I can be there in about twenty minutes. Can I come get you?"

"He left a note on the nightstand with my name on it. He called me in the middle of the night and told me to stop by. Rick, he wanted me to be the one that found him. I'm terrified to open it."

"Okay, stay put. I'll come. Stay at Duke's. Or you want me to—"

"No, no. Don't come get me. I have to deal with this."

"You have to take care of yourself. This isn't like last summer. This is Duke, for Christ sake."

"No, I... I need to deal with this."

"Bug, you need to take care of yourself. You were a wreck for months after Hank and Jane, and you're only now just healin'."

"Well, I'm basically in charge right now. I need to be strong, and I need to show them—"

"Why don't you let the team handle this one? Why don't you come home?"

"I don't know, baby. I need to... I need to call VSP."

"Oh, my sweet Cheryl."

"I'll call you in a little bit, okay?"

"Let me call you, how about that?"

"Okay. You talk to Skylar?"

"Yeah. She's good. We're good. Home when? Around seven?"

"Yeah, should be."

"Okay. I love you. You'll get through this. You're gonna be just fine. Okay?"

Cheryl sighed. "We'll see. I love you too."

She put the phone down on the step next to her, and she let her head sink into her hands. The woodpecker tapped on.

. . .

Much to the dismay of shopkeepers longing for something festive and children hoping to frolic outside after school, the snow had completely evaporated by the early afternoon. Not long for Bensalem was the catharsis of a thing new and beautiful, a hint of winteresque purification after a summer of sweltering pain. Instead, the town found itself in a place it knew so well, trudging through muddy brown muck under drizzling slate-colored skies, weather just warm enough to melt snow but still cold enough to chill bones.

Cheryl and her flip phone withstood an onslaught of calls throughout the day—Virginia State Police, the coroner's office, other sheriffs offering condolences, friends of Duke's who wanted just to talk. She became the funnel and the focal point of Duke's suicide, and the jarring memories of her week from hell four months ago crept out of their caves, sizing up the mental barriers she'd constructed to keep them out.

When she told Deputy Monica Nelson the news about Duke, Cheryl saw the same fear she'd seen in her young officer's eyes when they marched up the hill at Hank's Horse Farm together. And she couldn't shake the comparison of Duke's mangled skull to that of Jane Harcourt's, who she found splattered all over the meadow by Wickham Road after the Dreyers had exacted their revenge upon her.

That memory picked open the scab of her frustration that she and Duke had let Aaron take the fall for Jane's murder, when it was clear as day Ellen was the one who pulled the trigger. And the gnawing, seething anxiety that besieged her when Caleb went missing crawled over every inch of her skin when calls from every Tom, Dick, and Harry in the state of Virginia poured in. This time, of course, Duke wouldn't be back from a vacation in a few days to help. One by one, the memories returned, and one by one, she tried to beat them back, banishing them to the dark corners of her mind where things only became real if light was shed upon them.

But even though these memories brought her pain and discomfort, they existed in the material world, the realm of the rational. They were mere physical symptoms of a more potent but unknowable problem. It was this problem—the real problem— that she had procrastinated to solve even after vowing she would. So, when gray skies finally faded to night and Cheryl sped past black blobs of trees and lamp lit houses on the way home, she thought not of simple matters like skulls or corpses or murder charges knocked down to manslaughter. She thought about what Duke said, about what Aaron said, about why Jane took Caleb, and rituals in which boys were forged into beasts. She thought about what little she knew of something Duke called "the Order" and the fantastic notion that it served to protect—by the most dastardly means necessary—the town of Bensalem from a demon of Hell or some otherwise diabolical origin. These were matters her mental defenses simply could not withstand, and now, they were battering their way back in.

It had been dark for some time when she finally arrived home. Light from the porch lamps lay in stains on the front yard as she peeled off her mud-caked boots and tossed them aside before entering. Rick was waiting, and he threw his arms around her before she could even close the door. She left it open and gripped him back.

"I'm so sorry," Rick said, his lips pressed against her neck. "I'm so sorry, bug."

She released him and pecked him on the lips. "How are you guys?"

"We're okay. We're doing okay. How are you?"

Cheryl marched past him up the stairs, where the din of rock music echoed through the hallway. She knocked on Skylar's door, more of a warning than a proposal before speaking. Skylar lay on her stomach on the bed with her feet in the air, reading something.

"Turn that down, please?" Cheryl said, leaning on the door-knob.

Skylar rolled her eyes, and only after great effort, slinked off the bed and turned off the music.

"Where were you last night?" Cheryl asked.

"At Ram's?" Skylar said, implying her mother's question was a stupid one.

"What did I tell you about sleepovers?"

Skylar stared back blankly.

"Skylar, what did I tell you? You are seventeen years old. You do not sleep—"

"He's seventeen too. We're not having sex, if that's what you're worried about."

Cheryl pointed at Skylar with her other hand. "You're grounded."

The look of complacency on Skylar's face transformed to one of instant shock. "Mom!"

"No Ram for one week. No—"

"Bullshit, no Ram for one week!"

"No Ram for one week. No friends for one week. Give me your keys."

As if prepping for an impending apocalypse, Skylar threw her keys, her books, and some spare clothes into her shoulder bag. Red blotches broke out on her neck.

"Skylar! Don't you dare!"

"Fuck this," Skylar said under her breath as she brushed past her mother, stomped down the stairs, and slammed the door behind her.

Cheryl watched from the window as her daughter peeled out of the driveway and sped off westward—west toward Ram's.

Rick rushed up the stairs and was out of breath by the time he arrived. "The hell was that about?" he said.

"I just don't want her sleeping there," Cheryl said, her back still to him.

"Well, where you think you just sent her runnin' off to?"

Cheryl said nothing, only rested her forehead on the cold glass. Rick plucked the ranger-style police hat squished between her head and the window, took her head in his hands, and gently brushed his fingers through her hair.

. . .

Skylar practically strangled the steering wheel. Her freshly painted turquoise fingernails dug divots into its plastic, and her locked arms pressed the frame hard into its column. The chalky sound of molars grinding in her head joined the thrashier percussion of Minor Threat blasting from the car's blown-out speakers, an unintended modification her brother Lenny had made to the vehicle well before it fell into her hands.

At one point, Skylar screamed. She smacked the steering

wheel with her palm so hard it hurt, and she choked out breaths as mascara-stained tears rolled down her cheeks.

The temperature outside dropped as she sped down State Road 639. Damp blades of grass and dead leaves began to grow icy exoskeletons. Melted snow that had pooled in animal tracks began to freeze. And as Skylar's rage grew hotter, the rage of another, quite close to her at this very moment, grew much colder.

. . .

Maurice Bacon's rage was not built on a foundation of teenage angst. It couldn't have been, since his teenage years were stolen from him. His rage was a weapon, built from much older, stronger stuff.

It was forged when he was taken as a boy, without his knowing and very much against his will. The ritual shackled his young body in alchemical chains, and it exiled him to subsist, all alone, deep underground in the forest. For twenty years he dwelt there, his armor growing around him, his nemesis rising each night to find food, his sole task to use his weaponized body to stop it. All for the sake of protecting a town that soon forgot him.

His rage was then tempered into something sharp when he was finally relieved from his duty by the Order. He was gawked at and shunned by Bensalem's townsfolk and what was left of his family, all of whom were told he had simply gone missing to keep the secrets of the Sentinel and Nothus intact. There was a terrible scar on his forehead, and something was wrong with his jaw. It didn't work the same after being broken during the ritual and left unhealed for two decades. It would click loudly, drop out of its socket, and he'd pop it back in with his hand. Sometimes, he'd have to hold it in place when he ate. He walked with a jarring stiffness, as if his limbs had been welded into rigid poles. Little did people know that for a time, they were. Worst of all, the alchemy had altered his brain. He still had the vocabulary of a five-year-old, he never learned to exercise judgment, and the idea of joining a functioning society soon became untenable.

But it was not until recently that his rage, forged and tempered by the fires of exile both underground and above it, became unleashed. It happened when Jane Harcourt, the cleric of the Order's Bensalem chapter, whose own son had relieved Maurice's Sentinel duties, died four months ago. Jane took Maurice in when he wanted shelter, fed him when he was hungry, even made him a member of their chapter to give him something to belong to. Only Jane provided these things to Maurice Bacon because only Jane understood. Maybe a part of her compassion was to offset the guilt of allowing her son to succumb to the same fate. Maybe it was her disdain of the Order's leadership, who constantly questioned her "old ways."

Regardless of how or why, Jane had become the single stabilizing force in the ex-Sentinel's fractured life, and without her, little remained to tether him. The Order's Bensalem chapter, its members advancing in age and its ranks dwindling even before Jane's death, had effectively disbanded. Those remaining lacked the energy or alchemical skills to maintain the cycle of the Sentinels the way Jane did. It would be well enough to let the Order's leadership right the ship in their own way and on their timeline.

Alone, Maurice persisted. His faith grew more zealous, more unhinged, and only in brief and infrequent moments of mental clarity, he lamented how he had become what his old friend, Jane Harcourt, feared most.

Donning Jane's old brown cleric robe, he stood barefoot on the frosty earth of the glade, a lone acolyte folded between layers of the forest's shadow. Faint whiffs of Jane's dried blood floated into his nostrils, and he smiled, knowing he was consuming some fleeting part of her. He stood this way for hours, simply waiting, a skill he had grand-mastered over the last sixty years. The glade was soundless, as the forest's more natural inhabitants had learned long ago not to go anywhere near it. Even the wind was still. Maurice just stood there, quiet and freezing.

The encounter began when his right index finger started waving, slowly and methodically at first, as if tapping an invisible keyboard. After several minutes, its pace accelerated to a twitching, the knuckle rocketing back and forth in its socket. His smile widened, feeling his master approaching.

Maurice's ring finger started to move, then the pinky on his other hand, then both of his thumbs. Over the course of a good hour, each of his fingers became alive, moving at velocities unsustainable by human muscle alone. It was also during this time his eyes, set deep in a scraggly bearded and weather-worn face, faded from pale blue to completely white.

He gasped in wonder when two faint red lights appeared in the distance.

The Nothus' eyes splintered in the cold winter night, like two bloodstained orbs, the sheer mystery of their presence deterring the advance of any creature cursed enough to notice them.

Maurice whispered, "The kingdom, and the power, and the gl—"

The Nothus' rapid and sudden movement shocked Maurice back into silence. Its eyes dropped into the ambiguousness of the forest floor and within seconds re-appeared as two raging lamps of fire above him. Maurice craned his neck to meet the gaze of the Nothus as it stood towering over him. The light from its eyes coated its snout and sprawling antlers in a soft vermillion glow.

The glow did not, however, reach the Nothus' fingers, those sharp and hellish hooks of death that had butchered so many over the centuries, as they, too, twitched in rapid succession. Maurice and the Nothus faced each other, one looking up and one looking down, white eyes gazing into red.

And then it stopped.

The Nothus was suddenly gone. The forest was black. Maurice was alone, his eyes and his fingers as they were when he arrived.

"Yes. Yes, my king," Maurice said, grinning. "I will find it. Your will be done. I will find it for you. Your will be done. Your will be done."

DAY 3

"Have a seat, Deacon Pierce," said the Grand Elder of the Order of the Old Roses.

Roland Pierce took crisp steps across the Grand Elder's 110th Floor office, *click-clacks* of his shoes reverberating off the mahogany walls. He unbuttoned his tweed jacket as he sat in one of two gargantuan leather chairs facing the desk, being sure to expose the brilliance of the gold-plated cross around his neck. With the cuff of his sleeve, he wiped the red rose in the center of the cross to enhance its shine.

The Grand Elder stood as he typically did, back to his guest, exacting gaze lasering the Manhattan streets a thousand feet below. Pierce had only seen the Grand Elder's eyes once in his entire tenure—four months ago, when in the aftermath of the Bensalem incident, he turned around to display their power of transformation. They had morphed from gray pebbles to beaming stone-white spotlights, and the illusion of their scale seemed to extend far beyond their sockets.

"Don't be afraid, Deacon," the Grand Elder had said, "the

New King Salomon lives through me."

It was those words about their fabled New King Salomon that had stuck like a thorn in Roland's foot since they were uttered four months ago.

"Good morning, sir," said Roland.

"Did you have much of a problem in Oaxaca?"

"No, sir. The local chapter was very understanding."

"Because the mayor's in our pocket."

"Yes, sir."

"And Cotingac? Was that situation handled?"

"It's ongoing, sir. I assure you, it will be."

"That one worries me. It is not so dissimilar from the one you experienced in Bensalem"—he put his fingers through the blinds and inched his face closer to the window—"which, unfortunately, is why I've summoned you. Sheriff Duke Quinlan is dead. I'm sure you remember him."

"Oh. Yes, I certainly do."

"I believe his passing may present us with a problem. He allowed the cycle to continue without disruption. Your report mentioned his second-in-command. What was her name again?"

"McNamara."

"Right. What's your sense of her?"

"Hard to say. At the time, it seemed she had been kept completely in the dark. I think the events shocked her in a way that may not be... beneficial. Quinlan was away when the Nothus attacked and the transition was attempted."

"And we've lost touch with the chapter?"

"As far as I know, they're gone. In fact, my last correspondence was with Quinlan, and he asked if headquarters would handle the situation going forward. He said he would allow a transition if we could sponsor one, but he wanted no part of it.

No culpability. Said that if we came, he wouldn't even want to know we were there. That was at least a month ago."

The Grand Elder released his fingers from the blinds, snapping them back into place. "I fear something terrible may be about to happen."

Roland fidgeted in his seat. "What do you mean?"

The ticking of a grandfather clock in the corner of the office kept time in his silence. "I've lost touch with the New King."

Roland reciprocated his boss's hesitation, and after a long pause of his own, whispered, "Oh?"

The Grand Elder, back still turned, tapped an index finger to his temple. "I no longer have the ability to channel his vision."

"I see. I'm very sorry to hear that, sir."

"It was both a gift and a punishment." The Grand Elder shrugged. "But I'll have to regale you with the details of that procedure I underwent to get it some other time. You'll want to make sure you're on an empty stomach. We have more pressing matters to discuss today."

"Yes, sir."

"There are several things now working against us. The cleric is gone. The Sentinel will surely expire soon. As much as I hate to admit it, Quinlan may have been the only fragile thread holding it together. Action through inaction."

"I see."

The Grand Elder reached back for the arm of his desk chair and sat. Now, all Roland saw was a wall of leather.

"The last thing I saw before I lost my vision was the transfiguration of a man into something diabolical. It was he who severed my connection with the New King. Whether under his own free will or the Nothus' charge, I can't be certain."

"I don't understand. Who could that possibly be?"

The Grand Elder took a long pause. "I fear, Deacon, that the local chapter is not as dead as you believe it to be."

Tick, tock, tick, tock, tick, tock. Each oscillation of the pendulum seemed to progressively amplify the silences between.

"I think now is the time for action," the Grand Elder said. "Bold action."

Roland did not respond. He just glared at the leather-backed chair.

"There is a very old book," the voice behind the chair continued, "written mostly during the time of Bensalem's foundation. It contains the full history of the pilgrimage. The New King's ascension. It details the methods of transformational alchemy they used to create the Sentinel. It's all there. The founders of that town were very traditional. Everything you've sought to know, it's all there."

Something hitched in Roland's throat as he tried to make sense of what he was hearing. For so long, after so many rituals and missions and personal sacrifices, the most intimate secrets regarding the New King still had not yet been revealed to him.

"Long ago, the New King showed me what the Nothus did to his people. It unleashed unimaginable pain. Violence. Insanity. Death. It decimated Bensalem's population. The cycle of the Sentinels is an imperfect solution, and it's not evolved since it was initiated." The Grand Elder rose and again faced the blinds, hands clasped behind him. "But the world has evolved. Bensalem is obviously no longer an isolated settlement in a new world. If the Nothus were to roam unfettered again, it would... well, I loathe to think of what it might do."

"You want to end the cycle, don't you, sir?"

"I don't want to. I believe we must. Because if we don't, it may be ended for us."

"How do we end it?"

"The foundational question, Deacon. That's why you must go back to Bensalem. Find the book. A cessation of the cycle has never been attempted. The book may not even tell us explicitly how to do it, but it's the only source that would."

"Do we know where it is?"

"It may be where the cleric operated. It may not. We must try to find it. Not only for our own sake, but for the sake of the Order. I know I don't need to tell you how important this is. The vision of a prophet that started in the Old World hundreds of years ago has become a worldwide network of influence and power. The sanctity of Bensalem's secrets remains central to that vision." He raised one hand in the air, his back still turned. "A whole New Atlantis is waiting for us. A utopia of universal enlightenment."

"Will I have any help?"

"No. This is incredibly sensitive, and I trust only you. You're to speak of it to no one except me."

"I understand. I'll find the book."

"You're looking for the Grimoire Perantiquarum Rosarum. The Spells of the Old Roses."

"What does it look like?"

"You'll know it when you see it."

. . .

Three hundred miles southeast, Bensalem rose under another sulky winter sky. Cheryl's breath clouded as she chipped away the icy crust that had formed on her windshield overnight. Two reports of car accidents already today, which was two more than she'd dealt with since last year's first icing.

"This fuckin' shit," she muttered to herself as she rammed

the ice scraper. When her windshield was finally clear, she opened the back door, and a mix of frustration and relief propelled the scraper a touch harder than she intended. It flew across the back seat and clunked off the opposite side door.

Not ten seconds into her patrol car's reversal out of the driveway, the brakes locked, and the car slid backwards into the street. Cheryl kept it there for a moment before taking a deep breath and driving forward. She took the icy roads slow, assessing their perilousness and attempting to project how many more accidents to expect.

Her flip phone rang, and she swatted at the passenger seat without taking her eyes off the road. A *thunk* and another perfunctory curse uttered as her hand brushed the phone into the passenger-side wheel well. She let the phone ring out, and she pulled onto the shoulder of another nameless state road to retrieve it.

"Oh, good morning, ma'am. I was just leavin' you a voice-mail," Brady said when he answered.

"Whatcha got? Another one?"

"Lordy! We do, and Highway Patrol says they can't send another car out our way. They got their hair on fire this morning."

"Where?"

"Clarendon and Main. Sounds like nobody's hurt. Just a bunch of car parts in the street."

"Roger. I'll swing by."

"Ten four."

A low-riding sedan blazed past her as she eased onto the road, and she jerked the steering wheel back to the shoulder to avoid it. A trail of dirty exhaust bubbled in its wake as it sped on. She reached for the radio.

"611 to dispatch," she said.

"Mornin', ma'am," Deputy Monica Nelson called back, her

voice cracked and muffled through the radio.

"Scoot Hamilton just sped by me like a freakin' banshee. Headed northbound on Route 45. He's driving on a suspended license."

"Oh jeez. Okay. You gonna give chase?"

"I'm liable to end up dead in a ditch if I do. We got anybody up that way that can intercept?"

"I'll check, ma'am."

"Ten four."

Cheryl shook her head and got back on the road. Her phone rang again. This time, it was within arm's reach.

"Now fucking what?" she barked into the speaker.

"Is this Cheryl McNamara?" said a formal and unfamiliar voice.

"Yes. This is she."

"Well, good morning. This is Attorney General John Pickett. How are you this morning, Deputy?"

"Oh. Oh, my goodness, sir. I'm so sorry. We're just... we're just fine here. Sorry about the way I answered there, I'm just cleanin' up a few early morning fender benders. Seems like every year, people forget how to deal with a little ice, don't they? Gosh, I'm sure sorry about the f-bomb there."

"Don't sweat it. If this wasn't an official conversation, I'd drop one every other word."

"Ha. Well, that's a relief. What can I help you with, sir?"

"Well, I'm calling to follow-up on the terrible news about Sheriff Quinlan. I'm just so sorry about that. He was something of a legend around here. I can't imagine the hole he'll be leaving in your community."

"Oh, thank you, sir. Yeah, his loss is hitting us pretty hard. We're gonna be just fine, though. He left a good force and a good town behind him."

"I hear you discovered him?"

"Yes, sir, I did."

"That's just terrible. I'm so sorry you had to find him, but I'm glad it was you."

"Ah, well, thank you, I guess."

"Anyway, I'm calling because we're appointing you sheriff until the elections."

She slammed on the brakes as a rocket of warmth shot through her chest. "Are you serious?"

"In fact, you do a good enough job, we'd be pleased to back you if you wanna run."

"Run?"

"We'll be sending over some paperwork. It'll have to get done rather quickly, I'm afraid, since this happened so suddenly. Y'all have a fax machine over there?"

"Oh. Yes, sir. Absolutely, sir. We have one at the office. It's a great one. We... well, we don't use it that much, really, but I'll have Monica test it right after I get off the phone. I'll have her look out for it, sir."

"And we'll need you to come up to Richmond sometime soon for a swearing-in ceremony. Not too big of a deal, really. More paperwork, actually. Bring your family if you think they'll get a kick out of it. Your call."

"Certainly, sir. Gosh, I don't really know what to say. Thank you. You are being serious, correct, sir?"

He laughed. "You sound surprised, Sheriff."

That word hung in the thick air of the unit's manufactured heat. Cheryl didn't even realize she had pulled over again. A pickup truck clunking by her on the road offered a double honk of 'hello'.

"I'm sorry, sir, I am. Quite surprised. Wow. Thank you, sir."

"Your surprise surprises me. Duke sang your praises! Your record is… well, frankly, it's impeccable."

Cheryl tried to coax her face muscles out of their grin to form words. "I don't know about that. I don't know what to say. Thank you, sir."

"And the way you dealt with everything last summer… I don't know if Bensalem has ever dealt with anything like it before. Certainly not in my lifetime."

"Yeah. Yeah, it…" Her eyes were drawn to a copper-colored hawk floating through the quilted sky. It soared over the brown and barren topography, not looking down, but looking up and looking ahead. With a great flap, it soared beyond the trees. The edges of her eyes lined with tears. "We're okay, though, sir. We got through it, didn't we? We're a tough little community down here."

"You've got to be in today's world. I have every faith in you, Sheriff. Call my office if you run into any problems with that paperwork."

"Roger that. I won't let you down, sir."

As soon as she ended the call, a vulture sailed into view, tracing the opposite path of the hawk. For a moment, Cheryl couldn't tell if it was the same bird she had seen before as she zeroed in on its boiling head. The flying beast extended its white talons as it tilted backwards, and it landed on an ambiguous black lump in the shoulder brush.

She reached for her phone to tell Rick the news but stopped herself and instead drove on toward downtown Bensalem.

A sleety white haze now hung over the valley, obscuring the hills and dimpled slabs of granite buttressing the mountains. It thickened as she drove through it, as if an invisible hand pulled her on a string through an alternate dimension, a zone only discoverable upon a leader fully realizing their inherent loneliness.

"Sheriff McNamara," she whispered to herself. "Sheriff Cheryl McNamara. Hi, I'm Sheriff McNamara. Yes, good morning, this is Sheriff Cheryl McNamara. Sheriff McNamara." She flicked on the wipers as gentle drops of winter stippled her windshield.

The rain did not seem to deter a vested young woman hanging Christmas lights on her storefront at Main Street's southwest corner. It did, however, sting the faces of two old men walking together as briskly as their bodies would carry them, their hands shoved into coat pockets and eyes squinted down at the pavement.

The creeping hand of fear clutching Cheryl's core each time she drove down Main Street began to tickle her insides. Almost instinctively, she began to turn away from M&J Fine Gifts as she approached it, but this time, she caught herself and turned her head right toward it. She tightened the grip on her steering wheel and slowed the unit to a crawl. Jane Harcourt's storefront skulked through the frame of Cheryl's passenger window, a drab and tenantless husk, a fissure into which so much of the blood from Bensalem's wounds had fallen.

In a sudden movement, she pulled into the parking lane and stopped. She closed her eyes, and rather than channeling mental energy to bolster the defenses she'd erected around that week from hell last summer, she yanked them down and invited the pain to ambush her. Yet to her relative surprise, no bloodthirsty army of memories and traumas and regrets advanced. Instead, there was a single image, an image she had not for a second considered since that day.

All that came to her was the mental snapshot of that ghastly portrait hanging high in Jane Harcourt's lab, as if it had been waiting for this very moment to reappear. As if all those awful memories—the search, the stress, Hank's corpse, Ellen's screams,

Aaron's tears—had laid down their arms and anointed the painted visage of that white-eyed, puritanical man, with a thin moustache and an even thinner smile, to wield their collective power. Cheryl didn't understand it, and from that lack of understanding rose a new faint chill of fear, something colder and sharper, something closer to an ambiguous truth.

Sleet pelted the windshield, and she tried to reason why this wraith-like man was all her mind's eye could see. Her eyes jolted open, and peering at M&J Fine Gifts, found the razor-thin outline of the secret door she'd discovered behind Jane's counter. Cheryl looked not at the door, but through it, putting herself back in the garish laboratory it led to and the portrait of the man inside it.

"Dispatch to 611," Monica said over the radio.

Cheryl didn't answer. She didn't move.

"Deputy, you there?" Monica said.

"Yeah, go ahead," Cheryl finally answered.

"Another one. Northbound on 45 by Wilkinson's Ridge. It's that sedan you mentioned."

"Shit. Scoot?"

"Yes, ma'am."

"Is he hurt? Is anybody hurt?"

"Don't know yet. By-stander just called it in."

"Who's gettin' it?"

"Derek's headed out there now."

"Can you have him buzz me when he does?"

"Ten four. You still headed to Clarendon and Main?"

An even denser fog now covered the road, cloaking the entire world in a ghostly gray veil. Even M&J's broken windows and barren shelves were less clear to her. She took a deep breath.

"Yeah. On my way."

. . .

Roland had already determined the first place he'd visit in Bensalem before he left the Order's gilded Manhattan headquarters.
There would be much to learn and many places to see in the town
he'd hoped never to see again, but none more important than the
heart of the forest where the rituals took place. His commander's
notion of nefarious activity in an area of his responsibility gnawed
at him as he rode the elevator down from the 110th Floor, ears
popping along the way.

  Roland took the elevator straight to the Order's library,
devouring all the official Bensalem records he could find. He
reviewed the list of Sentinels, the names of clerics and chapter
members, police reports of missing persons as far back as Bensalem had an organized force. But these documents held limited
value, their classification level too low to yield value, not like the
sealed archives upstairs. The more he read, the more he yearned to
immerse himself in the darker elements of his assignment.

  By the time he finished with the library and made for the archives, the burnt orange beams of a setting sun refracted through
the glass of the elevator. But the archives, too, held nothing of
value, and by the time he got in his car, his hunger for truth had
grown into starvation.

  Only the town itself would satiate him. The evidence he
sought would be empirical, not historical. His hands would have
to get dirty and cold, and his heart would have to surge with visceral fear as he sought out that which had been locked away—evil
lurking in the black depths of the forest, zealots feasting on the
scraps of a backwards town, veiled truths that might shake the
very bedrock of the Order to which he had given his life.

. . .

As soon as Skylar arrived home from school that afternoon, she trudged to her room, wrapped a comforter over her shoulders, and collapsed on her bed in a malaise of boredom and exhaustion. The chill of the day had burrowed into her very marrow, and her body sank rapidly toward sleep as she waited for Ram to reply to the text message she sent, asking if she left her portable CD player at his house.

Her cell phone's chime brought her back from the brink, and she flipped the screen up to read the incoming text message.

It's not here, his message said.

She typed back, *Ughhhh my mom is moving all this shit around...*

Ram replied almost immediately, *<3*

She lay there for a moment, wondering if she would ever, in her entire life, conjure the strength or desire to peel her carcass off her bed. A half hour passed in which she drifted in and out of sleep, and only after her head stopped swimming, she rolled off the bed and stumbled to her parents' home office.

An early evening sky, scant with color and movement, spilled through the room's windows and onto the tops of several packing boxes in various states of closure. She pawed through the contents of the widest open box, sifting through various police manuals, binders, and papers. Nothing. Clear packing tape lined the top of the next box, and she peeled away one end of it to open a crack in the seal. Something shiny struck her eye, and she pulled the tape back further.

Upon first sight of the gold-plated letters—GRIMOIRE PERANTIQUARUM ROSARUM—the gaudy trefoil cross, and the leatherbound tome they were stamped on, an inexplicable zest of curiosity coursed through her veins. Her first attempt to lift the book failed, so she leaned over the box and pulled carefully, wrapping all ten fingers around its clammy and organic edges.

Skylar held the book out, trying to pronounce its alien title in her head and letting the last light of the day frame it in the window in front of her. Sitting cross-legged over it on the floor, she traced her index finger across the sharp contours of the red rose in the middle of the cross. A mildewy stench wafted up when she lifted the cover with a delicate hand, and the old yellow paper crinkled as she flipped to the first page. Her eyes skimmed the text, and her heart began to beat faster. Something about this book sucked her into its odd words.

I. FUNDAMENTUM

1. In the year of our Lord, 1611, our New King Salomon, seeking the newness of life, abandoned the foulness and pollution of the old world and set forth—; not to India, or China, or Japan—, but to the Virginia Colony to build a New Atlantis. Our New King Salomon did testify unto us his Great Instauration: a land with people set apart, a commonwealth upon which his renovations will usher in a golden age of peace and plenty, and upon which he will build his House on a rock in the eye of the new Kingdom, and it will light the path to enlightenment of all alchemy and sciences. 2. Our journey, beset by hardship, which made a great number of his Children renounce their faith and from which a great number of Children did perish, continued for two-and-one-half months through blue seas as a beacon of our Lord set adrift in the wastelands. On

the seventy-eighth day, the darkness cleared, and there-
upon our New King Salomon looked out over the bow
and saw great stone walls, and rivulets of light in the
sky, and the pillar of light in the sea, and upon that pillar, he saw the cross of light that burned brighter than
the sun of the old world, and the light burned our New
King Salomon's eyes so that they became as of ivory or
pearl, and he said, "We give thanks to God." 3. When
our boats could go no further, our new King Salomon
went to land and found the Sacred Texts wrapped in
linen, and the texts could be read in any man's native
tongue, and the light of God manifested from them,
and among them was the letter from Bartholomew,
disciple of our Lord and Saviour, Jesus Christ, to which
he revealed the secret of his salvation. We settled these
lands by the light of our new sun, and we gave thanks
to the Lord, and we called the land Bensalem.

Skylar suddenly felt the presence of another being behind
her. She whipped her head around the room.

"Is someone there?" she said, loud and clear. Her voice was
deep and textured in a way that her mother's wasn't.

No one was, and no one answered besides the drone of the
local news from television downstairs.

She scanned the room again and read on, skimming lofty
pseudo-Christian prose, trying but failing to make sense of runic
symbols, staring at equations of chemical compounds and math
problems her trigonometry and statistics classes didn't even begin
to qualify her to interpret.

Not knowing how much time had passed, forgetting she

even owned a portable CD player in the first place, she reached for her phone and called Ram.

"I just found the weirdest thing in my mom's stuff," she said.

"What?"

"This crazy book. I think it's hundreds of years old. There's, like, all this shit about... I don't know... occult stuff. There's weird symbols. This thing is so... I don't know."

"What kind of occult shit?"

She flipped a few pages. "I don't know. Talking about some weird religion. It talks about Bensalem. They keep referencing something called the New King Salo—Solomon? I don't know how to say it."

"What's it called?"

"I don't know. Something long, and I think in Latin?"

Ram paused. "I don't understand."

"What don't you understand?"

"You found an occult book about Bensalem? In Latin?"

"No. Well, yeah. I... " Skylar lost herself on a page showing what looked like a table of elements. She didn't recognize any of the letters or symbols.

"Sky?"

"Sorry. I don't know. I think it's Latin. It's in my mom's stuff."

"Your mom wouldn't have a book like that."

"I know, right?"

"Can I see it? Maybe I can read parts of it."

"I don't think I can get it out of here." Still kneeling over the book with her back to the door, she once again scanned the room, assessing it. Her eyes traced the corners as if there might be a more clandestine exit than the door or the window.

"Want me to come over?"

"Oh! I know! I'll take pictures of it. I'll take pictures of the pages and we can look at them tomorrow. Won't that be fun?"

"What did you say it was called?"

"I don't know if I can pronounce it."

"Can you spell it?"

Skylar closed the book and read the title. "G-R-I-M-O-I-R-E. New word. P-E-R-A-N-T-I-Q-U-A-R-U-M. New word. R-O-S-A-R-U-M. That's it."

"Grimoire Perantiquaram Rosarum. That is Latin. I think that's, like, book of old roses, or something. Something about old or ancient roses."

"Really?"

"Pretty sure. See, I dropped out, and I'm still smarter than you!"

"Pretty sure? Pretty sure you're a dumb ass." With the phone sandwiched between her cheek and her shoulder, she cradled the book in her forearms to feel the weight of it. "It's huge and heavy. It's just a book, but it feels... I don't know how to describe it."

"What do you mean?"

"You know that feeling when you hold a gun? Like, it's just not just object, but something more powerful?"

"Yeah."

"It's sorta like that, I guess."

"Why would your mom have that? Dude, what if she's secretly a witch? Could you imagine?!"

"She's the last thing from a witch. She's, like, the most boring person ever born."

"Where did you find it?"

"In these boxes. Stuff I think she's moving into her new office at the station."

"So maybe it has something to do with that?"

"With what?"

"Your mom's work. Maybe she's investigating a cult."

"I fucking wish."

Rick's heavy footsteps echoed up the stairs.

"Shit, my dad's coming. I gotta go," Skylar said.

"Take some pictures?"

"Yeah, yeah. I will."

She hung up on Ram and silently placed the book back in its box.

. . .

Cheryl struggled to lift the moose antlers off the wall behind Duke's desk, now her desk. The mere sight of them disturbed her ever since the day, four months ago, when he revealed the secrets he had hidden from her. Those blooming brown horns lined up perfectly with the back of his head, as if crowning him king over the twisted rituals of which he spoke. Removing the trophy was the opening gambit in a wholesale refreshment of the sheriff's personal office at the station.

She glanced around, unable to identify a single object that appeared to have been touched in two decades. The room's retro array of wood paneled walls, yellow furniture, and off-white tile all seemed to blend into a single vomit-colored shade.

"How's the new digs, Sheriff?" Brady's voice called from the door behind her.

"Oh, hey there, Derek."

"You want a hand with that?"

She shot a mean look up at the antlers. "You mind?"

He stepped right up, and together, they lifted the trophy from the wall. Off with it came a silky film of eons old cobwebs. Its absence revealed a wholly darker section of wood paneling untouched by sunlight.

"Jesus," she said as cobwebs flaked to the ground.

"No kidding. This place is in sore need of a makeover."

"Wish it didn't have to happen like this, though."

He scratched his head, rubbing stray cobwebs through his hair. "I don't know. Had to happen eventually. Old Duke had one heckuva life, didn't he?"

It was as if all his old objects—photos from the Vietnam war, guns mounted on the walls, honors and awards framed on the desk—pooled their invisible voices together in a resounding, "Yes!"

"You okay with all this, Derek?"

"Okay with what?"

"Well, I'm just here until the election. And listen, if you wanna run—"

He shook his head. "You kiddin'? I'm glad you're sheriff. Think I want it?"

"Kinda thought you did."

"Listen, no offense, but I got plenty of time."

"Oh, come on, now! You're only what? Twenty? Twenty-five years younger than me?"

He blushed. "Twenty-seven, if we're countin', ma'am."

They shared a laugh.

"I mean it, though," he said. "We're all behind you, Sheriff. You'd know if we weren't. Pickett made the right call, and I'm serious, I do have plenty of time. Yeah, I do wanna be sheriff one day, but not any time soon. I can guarantee you that. I'll even support your bid if you wanna run."

"Hell, don't even get me thinkin' about that. People hate me here. Been here most of my life now and still feel like an outsider. Once a transplant, always a transplant."

"Now, you know that ain't true. People are gonna be glad you're in charge. I think."

"We'll see."

"You want any more help with this stuff?"

"Nah, that's okay. I got it."

"Ten four, Sheriff," he said as he shuffled out of the room.

She peered down at the antlers, now mounted to the linoleum floor. They stared back at her.

"Hey!" she shouted. "Derek?"

He leaned back in through the doorway. "Yeah?"

"I wanna talk to you about somethin'. You got a minute?"

"Sure."

"Have a seat," Cheryl said. She opted not to sit in Duke's creaky old roller behind the desk, but in one of the two foam armchairs in front of it. Brady sat in the other.

"What's goin' on?" he said.

"Well, first of all, this stays between us. For now."

He squared his eyes and nodded. "Of course, Sheriff."

She sighed. "Do you know anything about, uh, occult activity here in Bensalem?"

"Occult activity?"

"Yeah."

"What kind of occult activity?"

"Well, according to Duke, our town's got a little bit of a secret. Now, I didn't know about any of this until he told me a few months ago, only after Hank Teakle died and Caleb Dreyer was kidnapped. He said he wanted to tell me earlier but never did."

She waited for a response but didn't get one.

"That's why I'm tellin' you now," she said, "I don't wanna make that same mistake."

"Mistake?"

"Duke said... and the Dreyers also said this when we questioned them... that there is some kind of... I don't know... supernatural entity that"—she closed her eyes and shook her head—"that lives in the woods off SR 639. They say it's this huge, monster-lookin' thing. I know that sounds crazy."

He took his elbows off his knees and leaned back in his chair. His gaping mouth asked a thousand silent questions. "Duke said that?"

"He did. He also said there's some kinda cult that was run by Jane Harcourt. I guess they go back hundreds of years or something. What never came out in the report was that Jane kidnapped Caleb Dreyer, and that's why his parents shot her."

"Oh. No shit?"

"No shit. The Dreyers said Jane wanted Caleb for some fucking cult ritual thing. Duke corroborated it."

"My God. Are you serious?"

"It gets weirder."

Brady's eyes widened. "Uh. Okay."

"Now, I haven't witnessed this, mind you, but this supernatural monster is apparently a mutated version of Jane's other son, Mark. The boy who went missing way back, way before you were born."

"What in the blue hell?"

"I know. I know how this sounds. I had the same reaction. In fact"—she pointed—"I was sittin' in that same exact chair when Duke told me. I just need to get all this out in case it's actually true. I don't know if it is. Let me be clear about that. But if it is, someone else needs to know."

"This all sounds insane."

"There's also this other monster, something called... gosh, I think he called it the bastard."

"The bastard?"

"Yeah. This thing is apparently what killed Hank Teakle. Duke said it kills people that... I don't know... get too close to it or somethin.'"

Brady shook his head. "How could any of what you're describing exist without us knowing about it? Without anyone knowing about it? A cult? Monsters in the woods? Surely, my dad must know."

"Well, if he does, I guess he didn't tell you."

He scoffed. "Think about what you're saying. There are monsters in the woods that kill people? Only things killin' people here are heart attacks and heroin."

"No, I know. I—"

"The Dreyers tried to tell me something about this. They said there was a monster in the meadow across from their yard."

"Wait, really?"

"Oh yeah. You don't remember? Ellen drove to the god-damned station in the middle of the night and freaking demanded I follow her back to her house to show me. Of course, there was no monster when I got there, but both she and Aaron... man... I've never seen people so wired. They were hysterical. They were insane."

"Shit, I do remember that."

"Sheriff, with all due respect, it sounds like a crock to me."

She leaned forward and lowered her tone. "Derek, I know how this sounds. I know. Again, I have not seen any of this myself. I don't know if I believe any of it. Duke laid all this on me like a ton of bricks while all that shit was going on, and I didn't know what to do with it. Still don't. But what I can tell you is that I still have no goddamned idea what killed Hank Teakle. You saw that corpse. You saw the way his chest was carved out. Remember how deep the hole was? I know of no person or thing capable of that. I think about it every single night before I fall asleep. I ask myself what could have possibly done that and why. What could have done that, Derek? What could have done that to him? Do you have any idea?"

"I'm not a homicide detective. I just police a little town in the woods. That's all I aim to be."

"But think about it for a second. Two murders and a kidnapping, all in the span of a week? In a place that doesn't see that kind of violent crime in a lifetime? Does that really feel... random?"

He bit his upper lip and stared at the drop panel ceiling.

She leaned in closer. "See? Something's just not adding up, Derek."

"Why you bringin' this up now? I thought we moved on." He gestured with his hands before smearing them down his face. "You think you're the only one it hurt? Can't you just let it be?"

"Duke wrote a note, you know. He wanted me to find it, and he addressed it to me. It read like the ravings of a madman. He mentioned some of the stuff I'm talking about. Why would he do that? I truly think he was way more connected to this than I ever realized."

"A cult, though? Really? Couldn't it be that he was just a crazy old man? C'mon, you and I both knew he had lost a step. Well, a few steps, really. Those crimes were hard on everybody."

Cheryl shook her head. "I don't think so," she whispered, glaring at him. "Let me put it to you another way. We don't know a lick more about this than we did four months ago. Right? State's got nothin'. We got nothin'. Just at face value, didn't it feel a little more than random?"

Brady sighed.

"What was motivating the Dreyers back then?"

"Their son was gone."

"Exactly. Their son was gone. Imagine if that happened to us. What if someone hurt Lenny or Skylar? What if something happened to your little Noland?"

He shifted his eyes down, away from her.

"You'd do everything and anything. Wouldn't you?"

"Of course. I'd do anything for Noland."

"Something hit me when I got the call this morning, Derek. Something hurt this town real bad, and as far as we know, it's still out there. You know what I'm saying? If you really want to protect something, don't you demand to know everything you can about everything in the world that could possibly hurt it? No matter how dark and unbelievable it might be? Don't we owe Hank that? Caleb? Even Jane? There are missing pieces here. Big ones."

"Well…" He glanced over her head and out the window, where the shadows of trees had grown long and the world had dimmed to its darkest shade before night. "I sure hope you're wrong," he said after a long time.

She nodded. "Me too."

. . .

Not until well after her parents were asleep did Skylar venture back to her mother's office. Shades of a dreary midnight cast the boxes in almost blue shadow, and the thin slice of a new moon cut the window sash like a cosmic sickle. Only the strained hum of a steam radiator accompanied her.

The Grimoire wasn't as heavy as it seemed that afternoon. It could have been that, in the hours since her discovery, the very idea of it had become more palatable, the contents of it a bit less arcane, the weight of it somehow more manageable in both her mind and her hands.

One by one, she took flash pictures of the pages on her digital camera until her memory card was full. She texted Ram.

It's too long.

What is?

My mom's book. I'm not even halfway through, and my card is full.

Two meager black objects—maybe birds, maybe bats—darted past the window, squawking one-note battle cries. As their desperate expression of language evaporated into the night, Skylar consumed the Grimoire's words, pictures, charts, and diagrams. She spent a good five minutes scanning a hand-drawn picture titled "New Atlantis." The lushness, splendor, and grandiosity of the city was not lost through the artist's monolithic pencil strokes. It was a gorgeous display of columns, towers, turrets, and gardens.

As for the book's text, lines not written in Latin were written in a version of English she could barely understand, and it baffled her that the two old, odd languages were used almost interchangeably, sometimes switching in the middle of sentences.

Countless references to Christianity and the Kingdom of God early on reminded the reader in an almost nagging manner of its inherently religious intent. But as she turned pages, skimming more for a feel of the work as opposed to mastery of its contents, the religious references thinned, and the tone of what she could understand seemed to sour. Near to its midpoint, a diagram spread across two pages showed some kind of registry or family tree. Sprawling clumps of tiny-texted surnames were connected by a web of arrows and lines branching off into hundreds of directions. The handwriting varied greatly, implying the list was not the work of a sole author, but many over time. Skylar's eyes narrowed, and she began scanning the names for anything that looked like McNamara.

When she flipped to the back of the book in search of an index, she instead found a ripped-open envelope plastered to the inside of the back flap, and she held her breath for a moment when she observed two drops of blood and the word "MAC" on its cover.

She retrieved the note inside, written on Sheriff Duke Quinlan's official letterhead.

It is now time. The seed has grown and consumed me. The boy awaits. I have failed the boy. And the KILL YOURSELF. It sends its envoys. It will send more envoys. One with me now. I cannot help KILL YOURSELF you. I can help you by getting out of the way. KILL YOURSELF They are looking at me and they run in the back of my dreams. The pestilence sent the one in the corner. He is going to kill me. I am going to kill myself before he can kill me. I am going to kill myself kill myself kill myself because I am afraid that KILL YOURSELF KILL YOURSELF if they kill me I will become like themKILL YOURSELF. They walk at KILL YOURSELF KILL YOURSELF night. Their footprints are KILL YOURSELF KILL YOURSELF KILL YOURSELF. You KILL YOURSELF must cure us from N. N sees all. N SEES ALL!! It will KILL YOURSELF   KILLYOURSELFKILLYOURSELF KILL YOURseLF send more and they will walk among you. The New King Salomon has fallen into dull darkness.

Skylar's blood ran stone cold. A veil of wind slapped the

window. She yelped and jumped back, but quickly collected herself and re-read the note three more times, her mouth no less agape than it was the first time she read it. From the fuzzy pocket of her pajama bottoms, she delicately retrieved her flip phone and called Ram.

"Ram," she whispered. Her tone was as soft as it could be, fearful of unseen eavesdroppers in this world or the next. "There's a piece of paper that's the most fucked-up thing I've ever read."

"Oh shit. What was it?"

"I think it's Sheriff Quinlan's suicide note. It's in the book."

"The Grimoire?"

"Yeah. It's super fucking weird. It says 'kill yourself' like a hundred times. It's written so weird, like there were two people writing. He talks about envoys and this thing, the New King Salomon. Something about failing a boy."

"New King Salomon?"

"He must have had this book before my mom. He addressed the note to her." A sudden chill pricked Skylar's skin. Goosebumps formed on her arms, and her jaw tightened. "This book is so weird. It's talking about these... I don't know... something called the Order of the Old Roses, something called New Atlantis."

"Order of the Old Roses? There's something called the Rose Cross. Or maybe it's the Rosy Cross? I forget, something like that. I don't know much about it. I think it's, like, the Knights Templar. Remember the old, Medieval guy at the end of *Indiana Jones*?"

"This book must be written by them."

"Who? The guys from *Indiana Jones*?"

"No, the Order of the Old Roses. Didn't you say that was what the title said? Can you take pics and show me?"

"I'm not even halfway through, and my memory card is already full." A long beat passed between them before Skylar followed up. "Ram? You there?"

"Do you think the sheriff killed himself over this book? Or what's in it?"

"I don't know."

"Do you think this has something to do with all the shit that went down in the summer?"

A third voice entered the conversation, this one from right behind her.

"Sky?" it called.

Skylar spun around and snapped her phone shut in a single motion. Cheryl stood in the doorway, her tiny body swimming in a white nightgown and blond curls floating, her eyes more closed than open.

"What are you doin', sweetie?" Cheryl said.

"Nothing. I'm sorry. I—I'm looking for my CD player. I can't find it anywhere, so I just wanted to check."

"Oh, I'm sorry, sweetie. I haven't seen it."

"I'm sorry. I'll get out of your stuff. I just couldn't sleep and thought maybe it was in here for some reason."

"Yeah? You doin' okay?"

"Yeah, of course."

"Why aren't you sleepin'?"

"I don't know. I think I'm just stressed about midterms."

Cheryl looked out into the hall and nodded to herself. "Better get some sleep if you can, or else you'll be all grumpy in the mornings like me."

Skylar chucked. "Okay, Mom."

"Goodnight, Sky. I love you."

Skylar paused before replying. In that moment, her mother felt both closer and more distant than she'd ever been before. "I love you, too, Mom. Goodnight."

Skylar sat motionless until the click of the bathroom door reverberated through the upstairs. She read Duke's note one more time before placing it and the Grimoire back where she found them.

. . .

For six decades, the path Maurice Bacon traveled was a lonely one. It lay littered with the sins and the silence of his trespassers. He navigated it in a state of inhuman reclusiveness, almost feral, paying no mind to agents of sanity who might hinder him.

When Jane Harcourt died, the few elders remaining in the local chapter disbanded. They wouldn't weather Maurice's babbling, his increasingly unhinged lamentations. He pledged to carry on alone in the face of their heresy, in whatever way he could and in the company of whoever would have him. His zeal to enter New Atlantis—arms raised and bathed in the light of the New King Salomon's eyes—tugged at the very cords of his essence. It was all he had left.

In the glade that night, he had lost all feeling in his bare feet by the time he ran the knife blade across the top of his left hand. His jaw fell out of its socket when he gasped, not from pain but pleasure, as the cold steel scraped across his metacarpals. A burst of wind screeched through rows of immense trees and scattered drops of his blood across the frosted earth. When the wind died, he snapped his jaw back into place using a left hand now wrapped in a wet glove of blood. He dropped the knife, the latest in a litany of items he had taken from the lab hidden in M&J Fine Gifts, and it clanked on the frozen dirt between his feet.

He crouched and turned his palm faceup so the blood spurted out, gasping again as it covered a small pile of pewter-colored powder between his feet. The trees watched him stick-walk to another pile, where again he crouched, lowered his hand, and wet the powder with his blood. He liquified another in the same manner, and another, and another, until fifteen separate blankets of blood capped fifteen piles of pewter powder set about the glade. His jaw popped out, and he popped it back in again, smearing more blood across his face.

As the blood melted the piles of powder, his eyes, set tense below the jagged scar on his forehead, morphed into stark white stones, and his fingers began to twitch. Droplets whipped off the fingertips of his left hand while pale rods of bone pistoned up and down under the sliver of his open wound. All around the glade, funnel-shaped indentations now marked the patches of earth where powder mounds had been, and they expanded in size and depth as Maurice continued his seance. His jaw fell out again, but he ignored it. It just hung open, locked in a dead scream under cadaverous eyes.

A seed-sized object appeared at the bottom of one of the indentations. It rose from the earth and elongated to the size of a twig, and two more similar objects poked through in the surrounding area. All three rose higher in unison to reveal their rootedness to a much larger thing.

The other indentations in the glade underwent similar phenomena, each expanding from a few inches to several feet, each pushing a handful of long objects out of the earth, eventually revealing themselves not to be twigs, but sets of blood-soaked antlers attached to animal skulls. So thick was the blood that it did not drip, but hung, like shiny red tinsel from each antler point, and when the lanky hosts of such heinousness yanked their wild hands free from the dirt, dark streaks of blood flew from their long, thin fingers. Nothus fingers.

At first, they writhed on the ground, their maroon neonatal bodies glimmering in moon beams unfortunate enough to fall upon them. But as foam spilled from the corners of Maurice's mouth and ran down his blood-smeared jaw, these fifteen monstrosities, borne from some sadistic mixture of silvery powder, his own blood, and the earth itself, shook off their membranes and stood on cloven hooves.

As if counting off to assess the size of their brigade, they announced themselves by penetrating the forest with screeches. They lurched about the glade in awkward strides, finding their balance, judging the crushing power of their terrible fingers, screaming to each other in some language of hell. Maurice cackled.

When their blood cloaks were gone, either smeared on the ground as they writhed or strewn on the soil as they plodded, the only objects still red in the glade were the glowing, incendiary eyes set deep in each of their skulls.

Maurice's jaw wasn't set, so the words came out as a garbled mumble. "Yethhh! I will lead tthhhem, my king! I seekthh the light of New Atlanthisss!"

Two of the creatures walked up to Maurice and sniffed him. He wrapped his blood hand around one of their bone-thin wrists, and the creature let him hold it there for a brief moment before screeching and swatting it away.

With arms raised high, he dropped to his knees. He cocked his head to the sky, and his gaze warped beyond the hazy gray clouds toward a high and distant light visible only through the kaleidoscope of his delirium. Within the apex of that light, he bore witness to a city shimmering green and gold, where the enlightened walked on pearl cobblestone streets and inhaled an elixir-infused atmosphere, and in the center of the city stood a great temple, a temple whose ivory columns and spiraling turrets rose high above the skyline, whose patrons peered out for eternity on balconies lined with balustrades chiseled into the likenesses of great philosophers, whose energy pulsated with utopic realizations of both science and faith.

His entire body trembled. Soft grunts emitted from his slack-jawed, foaming mouth. When Maurice collapsed into a seething, hyperventilating ball on the bloodstained floor of the glade, the herd formed a tight circle around him. They stood completely silent, watching him through fifteen sets of fire-fueled eyes, and as twilight approached, they gathered his body up with their immense fingers. When the time was right, they walked, single-file and holding their master aloft like some heraldic device, out of the glade and through the Black Door of the Bastard where the Nothus awaited.

. . .

And so it was that night, as Skylar crossed a dangerous threshold of knowledge in her parents' home office, as Cheryl leaned on the bathroom sink and waded through the maze of her fears, and as Roland Pierce blazed down I-95 toward Bensalem, Maurice Bacon—eyes white, jaw hanging, heart void, mind gone—left the glade not as he entered it.

No longer was he an aimless outcast roaming the impenitent night. No longer was he a filthy and bloodstained supplicant beset by his heritage. No longer was he the one forgotten, the one discarded, the one stepped on and scraped off the boots of his brethren like an unloved and unseen scum.

Tonight, he was infused with divine mission and enlightened purpose, his New King's marching orders stamped onto his very soul. Tonight, he was a master of others—a thing he had never been before.

But behind that door, beyond long halls, and dwelling deep in the cave's innermost sanctum, another yet watched and waited. For while Maurice was master to these spawns, and the Nothus master to him, even the most powerful beings—devils and angels themselves—have masters still.

DAY 4

Ellen Dreyer opened her eyes.

Her mind swam through the tranquility of a distant recollection. A dark-haired girl bounding through the woods behind the farmhouse she grew up in. The inhalation of sweet summer air, the feel of fresh soil under her bare feet, symphonic songs of birds and insects. Playing outside past dark, lungs stinging as she ran home for dinner. Looking, listening, learning, feeling. All of it so vivid but so vague, fuzzier than a dream and more fantastic than a memory, just a sensation of softness and light.

Every time she remembered her childhood, it felt further and further away, as if tied to a rope that grew ever longer with each day, each wrinkle, each heartache. Those precious milliseconds in the mornings gave her just enough time to tighten her grip on the rope and inch it back toward her. Toward her, where it belonged, not out there in the frigid ether, not in a cobweb of her mind. No, not far but close, warming her heart and soothing her soul, reminding her that if things were good once, then maybe, just maybe, they could be good again.

Because once those precious milliseconds were over, the hooks of her recent past sank back into her flesh, and they remained there for the rest of the day—stabbing her, cutting her, slicing her, keeping her awake and alone.

Yet as she mourned the passing of her innocence for the day, the void inside her was quickly filled up by a warmth that spunky country girl could never have fathomed, and driven not by coherent action but by the single richest form of love, the muscles in Ellen's arms flexed around her little son lying next to her. Caleb stirred and tightened his grip on his mother's wrist.

She kissed the back of his head, his black hair sleep-matted to her cheeks. Three cracks in Ellen's back penetrated the silence of the bedroom as she sat up in bed.

"Caleb," she said. "Baby boy..."

Caleb rubbed his eyes in a slow and methodical manner. Suddenly, he stopped, gasped, and spun around in bed to face her. Cooper, the German Shepherd sleeping at the foot of the bed, peeled his weary snout off the carpet.

"Shh," Ellen said, cradling Caleb's head in her arms. "It's okay. It's okay. The night's over. The day is here. Mommy is here."

Sun danced on Bensalem's bleak landscape, and wide, white streaks of light poured into the bedroom Ellen had, until four months ago, shared with her husband. She slipped out of bed and past a pile of children's books lined up next to a bench by the window, and before reaching Caleb, squatted to ruffle the ears of a stretching Cooper.

"How were your dreams? Remember any?" she said.

Caleb shrugged and slithered off the bed. She hugged him.

Downstairs, Janis Marquart sat wrapped in a shawl at the kitchen table. She lowered the Washington Post from her face when Ellen and Caleb—mother in her scrubs, son still in his pajamas—walked into the kitchen with Cooper trailing behind them.

Ellen pecked her on the cheek. "Morning, Mom."

"Morning, dear," she said, kissing the air in return.

Caleb waved with a slight smile on his lips.

"Good morning, little sir! You have a kiss for Grandma?"

He threw his arms around her and kissed her in the same spot Ellen had.

Janis put the paper down and took Caleb's hands in her own while Ellen poured kibble into Cooper's bowl. "I bet you want some pancakes. That sound good?"

Caleb nodded, still smiling.

"Single today," Ellen said, hovering over the coffee maker. "The ER shouldn't be too bad."

The doorbell rang. All four threw their gazes toward the hallway, and then the three humans bounced glances off each other. Cooper plodded toward the door while still crunching a mouthful of kibble. Ellen followed him.

Something seared in Ellen's stomach when she opened the door and saw Cheryl standing there.

"Mornin', Dr. Dreyer," Cheryl said, tipping her hat.

Ellen stared at her for a moment before crossing her arms and responding. "Hello."

"May I come in for a moment?"

Ellen stepped out onto the porch and closed the door. The crisp winter morning sent a chill through her. "I only have a few minutes. Let's just chat out here."

Cheryl smiled. "Sure. Well, um, it's good to see you again."

Ellen didn't respond.

"I'm sorry to come over unannounced, but I was just wondering if you might be interested in helping me with something. I wonder if I might be able to chat with Caleb for a few minutes sometime. With you present, of course."

"What do you want with my son?"

"Not sure if you heard this, but Sheriff Quinlan just passed. Funeral's later this morning, actually. I'm sure it's just temporary, but I'm the interim sheriff, and I'm trying to get my arms around some of the unfinished business from last summer."

Ellen shivered and wrapped her arms tighter around herself. "Can we talk about this later? I really have to go. I'm not really ready to have this conversation with you."

"Yes. I absolutely respect that. I'm very sorry to disturb you."

Ellen turned around and opened the door.

"It's just—" Cheryl said, and Ellen stopped. "I want to make things right. I don't quite know all the pieces of this, and I know you—and of course, Caleb—learned a lot about how this town works. I got a little bit of it from Duke before he died, but I really know very little about what happened. I don't know if it's because I'm in this temporary position or what, but it's been eating at me."

Ellen chuckled. "Oh, now it's eating at you?" She turned around and faced an open-mouthed Cheryl. "You know what's eating at me? My husband is still in jail because of you. He doesn't get out until August. My mother has to live here to help me raise my son."

"I—I'm sorry, ma'am. I unders—"

"No, you don't understand. You can't talk to my fucking son because he still hasn't spoken a word to anyone besides me or Mark. He hasn't said a word to his own grandmother in four months. There's no way in hell he'll talk to the cop who took his daddy away."

"Mark?"

"He can't go to school. He can't see friends. His therapists are pulling their hair out and—and do you know how much all that costs?"

"I'm sorry, are you referring to Mark Harcourt?"

Ellen paused. "Yes. Mark Harcourt. He's still out there. He's still in the ground, and I don't know how much is left of him."

Cheryl put a hand up, as if attempting to tame a wild animal. "Now, see, that's what I'm talking about. Can we help him? Is he alive? Can we get him out of there?"

Her words physically moved Ellen a step backwards.

"I want to help him, Ellen. Can we save him? You and me? I really want to end this."

"You have no idea what you're getting yourself into."

"Ma'am, I know that. That's exactly why I'm here. I have to start somewhere, and I want to try to earn your trust."

"Mark is the least of your problems."

"Why's that?"

Ellen exhaled a cloud of breath into the cold. "Are you gonna call me fucking crazy again?"

"No." Cheryl gestured with her hands. "I am truly trying to help and keep an open mind here. What else is out there? Duke said there's one good one and one bad one. Is Mark the good one? Or is he the bad one?"

"Mark's the good one. The Sentinel."

"Okay, and what's the bad one? Is that called the New King Salomon? Is that what you think killed Hank?"

"I don't know what it is, and I don't know what killed Hank. I—" She turned around in response to the distant call of her name from inside. "I have to go. I have to go to work."

"Can we please keep this conversation going? Even what you just told me is very useful."

But Ellen left the question hanging as she closed the door behind her.

By the time Ellen had packed her bag and said her goodbyes,

Cheryl was gone, and Ellen was the only person for miles able to hear the driveway's gravel crunching under her feet. She got into her car but, before turning over the engine, texted Cheryl.

Come back at ten mins before 4AM if you're serious.

. . .

Roland's heart slammed in his chest as he guided his gray sedan onto the shoulder of Wickham Road. The crunching of dead leaves underfoot welcomed him into the forest, and red and brown finches flitted through the branches above him. He dug his fists deeper into the pockets of his parka, as if reaching for some warmer place, but reluctantly removed one to retrieve the map and compass from his back pocket.

A little further north, and a little more east.

A close and sudden rustling stopped him in his tracks. Dead ahead and framed against a dark and mangled thicket, a great buck drilled holes into Roland's soul with its eyes, dark and beady little things, hollow like gun bores. Brown blobs shuffled in the foliage behind him. The buck stood handsome and tall, its chest up and accented with a tuft of snow-white fur, its legs rigid, its eyes firm. Roland didn't want to take off his glasses because he didn't want to move, but in locking eyes with the buck, he swore he saw—even sensed—a slight quiver in its jaw. No other muscle moved within its regal body, not even an ear twitch. One by one, two spotted fawns and a doe emerged from the foliage behind it and skirted off into a grove of maple trees.

The buck remained for some time after its family had fled to safety. It would not release Roland's gaze, even after taking two steps in the direction of its family and holding one hoof aloft in anticipation of a sprint. Something held it there, offering a part of itself in exchange for a part of Roland's, sending a message the mortal man couldn't receive. Roland opened his mouth to speak, but nothing came out. When he blinked twice to reset his sight, the buck was gone.

Roland looked at the map and the compass, and determining he was close, trekked on. His breath clouds, like the pines he now entered, grew heavier and more frequent. His toes hardened, and his face stung in the debilitating cold.

In this deeper realm of wood, his footsteps seemed to echo in a way they hadn't before, ticking his anxiety up a notch and goading him into incessantly glancing over his shoulders at nothing. For a moment, he considered his state of isolation and his paltry selection of options if something happened out here. A brighter patch of land ahead refocused him.

He didn't know what to expect upon reaching the glade, but it wasn't this. Roland first thought its surface was composed of clay, before realizing it was completely covered in dried blood. Hoof marks, much larger than the deer's or any creature he knew, littered the ground in chaotic patterns. Fifteen funnel-shaped divots, as if swaths of dirt had melted into the earth's core, dotted the otherwise smooth landscape. A rusting folding chair, there for who knows how long, lay tossed to the edge of the tree line.

In the center of the glade, right between two of the divots, something shiny glinted in the sullen morning light. For some reason, Roland thought about his encounter with the buck as he reached for the bloodstained knife on the frozen earth. He tweezed the butt with two fingers before wrapping his right hand around the hilt, squeezing it, getting a feel for its weight.

Holding the knife in his hand, he glanced around the glade, mapping its edges, studying its intricacies, fearing its unknowns. He searched his surroundings for things that could not be seen but felt, and he searched himself for answers to questions even the Grand Elder dared not ask him. He looked at the knife again, zeroing in on the thin line of blood running the length of the blade and the handful of streaks stained on its width.

Two flakes of snow landed on the outside of his glasses.

. . .

A half-inch rim of snow padded Duke's casket when they lowered it into the ground that morning. The circle of bereaved shivered and pelted each other with stony glances through cascades of heavy flakes. His funeral was widely attended, not just by residents of Bensalem, but by a veritable smorgasbord of state and local police. They dressed not in black, but in formal iterations of their uniforms. Cheryl tried not to stare too long at the ones she knew—the Martinsville sheriff and his deputy in their navy blues, Sperryville's sheriff in his brown. It was not lost on her how quickly the wake turned into a gladhanding session amongst these old, white men, and she couldn't help but sense a twinge of doubt as they all congratulated her through toothy grins.

The tight ball of tension building in her skull over the course of these conversations immediately evaporated when she stepped out of the funeral home and noticed her team—and only her team—huddled together under the building's awning. Monica bearhugged her, and Brady clamped a hand on her shoulder and jostled it with a force that seemed to forget he was twice her size. His face was beet red and puffy with tears.

"Gonna say anything, boss?" he asked.

"Aw hell," she said, not looking at him.

All stood and watched her, wanting but not expecting.

"Well, I, uh, I guess I'd just say thanks. Thanks for being so mature and professional about all this. I know it's been a hard coupla' days." She stopped to absorb their faces again and cleared her throat. "Actually, I know it's been a hard few months."

A slight change in Monica's disposition triggered Cheryl's memory of their fateful walk up the hill at Hank's Horse Farm. She remembered the ghastly smell of Hank's corpse. The squishy pop his errant eyeball made when Monica accidentally stepped on it in the driveway. The tears in Monica's eyes that early morning, not unlike the ones forming now.

Cheryl looked at Brady and remembered his dispatch call during her graveyard shift. She remembered chiding him over using the words "kinda nasty" over public radio, thinking that would be the worst thing to come out of it. Staring at him now, she wished like hell to go back to that moment, as if maybe another version of her timeline would have omitted the tragedy. That maybe Brady would have just called in a burglary or a fire, or maybe Hank would have just had a heart attack. She considered for a moment what a nice world that would have been.

"Listen, guys. I wanna tell you all something," she said. "I loved Duke as much as anybody, but I wanna do things a little different. Okay? I wanna... find a way to get to the bottom of this. To the truth. It ain't right what happened to this town, and somethin' tells me it ain't over."

A couple of them nodded.

"And God love him, but I don't think Duke was really goin' about it the right way. I don't think I've ever said that out loud before, but... well, that's how I feel. It's how I felt then, and it's how I feel now. Thing is, if he was somehow avoiding the truth in all this, I'm certain he chose that path for a good reason. He was a good man. A very good man."

She glanced over her shoulder to see if anyone else was in

earshot. No one was, but she leaned in and softened her voice anyway.

"Guys, I think we're up against a very difficult challenge here. A dangerous one. I don't quite understand it, but I'm trying to. And just like last summer, I'm gonna need y'all's help." She went around the circle with her eyes, locking on to each one of them for a second before moving to the next.

"We're with you, Sheriff," Monica whispered.

They all nodded.

Cheryl did not. She maintained her focus and kept talking.

"I'm gonna need that same professionalism, that same maturity. I'm even gonna go as far as to say I need you all to be brave. Trust each other, trust me. If you see somethin' you don't like, this is our circle of trust. Right here. Y'all got that?"

Everyone affirmed her.

"We're gonna figure this shit out."

. . .

Skylar's phone pinged during her AP Biology teacher's opening monologue. The students surrounding her turned their heads. One of them snickered. She didn't return their glances.

A text message from Ram: *I think I found something.*

She slung her bag over her shoulder and strode past her classmates, all still trapped in their boxy wooden desks. The claps of her Dr. Martens trampled the teacher's drone, and she offered a fleeting, "I have to go to the bathroom," without turning around as she left the class.

Twenty minutes later, she half parked, half slid into the New Colonial Heights parking lot. Her boot heels sunk completely through the snow, and powdery trails flicked from her toes as she brushed across an otherwise pristine white canvas.

Ram was the only one home when she opened the unlocked door. He was huddled over a stack of notebooks while Alice in Chains blared through stereo speakers. Two of Skylar's Grimoire pictures lit up two computer screens next to another stack of notebooks. One of the notebooks was open to reveal pages packed with handwritten scrawlings.

Skylar didn't say hello. She just wrapped her arms around him from behind and kissed his cheek. He reached for the volume knob and turned the stereo down, and then he kissed her on the lips. Ram's long, straight black hair seemed to blend seamlessly into the black T-shirt he wore with the words "SO FUCKING WHAT" stamped in bold white text.

"All right, you ready for this?" he said, grabbing a notebook from the stack.

"What'd you find?" she said.

"Well, I haven't read everything. I think there's a lot of missing info in the second half of the book."

"I can get it tonight. I'll clear my memory card."

"This might be hard to hear, Sky." He closed the notebook and looked up with concerned eyes. "Your mother is in a cult."

"Shut the fuck up. No, she's not."

"No, she is. They eat babies every third Monday of—"

Skylar punched him in the arm. Ram laughed.

"Okay, okay," he said. "That's not it, but it's kind of close."

"Come on, stop fucking around."

He opened the notebook again and ran his fingers across the pages as he spoke. "So, long story short, it sounds like there is actually a very strange cult, order, religion-type thing here, or was at one time. It revolves around this figure called the New King Salomon and the idea of New Atlantis." He made air quotes as he said the last phrase. "And just to be clear, I don't think your mother is involved."

"That name. New King Salomon. It was in Sheriff Quinlan's note."

"Whoa, shit. Really?"

"Yeah."

"So then, it must be still active, right? In some form? From what I can tell"—he flipped a page—"New King Salomon was some puritanical guy from England who brought a bunch of people here and founded Bensalem. It sounds like he was very interested in alchemy, and they thought Bensalem would be a kind of utopia using alchemy, or some shit."

Skylar cackled. "Utopia? Clearly didn't work."

"Well, it sounds like he was a real historical figure. Have you ever heard of Johannas Kelpius?"

"No."

"Back in the 1600s, he came over from Europe and founded a fundamentalist commune in the woods of Pennsylvania."

"The Amish?"

"Dude, no. The Amish are super mainstream compared to these people. Kelpius had this weird little pseudo-Christian society that worshiped spirits in the woods. They lived in caves. Some of the writings say he floated on rivers and shit."

"What?"

"I know. It's probably all bullshit, right?"

Skylar studied him for a moment before responding. "I don't know. Is it?"

Ram shrugged. "I'm not sure. A bunch of these guys came here, trying to advance their religious beliefs, and they saw the study of nature as a holy act. Some of them strayed pretty far from secular religion. In Colonial America, they had these networks of books and knowledge exchanges that were very popular among the wealthy and powerful. John Winthrop was a founder of Connecticut, and he was obsessed with the idea of a city on a hill—which kinda sounds like this New Atlantis thing. George Washington and Benjamin Franklin were huge in the Freemasons. Did you know that? They're still one of the most secretive societies in existence."

"All the Puritans thought that way, didn't they?"

"Well, there were, like, hundreds of different belief systems. There was a lot of disagreement, and a lot of them died out. Some of the shit these people believed was extremely fucked up. And I gotta say, if this Grimoire is true and it's talking about our Bensalem, it's super-duper fucked up." He wheeled to his computer and clicked through several photos. "Did you read the part about Judithe Peel?"

"No. Who's that?"

"Here. Take a look at this."

Skylar leaned over his shoulder and read the words etched in the picture on his screen.

148. Judithe Peel, daughter of John, did on her own volition and not in consultation with the New King Salomon release a pestilence unto the chaste Bensalem. Hereupon, four of our men answered the call of God and went into the wood to confront the pestilence. 149. The morrow after two days passed, only Matthew Aubrey, aged sixteen years, returned to Bensalem. We heard his screaming from the edges of the wood. He was unclothed, and he looked upon us with great fear, and he cried for his mother to open his skull and remove the daemon out from the inside. The boy gave his

account unto the New King Salomon, declaring that the pestilence extinguished the other three men, and Matthew Aubrey said it spoke to him these words. 'I am the manifestation of darkness, I am the bastard son of the one you meant to call, I drink the souls of the living, and it is from my darkness which your Kingdom will perish, and you will lay with me to-night.' 150. The boy would not describe the physical state of the daemon, only screaming when asked to do so, only saying its head was forked and that it communicated, not by spoken word, but in silence with its fingers. The boy said that when it laid with him, it was not carnal, but it pulled the boy under the ground where it lay beside him, and there it infected his mind, and the boy could not look away although he wanted to. 151. The girl, Judithe, beseeched the New King Salomon that she had noble intentions, and that she sought to call forth Herne the Hunter, the spirit of our Father's wood, wherefore his protection safeguard the chaste Bensalem from the impurity of the darkness beyond its borders. Hereupon, the girl, Judithe, was put to death by fire under conviction of witchcraft.

Skylar sat on the ground next to Ram's chair.

"Fucked up, huh?" he said.

"Is this real, Ram?"

He looked at the screen and then back at her. "I don't know. I kinda think it is."

"The pestilence?"

"Yeah. In one verse, they call it a pestilence, and then they call it a demon. Whatever it is, I think it killed off a lot of the settlers."

She lowered her tone to a whisper. "He mentioned that too."

"Mentioned what?"

"Sheriff Quinlan. In his note. He said the pestilence was going to kill him."

"Wait. Are you fucking serious?"

She nodded.

Ram clicked his mouse several times and backed away from the screen when he found the picture he was looking for. "Read this part."

55. By the Grace of God: Although our New King Salomon is slain, our dowry-men, and benefactors, and pioneers, and miners have together advanced his methods, and achieved an enlightenment of scientific and spiritual nature, only foretold in the sacred texts. 56. Our joy is measured, wherefore this enlightenment was not achieved in pursuit of a New Atlantis, but in response to our circumstance, wherefore the pestilence, the bastard of Herne the Hunter, summoned to the chaste Bensalem by Judithe Peel, a witch, who by the Grace of God was burned, has poisoned the light of our Kingdom beyond repair. 57. This enlightenment, through strict adherence to the seven steps of transformational alchemy, and guided by scientific and spiritual rigor, yielded the mechanism, which we call the Sentinel, by which we now defend ourselves against the bastard, and the bastard has not eaten in sixteen days. Indeed, the Sentinel is gruesome, and unto the parents of the child required, regrettable, but it is God who teaches us that all actions necessary to pursue a habitable Kingdom are true in His name. We give thanks to the Lord.

Ram spoke into his computer screen. "So, a Sentinel sounds like their way of combating this pestilence. The demon."

"What is a Sentinel?"

"I'm not a chemist, but it sounds like they used transformational alchemy to create something to stop it. And I can't really be sure about this, but they talk about a ritual involving a young boy."

"Oh no."

"I think they're saying they used alchemy to turn a boy into this thing they call the Sentinel. I don't know if it's figurative or literal, but it—"

"Holy shit!" Skylar said, her eyes wide.

"What?"

"Remember that little boy got kidnapped last summer? And Mr. Teakle died? And so did that old lady who worked in the store downtown? Remember all that shit happened?"

"Of course."

"I remember talking to my mom about it. The sheriff was on vacation, but he somehow knew that boy was kidnapped. He knew the whole time, but my mom didn't know. She thought he just went missing, but he said he was kidnapped. And now this book that lays it all out? And then he kills himself? And his fucking suicide note—the last thing he would ever say to anyone—talks about the pestilence and the New King Salomon?"

"What are you saying?"

"I'm saying this shit is still happening. Some part of it must be happening. My mom must know about it!"

"Did you ask her?"

"No, I can't do that yet. I don't want her to know we're on to her."

"Could you imagine if this is still going on? A cult in Bensalem? Some demon killing people in the woods?"

"Wait, what was its name again?"

"What name?"

"It said the bastard of something."

"Oh, Herne the Hunter. Hold on." Ram grabbed another notebook. He rifled through pages until he found a computer-printed picture taped to the inside. He handed it to Skylar.

The picture showed a half-man, half-deer holding a spear and riding a horse. It wore a long brown robe covering what appeared to be a male body, but its head jutted downward like a snout, and huge, gnarled antlers sprawled from its skull.

Ram shook his head. "Apparently this. Herne the Hunter."

Skylar pointed at it. "Is that thing real?"

He shrugged.

She closed the book and handed it back to him. Nirvana played low in the background of their silence.

"Is there any way to stop it?" she said.

"Stop what?"

"Stop the pestilence. Whatever this bastard demon thing is."

"Well, it sounds like the Sentinel is stopping it."

"Apparently not. It killed two people last year."

"I mean, we don't know that for sure."

"But that little boy was kidnapped. Was he supposed to be a Sentinel?"

Ram turned back to the computer and slowly clicked through the photos until he reached the end. "How much more of the book is there?"

"A lot. Probably close to half."

"The answers must be in there." Ram paused to let Kurt Cobain sing to them a tale about a Lake of Fire. "If... they're anywhere."

· · ·

Cheryl felt as if something thicker than blood ran through her as she trudged down Main Street's snow-glazed sidewalk. Seeing no one, she placed a gloved palm on the aluminum door frame of M&J Fine Gifts. The tarp taped around the glass panel that was shattered by vandals last summer buckled in the wind when she inched the door open. It nudged the little old bell that for so many years joyously announced the entry of new patrons. She distinctly remembered the location of that bell, and she made sure not to clamor it, not only to mask her presence, but also because the idea of the bell seemed almost inappropriate now. Any joy associated with Jane Harcourt's store had been swallowed up in its owner's darkness, in the terror that had sent Bensalem into a frenzy and two shotgun shells through the back of Duke Quinlan's throat.

She suppressed whispers of that same terror bubbling under her skin as her boots tossed motes of loose snow across the glass-covered floor. Her pulse quickened while her footsteps slowed, and a film of moisture formed over her lips as clouds of warm breath passed through them. She took off her gloves. With one hand, she doused the corners of the store with her flashlight. Her other palm rested on the butt of her service weapon.

Shelves and end caps once cluttered with a million souvenirs and knick-knacks now held only dust. Jewelry cases that used to glitter in the crisp light of overhead fluorescents were dark and bare. Even Jane's paintings and tapestries had been taken, leaving the interior walls devoid of any texture, save for the occasional bent nail. M&J's only remaining color resided in the wallpaper strips along the edges of the ceiling. Cheryl shone her light up at that odd pattern—gold, trefoil crosses with red roses in their centers—and then back down at the three black lines on the wall behind the counter. Two vertical, one horizontal, stenciling a small door as subtle in the store as she wanted to be right now. She approached, unknowingly tightening the grip on her flashlight. Removing the hand on her gun, she spread her fingers across the unmarked door, planted her boots, and leaned into it with her shoulder.

That putrid, sulfuric smell gushed into her nostrils before the door was open enough to shine her light through. If the smell was bad four months ago, it was worse now, as if the books and chemicals in Jane's lab were rotting corpses, turning the place into a festering, alchemical morgue. Her light bounced off the brick walls of the corridor as she took slow and steady steps forward. She put an elbow to her nose and mouth to mask the odor but quickly pulled it back to grip her gun again, deciding olfactory displeasure was worth the proximity to her weapon.

From the corridor, the lab looked exactly how she remembered it. Jars and beakers containing mysterious substances packed three long tables running the length of the room. A massive, gold-colored cross stood watch over the tables from the back corner. Scribblings of a mad woman littering the walls looked like some kind of alien graffiti, and an explosion of books seemed to touch every inch of the chamber: stacks of books in the corners and on the tables, open books on the floor and in the aisleways.

But just before she reached the end of the corridor and prepared to step into the lab, the harrowing sensation of another presence stopped her dead in her tracks. The sensation sharpened into a pang of deep-seated dread, a dread escaping from the shackles of her memory, slithering up her spine, and triggering a sudden involuntary shudder. She took a deep breath, but it did not quell the uncanny feeling of company in her vicinity. Nor did it get her feet moving again. All it did was flood her lungs with air so rancid she nearly gagged.

"Fucking stop it, Cheryl," she said to herself in a tone not loud enough to be a whisper.

It was as if the portrait of the puritanical man hanging just above the lab's doorway, hanging mere feet from her right now, beamed its twisted energy right through the walls and into her bones. The portrait wasn't even in view yet, but the details she recalled from her first glimpse months ago raged like reignited embers in the charred rubble of her memory—his thin moustache, his thinner smile, his raised left hand, his white eyes.

In a single motion, Cheryl jumped over the threshold and swung both her light and her gun up at the wall behind her.

At him.

There he was, hanging above her in near three-dimensional glory. Glaring at her with white eyes like a bastardized Mona Lisa. Smiling. Holding his left hand aloft.

For the first time, Cheryl noticed the letters etched into the portrait's wood frame: N. K. S. She knew those letters. Not as they were written here, but in the initials of the name Duke had spelled out in his suicide note. As much as she wanted to look away, to run away, her desperation for truth practically begged the New King Salomon to stare at her.

He obliged. She stared back.

Cheryl's shoulders heaved. Her molars grinded under the pressure of her clenched jaw and his palpable gaze. The light and the gun quivered in her hands, and her heart raced. Some small piece of her, the worst piece of her, wanted to put a bullet straight through the canvas between his white eyes.

She paused her breath for a moment and released a long exhale through pursed lips before pacing backwards into the lab.

Cold needles tickled the back of her neck as she considered only the vaguest of maladies she might literally bump into behind her.

Cheryl whispered, "It's just a fuckin' picture," and then repeated in her normal voice, "It's just a fuckin' picture."

Something clattered behind her. A glass broke.

She spun and charged toward the sound. "Don't move! Sheriff's Department!"

Blood surged through her veins. Breath barely escaped her tight and seething jaws. The adrenaline in her legs carried her quickly and confidently, and she kept the light and the gun drilled down toward the disturbance.

The corner of her eye caught wisps of something skitter across the floor. She cocked the gun, knocked down a pile of books while rounding the corner of a lab table, and cast her light into the aisle. Two glassy yellow eyes reflected back at her. She fired a single round. A squeal of pain echoed through the lab.

"Fuck me," she said, walking over to the raccoon convulsing on the floor. Its back feet twitched once, before it fell completely motionless. A stream of blood flowed from the top of its skull and eddied around the corner of a book collecting more dust than an M&J store shelf. She put her light on the cover.

New Atlantis, A Work Unfinished by Sir Francis Bacon.

The title reminded her of words she had read in the massive book she grabbed as she fled the lab in fear last summer. What was it called? The Grimoire... Something Something? Over the last four months, she had promised herself a dozen times she'd try to read it, half of those promises coming in the last few days—the last one just this morning when she finally moved her boxes out of the house and into her new office at the station.

She picked up *New Atlantis* by its top left corner. Thin red drops plopped from the pages as she examined it in her flashlight's beam. She wiped what blood she could on the table's edge and stuffed the book into her back pocket.

Mere inches from where she wiped the blood lay a curious sheet of parchment paper. Drawn in thick, waxy strokes, the ink seemed to depict some kind of scientific process or diagram. Its labels were written in a language she couldn't understand but guessed was Latin, and it was separated into seven panels from left to right. Even though she couldn't read it, she believed it to be some kind of ritual, based on its arcane-looking visuals. The left-most panel showed a pile of colorless dust or powder. Over the next two, the powder turned gray and then black. Cheryl's lips peeled back as she shined her light on the fourth panel, on what appeared to be a young child surrounded by robed figures. In the fifth panel, the child turned black, and in the sixth panel, their arms and legs grew grotesquely long. Something crawled under the skin as she peered at the seventh and final panel, at the depiction of a massive creature with three yellow eyes sketched into a rough mound of a head and fingers extending down to its feet.

Cheryl took two steps back from the table and shined her light back up at the portrait.

She thought about the night of Duke's revelations, the night he spoke of rituals and little boys becoming monsters. About Duke's note, written in two eerily distinct voices and referencing the New King Salomon. About Aaron and Ellen Dreyer describing a creature with three eyes and long fingers. She even remembered the three giant yellow circles painted on the inside of the barn at Hank's Horse Farm.

Yet as a picture of truth slowly came together in her mind, the scourge of this horrid puritanical man continued to trample her thoughts. The novelty and historical misplacement of this man, the sheer idea of this strange pilgrim occupying a space in Duke's heart so large he felt compelled to name him in his last earthly message—a message addressed directly to Cheryl.

"Who the fuck are you?" she asked.

She strobed her light back over the raccoon and nudged it with a boot to make sure it was dead. It was. She picked it up by the tail and sighed.

"I'm sorry, fella. Let's get you outta here."

. . .

"Shit," Skylar said under her breath.

The dim glow of a winter afternoon wringing out the last of its light filled the window in the McNamaras' home office. Skylar shuffled across the carpet floor to the table where the boxes had been. She texted Ram.

The book is gone!! Think my mom took it to her office.

Downstairs, Rick lorded over a pot billowing with steam on the stove. He stirred its contents in methodical circles and leaned into the smell. Skylar opened the fridge beside him and pulled a cheese stick from the crisper.

"Learn anything worthwhile in school today?" he said.

Skylar sat down at the table and dangled a razor-thin slice of cheese over her mouth. "Did you know there's a cult in Bensalem?

"Oh. Is that so?"

She pulled off another slice, somehow thinner than the last one. "Yeah. They do human sacrifices and shit."

Rick turned around and peered at her over his glasses but still maintained his stirring. "Skylar Mary, we have discussed the dropping of s-bombs. Have we not?"

"Sorry. They do human sacrifices and other terrible things."

Rick turned back to his pot and pushed his glasses back up the bridge of his nose.

"Seriously, though," Skylar persisted.

"Is that what you learned in school today?"

The front door slammed, and Cheryl stomped snow off her boots in the foyer. Skylar had peeled many slices from her cheese stick by the time her mother walked warily into the kitchen.

"Hey," she said, kissing Rick on the cheek. "Hey, you," she said to Skylar.

"Could I talk to you for a minute?" Skylar said.

Rick and Cheryl looked at each other.

"Me?" Cheryl asked.

Skylar nodded.

"Sure, honey, what's up?"

Skylar bumped her father with her eyes, indicating she wanted to talk alone. "Girl stuff."

Rick dropped the wooden spoon and put his hands in the air, as if placed under arrest. "I'll see myself out."

He left, and Cheryl rolled her eyes while picking up the spoon. "You okay, Sky?"

"I actually don't wanna talk about girl stuff."

"Oh. Okay."

"I was looking for my CD player in your office the other day, and I accidentally found that old book. The Grimoire."

Cheryl stopped stirring but didn't look behind her. Her body just went stiff.

Skylar gave her mother a moment to reply but prodded when she realized one wasn't coming. "Are you mad? I'm sorry."

Cheryl resumed stirring at roughly a quarter of her original speed. "It's okay. Just… just stay away from that stuff, would ya?"

Skylar lowered her tone. "I also saw Sheriff Quinlan's note."

Cheryl dropped the spoon and turned around. Skylar expected a harder face than what she saw.

"Please," Cheryl said softly, "listen to me when I ask you to stay away from that stuff."

Skylar reciprocated her mother's soft tone, round plops of boiling water behind her voice. "It's true, isn't it?"

Cheryl pulled the chair across from Skylar and sat in it. "Skylar, I'm gonna ask you again. Please, stay out of this. I don't know if any of it's true, and I tend to believe it's not. Duke was not well. He was very old."

"But clearly he must have believed in it. At least some of it, right? I read some of that book. I wasn't trying to snoop or anything. I just... I just... for some reason, it was so interesting. It was like I felt connected to it somehow. Have you read it? Do you understand it?"

"Listen to me," Cheryl said, taking Skylar's hands in her own. The bones in Cheryl's hands stood out like striated steel rods. "There ain't nothin' weird goin' on in this town. You've been here seventeen years. You're not a child anymore. You've always been mature for your age. Think about it, Sky. How could something like that exist in this town?"

"Something like what?"

A sharp fizz on the stove tore their attention away from the conversation.

"Shit!" Cheryl said, rushing over to a pot overflowing with white fizz.

Rick stumbled back into the room a few steps behind her.

"Dad, did you hear that?"

Both parents turned around, Cheryl's face raked with concern. She discreetly shook her head while shooting daggers into her daughter's eyes.

"Did I hear what?"

"Mom dropped an s-bomb."

Rick peered at her under his glasses. Cheryl stifled a laugh.

"Come on! It was boiling over! There's a difference between an emergency s-bomb and a... I don't know... an editorial s-bomb!"

"See?" Skylar said. "I'm getting it from Mom. She's a really bad influence on me."

"Hey! Now—Hey!" Cheryl said.

Skylar got up from the table, swooped her hands through the arms of her hoodie, and kissed both parents on the cheek.

"Where you goin'?" Rick said.

"Ram's."

. . .

Roland stepped on the gas, and the sedan's back tires squealed again in the snow. He got out and frowned at the snowbound tires, stained in the red glare of the taillights. His sigh projected a breath cloud far and wide enough to obscure the entirety of the uphill driveway leading to Hank's Horse Farm.

Looking around and seeing nothing but darkness, hearing only the choked purr of the engine, Roland decided maybe it was better to approach quietly anyway. He turned off the car, closed the door silently, and started marching up the hill.

He couldn't put his finger on his emotions—a mix of anxiousness, eagerness, tiredness, and fear—and he tried not to imagine all the ways in which this could go wrong. Instead, he simply focused on the snowy gravel in front of him, putting one foot in front of the other, syncing his breath with his pace.

He brought no light with him, preferring to force his eyes to adjust to the darkness, and saw nothing lit at the top of the hill. He wouldn't have been devastated if stood him up, as meeting with the Elders felt more like a formality than anything. It was impossible to predict how they would react to such a senior ranking member of the Order of the Old Roses, never forgetting there was no love lost between his boss and the old cleric. He didn't even know what he would see when he got to Hank's house. How many Elders were there? How old were they? That they even received and responded to his message—a note he had left in the glade and returned to find scribbled with a proposed meeting time and place—was somewhat of a miracle.

Roland stopped when he reached the top of the hill. Hank's abandoned house and stables broadcasted a chilling lifelessness, a terminal stagnation known only by those relegated to unkempt prisons and purgatories, waiting to die, begging to die. A capsized crescent moon and an array of hanging stars bounced hard blue light off the snowy courtyard. He looked up, and his eyes traced the outline of the dipper, its handle burned into the sky like a witch's fingerprints.

He put a boot on Hank's first step and held it there, listening. There was no sound, but there was presence. Roland felt the vague eyes of another, maybe many, stitch themselves to his skin, and he walked up the remainder of the steps bathed in an invisible filth that was not his own.

The door's rusty hinges wailed in the night. Roland sighed silently and stepped inside. He stood there for a moment, door open, feet spread, taking in the place. Hank's house was a tomb, a frigid mix of decaying things and cold air. It was darker inside than it was outside, as only a few blue diagonal streaks of moonlight speared the eroding walls. Roland scanned the entrances to two rooms facing each other from the foyer. He took a long look at the carpeted staircase at the end of the hall.

"Hello?" he said.

The entrance hall's floorboards cried out in pain under his footsteps. Huge burlap sacks leaking grain lined the walls of the room to his left, what appeared to be a dining room that had fallen into disrepair. The room to his right was empty, too, a living room bracketed by bookcases and coated in an explosion of loose paper. He didn't step foot in the kitchen after walking past the staircase, electing to slink his head around the door jambs.

An old analog clock ticked above the sink. Its gruff, mechanical clicks found nowhere to hide in the stillness of the house. Roland watched the second hand chug upward with caution, as if almost knowing it was the last remnant of a living world, warning any other who would approach to flee or risk becoming part of the graveyard. But Hank's house wasn't even a graveyard. It was something worse, a place unmarked and unvisited, literally littered with memories that died along with their owner at the long, terrible hands of the Nothus.

He released the tension in his shoulders and turned around, but after a single step toward the door, his shoulders, arms, and jaw clenched in reaction to what he saw.

A shadowy figure now stood in the front doorway, draped in the blue light of the moon. The silhouette was completely black, a cutout of the night placed directly between Roland and safety.

"Are you the cleric?" Roland said.

Another figure stepped into the hall from the dining room. A creaking floorboard above him revealed another at the top of the stairs.

"My name is Roland Pierce, First Order Deacon." He tried to look at all three of them at once, hoping the faintest of movements from them might indicate some intent to communicate.

Two more stepped out from the living room.

A soft voice from behind echoed. "Hello."

Roland spun around to face a figure wearing a brown robe just inches away, and he took an instinctive step back.

"Are you the cleric?" Roland said.

The edge of the figure's hood extended well past its face. "We have no longer a cleric. Mortua est."

"Then, who are you? Are you the local chapter?"

"We are the envoys."

Roland glanced behind him. He had lost track of how many there were in the first floor rooms and on the staircase, but however many there were, it now felt like their number had doubled, all sliently staring at him. A moonbeam cast across the edge of one of them revealed long, terrible fingers dangling from the sleeve of a red robe.

"And are you the leader of the envoys? I'd like to help you. The Order can help you."

"Servus humilis sum."

Roland cleared his throat. "All right. If there's no leader here, then... who do you serve?"

"We serve the New King Salomon. We seek the light of a New Atlantis." The figure's voice had a way of slithering. It held consonants for too long and sometimes skipped over vowels, and its breathiness indicated a struggle to emerge, as if the owner wasn't used to speaking or did so with great discomfort.

"Good. Good. So do I." Roland peeled off a glove and extended a hand.

What Roland shook was not a normal hand. The palm and the knuckles felt like human flesh, but the fingers were hard and cold and extended nearly around Roland's wrist. When the figure pulled its hand away, that's exactly what Roland saw: a hand half-human, half-Nothus. He swallowed the lump of fear that had been building since he stepped foot in the house.

Roland glanced behind him again, and noticing the other hooded figures were closer to him, pivoted so his back was to the wall. He cleared his throat. "As—as I said, the Grand Elder and I would like to help you. We'd like to—" Roland paused to glare at a red-robed figure now within inches of his face. "We understand the Sentinel is weak. We'd like to help you by ending the cycle of Sentinels so that no one has to endure that pain again."

For the first time, Roland noticed the dark stain surrounding a hole in the brown robe of the one who spoke. It flapped slightly as snake-like words were spoken.

"I know the pain of the Sentinel. I, too, spent many years lying with the Nothus Noctis."

"The Grand Elder—"

"Senem magnum nōn servīmus. We serve the New King Salomon. We, too, wish to end the use of Sentinels, but we do not need your help. The king has instructed us that the Nothus Noctis will bear unto us New Atlantis' light."

Roland looked at the brown-robed figure quizzically. "What?"

"We have no use for spells and Sentinels. The New King Salomon has shown us the light. Lēgātī ei sumus voluptātemque eius adhaerēmus."

"And... what exactly do you believe to be the New King Salomon's will?" As soon as Roland asked the question, a question he had considered greatly in the icy silence, he slid his foot toward the front door.

The robed figures did not put hands on him or attempt to stop him. They just turned to keep facing him as floorboards creaked under his steps. The brown-robed figure raised its hands above its head and removed its hood. It stepped into the moonlight. Roland gasped.

Half of the head's features were human, half were something

else. One eye was a tranquil blue surrounded by white, but the other was a glowing red orb, twice the size of a human eye. Horns or small antlers sprouted from a head of scraggly gray hair. Loose and broken skin hung from its jaw, exposing the bone on the entire left side of its face. In some places, the bone had been stained brown instead of ivory white. It uttered one soft word from a snout-like mouth that extended from its face like a bloated tumor.

"Rēgnāre."

Its jaw dropped from its socket, and with a wiry hand, it pushed it back into place with a loud snap.

Roland brushed past the figure standing in the doorway, tearing the fabric of its robe in his haste. He couldn't make out the figure's finer features under the veil of the house's darkness. All he could see was a ripped red hood hanging from an antler on its head.

He scampered down the steps and bolted down the driveway, looking back only once to see the robed figures gathered on the porch, not pursuing, just staring at him in silence.

. . .

Cheryl closed her eyes and massaged the rims of her knee caps. They throbbed like stones pulled from the bed of a freezing river infused with the angry chill of winter, transmitting their cold, dull pain to the surrounding muscles and tendons. These first days of winter had wrapped their chilly tentacles around her, and even though her arthritis had long been an annual phenomenon, every year she held onto the hope the aching would spare her. Maybe her body would magically revert to its thirty-five-year-old state. Maybe this year, the winter would be warmer, or she'd finally build tolerance enough to put the pain out of mind. But every year, it got colder and it got worse. While her knees throbbed, she struggled to keep the rest of her body awake, nestled warm and weary in her down jacket and baking in the blast of the unit's heat vents. All that kept her awake was the lingering stench, the lab's rotten sulfur still lingering in her nostrils.

When the neon-green dashboard clock morphed from 03:59 to 04:00, she shook off her fatigue. The silhouette of Ellen Dreyer standing in her lit bedroom window stuck to Cheryl's rearview like a yellow and black postage stamp.

04:01

She kept her eyes locked on the meadow across Wickham Road. All the world ahead was bleak and frozen, and though the headlight control stick tried to seduce her into activting it, she remembered Ellen's strict instructions of no big lights. Small flashlights were fine. Car headlights were not.

04:02

Because even if they didn't quite know why, the Dreyers knew too much direct light on the Sentinel would paralyze it and prevent it from its nightly task of Nothus suppression. They had learned this the hard way four months ago, and Hank Teakle paid for their mistake with his life. Cheryl had heard all about it from Aaron and Ellen in separate accounts, and then again later from Duke. She didn't believe any of it back then, but she was starting to—

And then, at 04:03, whatever doubts Bensalem's new sheriff had about the twisted tales she'd been told evaporated. The pine trees to her right rustled softly, tumbling clumps of snow from their boughs, and a shadow of gargantuan size stepped into the moonlight.

"Mother of God," Cheryl whispered.

The Sentinel's head nearly crested the tree line, an impossible height for any organism she could imagine. The moon's glow cast a soft blue shine off its surface, a surface that appeared entire in its coverage of the creature. It was pewter-colored, almost silvery, but a dark mist shrouded its details and seemed to track its movement. Legs thicker than tree trunks plodded through the meadow, and hands and fingers dreamt up from some hellish nightmare swung by its sides. Cheryl found herself focusing on a triangle of yellow lights where a stump of a head bulged above its shoulders.

She glanced at the reflection of an unmoved Ellen Dreyer in the rearview, gathered her flashlight, and stepped out of the patrol car. Her boots crunched under the gravel of the Dreyers' driveway as she got out, and she stood behind her open car door, holding the flashlight on the creature. A cloud billowed forth from a jaw slack with the shock of the monstrosity before her.

The Sentinel crunched deep divots into the snow on its way through the meadow. Cheryl took cautious steps down the driveway, painting the Sentinel in her light and letting the sight of it—the belief of it—flood her eyes and her mind.

She could have sworn, for a split second, this largest of creatures offered the faintest of adjustments to its left, toward her, but her cognition was crudely interrupted by a shrill ring erupting in her ears. Cheryl winced and put her hands to her head, trying but failing to block out the razor-sharp ring. The muscles in her legs started melting under a now-racing heart and hyperventilating lungs. Ellen yelled something from the house.

Cheryl dropped the flashlight, fell to her knees, and clutched her chest with weakened fingers. Her hyperventilating turned to a coughing fit, and the brass clang of the ring hardened into a heavy drum pounding her brain.

"Mark! Mark! No!" Ellen yelled, somewhat closer.

Cheryl's racing pulse slammed on the brakes and tanked.

Her eyes rolled back in her head, and her world went black.

"No, sweetie! Don't hurt her, baby! Don't hurt her! Mommy's here!"

. . .

Skylar's eyes blasted open. Her neck and back prickled in an ice-cold marinade of sweat. Every muscle in her body felt like lead.

"Sky? You okay?" Ram was propped up on his elbow and gazing at her.

"What happened?"

"You were screaming. You had a nightmare." He put a hand on her cheek. "You okay, babe? You're freezing. You're sweating."

She reached for him. "Where's my mom?"

"What? Your mom? She's at your house. You're at my apartment."

"I think something's wrong. Something's really wrong."

Ram pulled both of them up to a seated position in his bed. He stroked the backs of her arms, trying to warm her. "What's wrong?"

"It's my mom. Something's wrong with my mom." Skylar closed her eyes. Waves of twisted shapes cascaded through her mind. They crashed and blended into each other, spinning and drowning into the centroid of her mind's eye. "I think it took place in the woods."

"What?"

"Something was happening to her. I don't remember faces or sounds. I think Hank Teakle was there too. He... he had no face."

"What... what were they doing?"

"I don't know. I just felt her there with others. Something about chemicals."

"You feelin' okay? You want me to drive you home? You're really pale."

"They were doing something to her. I felt her burning."

Ram released her arms and shifted back, his brow furrowed in confusion.

She looked up at him. "And there was something dark. Something so dark."

"The Nothus?"

Skylar shook her head. "Something else."

They stared at each other in silence, hearts beating together in the nascent dawn.

DAY 5

No sun greeted the day, only a sleepy mural of overcast skies. Gloom hung heavy over an intermittent landscape of snow and exposed ground. Whatever magic yesterday's snowfall had bestowed upon Bensalem was now sundered under a hard, white crust suffocating the grass, and dirty, melting boulders lining the roads. Even the deciduous trees—the poplars, maples, hickories, and oaks—had shaken away their white sleeves. Only the paper-white mountains, high and mighty in the lofty distance, seemed unfazed.

A murder of crows carved through the sky above the ice-coated eaves of Ellen Dreyer's hillside house and swarmed the branches of a naked red maple in the backyard. It was as if a divine hand guided them to this one and only tree set amidst the thousands. They settled there, and they picked at themselves and bristled in the frigid wind, a wind that cast about the malice of a young winter and penetrated even the most well-insulated dens.

It seeped through the cracks of Ellen's kitchen door and sent a shudder through Cheryl's shoulders, nearly upsetting the coffee mug she gripped with both hands. She was sitting at the kitchen table, and she'd been making small talk with Ellen's mother about the more mundane details of rural law enforcement, teetering on falsehoods regarding her presence in her daughter's home.

Ellen came downstairs with Caleb and asked her mother to watch television with him so she could speak with Cheryl alone. Her face sagged, and the bags under her eyes stuck out like fresh bruises.

Cheryl took a long sip of coffee. "I should be headin' out. Thanks again for letting me crash on your couch."

"It's all right. I'm glad you got to see him. I was hoping he wouldn't do that to you, but after what he's gone through, he doesn't think anyone's safe. He's just scared. He did that to Aaron when they first met. He did it to me. He'll do it to anyone who he doesn't know or trust. It wasn't personal."

Cheryl sipped again. "It's really okay. You warned me. I'm just fine."

"What did my mom ask you?" Ellen said.

"What have you told her?"

Ellen chuckled. "What have I told her?" She fumbled with the coffee pot, clanking it crudely in the coffee maker before filling a cup and taking a seat across from Cheryl at the table. "Have I told her about the monster that lives outside our house? Have I told her there's a boy, or maybe even a man, that's been trapped inside it for the last forty years?" Ellen put her mouth to her mug and held it there as tones of manufactured television happiness drifted in from the living room. She stared not at Cheryl, but through her, her sclera bloodshot and opaque, her gaze scalding some deep and latent layer of her soul. "Have I told her that I talk to him to keep him company? That I read him stories at night to give him an ounce of joy? If he's even capable of joy?" The muscles in Ellen's neck and jaw spasmed, and she seemed to suppress a hitching breath. "Does she know that I've... that we've become so close that I can hear him crying? That I think about him and what's happening to him and his pain more than I think about my own son? My son who—"

Cheryl reached across the table. She took Ellen's hand and inched her chair closer, leaning in close. "Help me get him outta there. Help me save him. I need your knowledge and your guts. Let's save him and bring him into our world, yeah? Let's get him out of there and kill whatever's doin' this. Let's end this fucking insanity. Because this is insanity. That a little, innocent boy has been trapped in that thing for... seriously, forty years?"

Ellen turned to an unassuming Caleb standing in the doorway. She beckoned him toward her, and she scooped him up and clutched him when he came. "I—I don't know if we can," she choked through tears.

"Why not?"

"I have no idea how to get him out. He has no idea how to get out."

"What do you know about how he got in there in the first place?"

"Caleb, could you give Mommy a minute to talk to her friend?"

Caleb offered something resembling a nod and spilled off his mother's lap.

"I don't know anything beyond what I saw when we found Caleb," Ellen said. "Jane must have known."

"What did you see when you found Caleb again?"

"He was—" Ellen winced and covered her mouth. "He was tied up in a burlap sack. This gray shit was smeared all over him. His jaw was dislocated, and there was a huge rock inside his mouth."

"Yesterday, I went to Jane's old lab. It's hidden behind her store. I saw this diagram of what looked like a ritual of some kind they must perform to create these Sentinels."

"Really?"

"I mean, it was just crude drawings, and I didn't understand the text, but it looked like a process to combine chemicals and a child to create a monster."

"She was preparing to do that to Caleb. She did that to Mark. She did it to her own son."

"Have you ever heard of something called the New King Salomon? Or something called New Atlantis?"

Ellen leaned back in her chair and took a deep breath. "No."

"Do you know anything about the thing the Sentinel goes out and fights? That's what you said, right? That he goes out every night at the same time and fights something?"

"Aaron and I followed Mark into the woods that night, the night we found Caleb. It was so dark we couldn't see anything. Mark led us really far into the forest. Aaron said he saw two red eyes, and then something happened to his head. Sort of like what happened to you last night but worse."

"Did the Sentin—Mark—did Mark do that?"

"I don't think so. I think Mark and whatever that thing is have this ability to crawl inside our heads. Aaron said he saw Mark in his dreams. He used the phrase 'running in the back of my dreams.' I think that means they can basically invade our minds and our dreams. I think they share a lot of commonalities."

"Did you see this other thing?"

"No, it was too dark. Aaron just saw the eyes. We heard them fighting, and we thought we were going to die. I actually thought Aaron was already dead. He dropped so incredibly fast."

"Where was it? Deep into the woods, you said? Do you remember where?"

"No, honestly. The only way to find it would be to follow Mark."

Cheryl released Ellen's hand and leaned back in her chair. She looked around the kitchen, its high ceiling, stainless steel appliances, marble countertops. "You have a beautiful home here, Dr. Dreyer. You have a beautiful and wonderful family."

Ellen kept staring straight ahead.

"I fear this thing is much bigger than Jane and Mark. There's some kind of odd following attached to all this, some kind of religion. I found this huge, old book in Jane's lab, something out of a movie, that I think is their Bible."

Ellen looked at her. "Jane's religion?"

Cheryl nodded. "Yeah. I think that's the root of all this."

Ellen shook her head and looked away again.

"If there's a ritual to create a Sentinel, maybe there's a ritual to reverse the process. Jane took Caleb because she wanted to save Mark, right?"

"I don't know. That's what Aaron said she told him in a dream."

"Was she in your dreams too?"

"Only Aaron's. I've never had dreams about this. I don't know why. I even asked Mark to come see me in my dreams, and he hasn't. I don't know why it happens to some and not others."

"What did Jane say about Mark and Caleb in his dream?"

"I don't know."

Cheryl stood and zipped up her coat. "Dr. Dreyer, I'd love your help on this. I'd love to see whatever this thing is that Mark is fighting. I'm getting to the goddamned bottom of this, but I don't know if I can do it alone."

Ellen sighed. "I don't know if I'm up for that. I'm weak. I'm not like I was back then. Something happened to me. I have to protect Caleb. I have to be here for Caleb."

"I understand. I really do. But if you change your mind, you know where to find me." Cheryl started toward the door.

"Thank you. I will."

Cheryl turned around once more before leaving. "I'm serious, you know. I want to get him outta there."

Ellen's glazed eyes just stared ahead.

. . .

Skylar had driven back from Ram's and slipped into the house before her mother came home that morning. Rick slept in on Saturdays, so she showered, raided the cereal drawer, and burrowed deep into the living room couch. Even fortressed in blankets, the morning's chill found her and touched her bones. After flipping through the basic cable channels twice over, she stretched out and closed her eyes.

Her body tried to sleep, but her mind wouldn't let it, instead projecting the murky dregs of last night's dream on the backs of her eyelids. Green and yellow blobs danced on a black floor. They swirled around a handful of blinking stars set upon an altar and slowly sharpened. She interpreted the yellow as a young woman, face blurred, knelt over the stars and in front of a green latticework of trees. The young woman's hands fiddled with the stars to adjust their brightness, as if the hands of God herself calibrated the conditions of an infant universe. As they did in the dream, the young woman's hands turned suddenly red and she lurched back from the altar. It was at this moment, too, that a surge of visceral dread, a dread entirely corporal to Skylar and taking no visual form, washed out the stars, the trees, and the young woman alike, and the red upon her hands bloomed into an immense napalm, becoming a prism through which her fear was amplified. Her vision saw beyond its bounds, and then, there entered at the edges of the napalm a pink glow that soothed the red, slowly constricting it, smothering it into itself. But as the pink glow grew, so too did Skylar's fear, as the sights and smells and sounds of her mother, some she had not sensed since her very first moments of life, surged through the catalog of her memory.

The snapping of the front door pulled her back to reality. She did not open her eyes. A shuffling of shoes, the jangling of keys, a whisper of footsteps, and a soft kiss on her forehead. Skylar could not read her mother's mind, but she felt with every fiber of her being the woman's heart as she stood above her. Flesh of my flesh.

More faint footsteps. The smack of the refrigerator's closing, the clinking of a glass, the screeching of a stool across the kitchen floor. A resigned sigh.

Her soft voice.

"Mornin', Derek. You good? Amber good? Noland good? Yeah. Yeah. Yeah, I'm all right."

A pause.

"So, listen. I saw it last night. The good one. The Sentinel. Yeah. Yeah, I did. The Dreyer place, yeah. Just like they said. Footprints might even still be in the snow."

Another sigh. A chance for him to speak.

"I know. I know. I can hardly believe it. No, not yet. Well, that's what's next. Ellen doesn't know where it is but said the Sentinel does. Mark, by the way. She's convinced Mark Harcourt is the Sentinel. That, I'm a little more skeptical of."

The smacking of an empty glass against the table.

"I'm gonna go out there again tonight. Gonna get eyes on the Sentinel and follow it. I need you to hold down the fort here, but be ready if I holler."

A barrage of incoming questions.

"I don't know. I don't know. Yeah. I don't think so. No. I mean, tell 'em if you want to, but I'd rather not at this point. Yeah. Okay. Okay, yeah. 4:00 a.m. I don't know. I don't know that either."

A softening of tones.

"Okay. Yeah, that's all good. I'll be here if you need me. Roger that. Okay, later, Deputy."

Skylar turned her mother's words over in her head for a quiet moment, while something scraped across the caverns of her mind in an attempt to escape.

...

Ellen strode down the corridor of the ER, whisking past a score of blinking, buzzing patient-filled rooms. Her hands were balled in her scrub pockets, and her sneakers squelched with each step on the waxy tile. A ponytail of long, black hair swung from shoulder to shoulder.

"Taking ten," she said to another doctor standing in the hall.

He didn't look up from his clipboard.

Ellen opened the refrigerator in the break room. Its shelves were bursting with condiments, brown paper bags, and single cans of various sodas. She snatched a glass container from the crisper and sat alone at the table in the center of the room. Before opening it, she put her hands on her lower back and arched her spine. A sigh of relief accompanied three loud pops.

Her cell phone rang in her pocket. She placed it on the table without answering after seeing "Cheryl Police" flash across the screen.

Those letters had not adorned her phone since that wretched day, and seeing them now sucked her right back into her person hell. Like reading something in a dream, she didn't process the actual words, just resurrected their pattern from a dimly lit cul de sac of memory.

Cheryl Police.

Those two words flashing across her phone brought her back to the forest, the sweltering heat, the hollow cries of "Caleb!" from Derek Brady and the rest of the search party bellowing through the trees, cries that carried on long after she had stopped shouting herself, long after she had decided her missing son wasn't there. They kickstarted the gears that had turned in her mind as she trudged through the pain and the sweat, as she sifted through the details and the chaos of that day, only to realize the "monster" Aaron had discovered wandering the meadow at night had some kind of connection to Caleb's disappearance.

When the phone stopped ringing, the screen went blank, and her mind jumped forward two weeks. Aaron had just accepted a plea deal of pleading guilty to manslaughter for Virginia's minimum one-year sentence—a slaughter Ellen had actually committed in an incandescent rage when Jane Harcourt came to their house and admitted to kidnapping Caleb. Her son. Her only son. Her greatest accomplishment in a life packed with accolades. The thing she loved more than her own life.

Ellen's rage in that moment was so true and precise, her conscience so utterly clear, that her muscles didn't even tense when she fired her father's old .22 gauge at Jane's abdomen, reloaded, and fired again at the base of her skull. She barely even glanced down at the red puddle growing on Jane's brown cloak or her decimated skull. To this day, neither Ellen nor her therapist knew whether it was fire or ice running through her veins in that meadow, but whatever it was, it was pure.

Yet instead of finding closure in her son's safety and his captor's demise, Ellen found only loneliness. Cheryl had taken Aaron away from her. Caleb still hadn't spoken a word since his kidnapping. She shuffled through the motions of her life in a soporific daze, never fully asleep or awake, drifting aimlessly through a world in which no one else existed. She finally broke down and asked her mother to come stay with her and her son and her dog in their house on the hill—a house she had begged for but had brought her nothing but sorrow—until she could get her head right, until Aaron came home.

Through all her excavation of emotions—sadness, anger, shame, fatigue—it took her the whole of those two weeks to uncover the one, true cancer pulsating at the core of her pain. Guilt.

The Sentinel had tethered itself to her when she first saw it. It didn't try to break her like it did Aaron or Cheryl. It tried to get inside of her, tried to talk, tried to tell her something. Jane and Aaron had both claimed a boy was somewhere inside that monstrosity, and Ellen didn't believe them until one night she sat under a starry late summer sky and went to him.

The Sentinel came out of the forest at 4:00 a.m. like it always did, but this time, Ellen let it inside her mind. It walked within feet of her, its gargantuan fingers nearly grazing her face and its cloak of flies drowning out all other sounds around her. It didn't stop. It couldn't stop, it told her, not through words but through the injection of clairvoyant sensations.

The Sentinel was able to tell her everything in an instant through its feelings and memories. It showed her his name was Mark, that he used to play with a toy firetruck, but that now, it was his job to stop evil, that this bizarre existence was all that he knew. That he didn't understand why he had to do this, just knew that he had to, and that he had some fuzzy recollection of his parents being responsible, but he loved them anyway.

Oh, he loved them more than anything.

Mark wanted to tell them he was sorry for whatever he had done. He would promise to be a good boy if they would let him come out, that he wouldn't shout, wouldn't run, wouldn't do any of the naughty things boys do ever again. Mark was so, so sorry. He'd even promise to take this duty freely for the rest of his days—to live out a solitary existence underground in diabolical pain, in this awful suit of alchemical armor, rising to fight a demon each night and withstanding its evil whispers each day—if he could have just one last taste of life—a toy, a piece of cake, a bedtime story. Even a hug would do.

Ellen's body seized, and she collapsed in the grass as he walked past. She screamed to the heavens as his experience poured into her, and the weight of taking his mother away from him—no matter what she was—crushed her like an avalanche. Ellen lay there, gripping clumps of grass as if her life depended on them. She heaved breaths and bawled tears, and her only sporadic moments of relief came when her lungs managed to suck down enough oxygen to release more murderous cries.

From that night forward, Ellen woke at 4:00 a.m. to talk to him. She started just by letting him know she was there.

"I'm here," she would say aloud, staring at him through her bedroom window. "I'm here. I'm listening, Mark."

Soon, it became, "I love you, Mark. Someone loves you," and somewhere along the way mutated to, "Mommy loves you. I love you, sweetie. I'm here. Mommy's right here."

Something deep inside that ghastly husk began to believe her, and something deep inside of her began to claim him as her second son. Even though he'd been in the ground for forty years and Ellen had no way of knowing if his body was a boy's or a man's—or even alive—they started making progress together.

His emotive flares gradually evolved into expressions and even simple words. Those words became more advanced when Ellen began reading Caleb's books to him, and something seemed to call back to her that he understood.

For weeks, Ellen hid her nocturnal activity. The sole focus of her days became anticipating their conversations. Much to the dismay of the hospital, she refused night shifts, demanding that she needed nights to be with her son, something she well and truly believed to be the truth. Little did the hospital know, the son she referred to was not the broken little Caleb Dreyer, but a supernatural oddity that roamed the forests by her house.

And then one night, while reading to Mark through her bedroom window, a small voice called out to her from the doorway.

"Mommy?"

Ellen dropped the book. Caleb stood there in his pajamas, clutching his stuffed dinosaur to his chest.

"Caleb! Baby! Did you just say something? Did you say 'mommy'?"

He plodded slowly toward her, his little mouth curved in a frown, and stopped within feet of the window.

"Are you talking to Mark?" he said.

A new type of tears streamed down Ellen's shocked face. She grabbed her baby and smothered him in kisses. Between his first words since his kidnapping and his acknowledgment of Mark, Ellen's heart erupted with a joy she hadn't felt in months.

Caleb would later reveal that he spoke to Mark while he was in the forest, tied up in the burlap sack, and under the spell of the transition ritual. Mark soothed the bedlam raging in young Caleb's mind. He told him everything would be okay and promised to be his friend.

Now, Ellen told Caleb they'd talk to him together. All three would keep each other company. They'd be a family. Even Cooper sometimes joined them, curling in a sleepy ball at their feet while they read children's stories to a fifteen-foot-tall monster in the woods. One thing was for certain, Ellen and Caleb agreed, that no one else could know. Not even Grandma.

No one else did know until Ellen told—and showed—Cheryl, but she decided not to tell her boys about Cheryl's intentions. She didn't want to get their hopes up.

Ellen opened her phone, dialed her voicemail, and listened to her only message.

"Hey there, Sheriff McNamara here. Wanted to thank you again for takin' me in last night. Man, I'll tell you, I had no idea what I expected when I came to visit, but I'm very glad I did. I've been thinkin' about all this, and I'm gonna try reading the Grimoire again. Stuff really doesn't make a whole lot of sense to me, but there's gotta be something in there, right? Maybe you know of a college professor or someone who can help me? Uh, but anyway, the real reason I'm callin' is, I'm gonna try and go see it tonight. The bad one. The Nothus. I'm gonna park out by your place on Wickham Road. And if you wouldn't mind maybe tellin' Mark I'm not gonna hurt him, maybe even ask if I can follow him, that might go a long way. Of course, thought you oughta be in the know, regardless. You know, if it doesn't work and I pass out in the meadow there. Guess I'm oh-for-one on that so far. Okay, you take care, now. Call me if you wanna talk. Thanks again."

Ellen placed her phone back on the table and covered it with her hand. She peered down at the untouched yogurt and apple slices in her glass container. Hearing that name again, The Nothus, sent a different sensation creeping into her. Her entire body flashed with a sharp pang of cold as she recalled Aaron collapsing in a heap in the blind darkness. The Nothus almost killing them both. The Sentinel beating it into submission, and both creatures mysteriously disappearing at sunrise.

"Dr. Dreyer?" The doctor from the hall leaned in through the break room door. "You okay?"

"Yeah. What's up?"

"Cindy said you were crying again. I just came to check up. You've been here for almost forty minutes. Want me to see if Dr. Mirsa can cover the rest of your sh—"

"No. No, I'm fine. Thanks, James."

He left. Ellen touched her cheeks. They were damp and red hot. She waited until he was gone before crying again.

· · ·

The sun dissolved behind a curtain of clouds around noon and never returned. The clouds, dense and weighty, dragged across the sky like an old blanket until their coverage was entire, and the day's shadows extended such to mask its early hour, as if the light of the world simply surrendered to the threat of winter. Squalls formed in the mountains and barreled through the town, some so strong they carried a rumbling, not like thunder, something guttural—the voice of winter forged from wind and rock.

Bensalem lay in a grayscale vignette, white on the bottom, gray on the top, black shadows and tree trunks in the middle. Heeding an invisible call of retreat, its citizens abandoned their Christmas shopping during what should have been a busy Saturday afternoon in December, opting for the comfort of fireplaces and college football.

Derek Brady yawned as the patrol car's wiper blades swished over its rain-speckled windshield. The blades left arced entrails of water that did more to obscure his vision than to aid it, but the northbound road upon which he traveled was long and straight. It vivisected the rolling white hills, like a chalk line snapped by a celestial carpenter preparing to cut the world in two. Up ahead, the faded red and white sign of the Old Rag Motel emerged from the drab horizon. It doubled as a motel and convenience store, drawing the patronage of those unable or unwilling to rest their heads in Bensalem or Sperryville to the north.

Brady pulled into the paved lot and parked next to a white SUV. The rain was light, but the cold cut right through him. He gritted his teeth, slammed the door shut, and marched through the reeling shadow of a colorless building. Benches butting the front of the building looked more attached to the ground by their wrappers of ice than the rusty concrete bolts hanging out of their sockets. Two withered potted plants stood sentry on either side of the door. He stepped inside with a huff, careful to close the door quickly to keep the heat in.

A woman at least twice his age leaned on the counter, holding a corded phone to her ear. A gust of wind pelted the windows and screeched through their razor-thin openings. Brady sat in one of four fake leather chairs circled around a magazine-covered coffee table. He didn't pick up a magazine, he just sat and watched the woman as she smacked gum between her molars and stared straight ahead.

"No, no, that's not it," she said. "You're gonna wanna back in and park on that gravel strip there." Her hands made a fruitless pantomime of the action she was trying to convey. "You know where it is back there? Go behind the garage and past the trailer. There's a trailer sittin' there, yeah. Go past that trailer, and you'll see a strip, a gravel strip, and park—" She grimaced at Brady and shook her head, so he shook his head back and smiled. "No, no, hon, the gravel strip. The—Jesus. Okay, hold on, Roddy, I got the police here waitin' on me. Lemme call you back in ten minutes. Okay? Okay. Don't do nothin' till I call back, now. Okay." She hung up the phone and glared at Brady. "Sheesh! Sorry 'bout all that. Dumbass nephew fixin' to get his damn truck towed."

Brady put his hands on his hips as he rose, the contents of his belt jangling. "No apologies needed, ma'am. Got me one of them myself."

"What's that? A truck or a dumbass nephew?"

He chuckled. "A dumbass nephew. He's only five, but he ain't exactly on the most promising path. Every day, I seem to get a call from my sister about some kinda injury or him breakin' somethin.'"

"Wish I could say it gets better from there, but it don't. This one started out like that, and he ain't straightened out yet."

He sighed. "What you gonna do?"

She emerged from behind the counter, cradling a purple down jacket. "Well, lemme show you why I called. I don't wanna waste your time comin' out here, but I simply ain't never seen anything like this and it's givin' me the creeps."

"After you, ma'am."

She opened the door and led him behind the office. Another blast of wind smacked them both, her gray hair flailing. "Sure is damn cold!"

"Yes, ma'am, it is. You get your Christmas shopping done yet?"

She didn't answer him, probably didn't hear him. They stumbled on through the snow behind the motel building, and they followed a back wall extending several hundred feet. With the motel wall on his right, Brady glanced at the dense trees to his left. He remembered this general area of the forest being the northernmost edge of his search party's area four months ago, a search that didn't turn up a shred of evidence indicating Caleb Dreyer's whereabouts.

He had mostly moved on from those dire days. Caleb was quickly recovered and Aaron confessed to Jane's murder. Some of the details between the two crimes were missing but none that warranted him losing any sleep. After all, it had been nothing but peace and quiet since then, save for the suicide of Sheriff Quinlan, and that was more unsettling than it was surprising.

The motel keeper stopped and pointed to the ground. "There."

Brady stepped around her.

Hundreds of saucer-sized hoofprints littered the snow. Their varied frequency seemed to form three loose concentric circles. An innermost core, the area of highest traffic, had displaced enough snow to make actual prints indistinguishable, leaving only loose clumps of snow and tufts of grass gasping for scraps of light. A ring of hoofprints pointing in all directions surrounded the core, and further out, a more sparsely populated ring formed a wide circle blunted on both sides—one by the building, the other by the edge of the forest.

Brady squatted and examined a print in the middle ring. It was cloven in shape, like two halves of a heart. He hovered a bare hand over it.

"It's bigger than my hand," he said.

"What the hell is it?"

Brady rose and plodded slowly through the outermost circle, stopping when he reached the trees. He gazed into that wicked foliage, thick and unkempt with weed and vine, searching for signals of life but seeing only shadow.

"Officer?" the motel keeper said. "Is it an animal?"

"I don't know. But it looks like they came from in there." He nodded at the forest.

"What's it doin' here? Only thing I reckon was some kinda food behind the motel, but besides that, there ain't nothin' back here at all."

"I don't think it's an *it*."

"Huh?"

Brady turned around and started back toward her. "I don't think it's an *it*. I think it's a *they*."

"Oh? How you figure?"

"Well, the prints don't look like they're all the same exact size. I mean, they're all really big, but you see how that one is a little bigger than that one?"

"What do you think did this?"

"Beats the hell out of me."

"I was thinkin' maybe a moose?"

"Ain't no moose around here."

"Hmph."

"And you ain't never seen this before?"

"Never in my seventeen years workin' here. Course, it don't snow all that often."

"How'd you come by it in the first place?"

She pointed behind her. "Dumpster's back there. I took out the trash a few hours ago and noticed the snow was all messed up, so I came over."

"Think they were nosing through the trash?"

"No. It's all still in the dumpster. Untouched."

"I wonder if something else attracted them."

"What do you mean?"

He didn't respond. After scanning the woods again, he pointed at the motel wall.

"Is someone stayin' there?"

"Beg your pardon?"

"What room does that part of the wall line up with? Is someone stayin' right there?"

"Shoot, I'd have to check. You wanna get outta this cold? I'm startin' to get frostbite."

"You go on ahead. I wanna stay out here a minute. Can you get me a list of who all's stayin' here?"

"I'm not supposed to, but I'll give it to you since you're police."

"Appreciate that, ma'am."

She left, and Brady struck out toward the other side of the motel. Ruminations of stories Cheryl had concocted bounced around in his head, and a nebulous dread fell over him as darkness tightened its iron grip over the land. He walked through a set of human bootprints that went the reverse of his path, rounded the other side of the motel, and strode through the parking lot. It held just three vehicles: his police cruiser, her SUV, and a gray sedan parked further away. Brady looked at the gray sedan and then peeked behind the motel again, sizing up the approximate direct distance between the car and the prints.

At the other end of the parking lot, the silhouette of the woman in her purple jacket appeared. She and Brady walked toward each other and met at the gray sedan.

"Thought it was the case, but only one guy stayin' here. That's his car," she said.

"What's his name?"

"Reservation says Roland Pierce."

"Roland Pierce? Feel like I know that name from somewhere. You know him?"

"Sure don't. Little bug-eyed guy. Quiet. Only saw him checkin' in a couple days ago."

"Plates are from New York. Know if he's in there?"

"He must be if his car is there. Do you wanna talk to him?"

Brady looked at his watch, numbers on a face he could barely read in the darkness. "Nah. It's gettin' late. I don't wanna freak him out. You just wanna keep an eye on the back of the building for me?"

She recoiled, as if physically struck. "Hell no! I ain't goin' back there alone! Especially not when it's dark!"

"Suit yourself, ma'am. I don't really know what to tell ya'. Try not to worry about it. I'll ask my buddy who hunts these woods more regular, see if he has any ideas. Sound okay?"

She grunted and walked back to the office.

. . .

Cheryl, in her sweatsuit, sat with her feet tucked underneath her on the couch. Rick was fully prone in his recliner but twitched in reaction to the football game on television.

He scoffed. "Mother of freakin' pearl. Can't stop the damn run to save our lives."

She flipped a page in the book she was reading, *A New Atlantis* by Sir Francis Bacon, with a look of consternation jackhammered across her brow. Cheryl cocked her head, the way a dog might when called to attention, and flipped back to the previous page. "The hell?" she said under her breath.

The football announcer called a touchdown for the other team. Rick threw the recliner's lever forward and sprang to his feet. "We can't tackle. Can't blitz. Can't cover. Heck with it all."

Rick might as well have not existed to Cheryl. She kept

flipping the same page back and forth, mouthing words under narrow and focused eyes.

"What you readin' there, bug?" Rick said.

It took a moment for Cheryl to look up and respond. "Well, I'm not too sure, but I think it's a story about how Bensalem was founded by a cult hundreds of years ago."

"Oh. Is that so?"

"Sure as shit hope not." She thumbed back to a page in the beginning of the book.

"Always found it odd we never had any churches here. Does the book talk about that?"

"I don't know. I can barely read it. So far, all they're talkin' about is a city with a temple and all these people in some kinda utopia."

"They must be writing about a different Bensalem then."

Cheryl snorted.

"Where'd you get it? Library?"

"No. No, I got it from a secret laboratory hidden in Jane Harcourt's old store. She was a mad scientist, and I think she was part of a cult called the Order of the Old Roses. Remember how her store had that wallpaper with all them gold crosses with roses on 'em?"

The football commentator practically jumped out of the television speakers with excitement over a long touchdown pass by the home team. Artificial cheers and hollers filled the room, but Rick stood still, hands on his hips and face screwed in confusion. "Mother of freakin' pearl!"

The front door opened. Cheryl stashed the book between the couch cushions.

"Hey there," Cheryl said.

"Hey." Skylar pounded snow off her Dr. Martens.

"I thought you were grounded."

Skylar hung her coat and shuffled over to the couch adjacent to Cheryl's. "I am grounded."

"Where were you today?"

"At Alexandra's house with Ram and some friends. We just watched TV. It wasn't a big deal." Her attention drifted to the football game's halftime commercials, but she turned to face Cheryl after receiving no response.

"And how does my princess plan to defy me this evening?"

"No plans," Skylar said softly.

The two of them watched intently as a local car salesman burst with excitement over an upcoming holiday savings sale. A ball of a man, the bright rouge of his face was outdone only by the blazing crimson of his polo shirt. His balding hair was pulled back in a ponytail, and heavy silver bracelets gleamed as he flailed his hands.

"Ron Cleverly," Cheryl said. "Cleverly Chevy. He's been doin' these forever."

"He looks like the Kool-Aid guy," Skylar said.

Rick, back in his chair, muffled a laugh.

Skylar turned to her parents, gripped the arm of her couch, and opened her eyes wide. "Oh yeah!"

Cheryl and Rick burst out laughing. Skylar turned back to the television with a smirk stitched on her face.

"He called me about a break-in a long time ago," Cheryl said after the laughter died. "He didn't look like that back then. You were real little, Sky."

"Nobody looks like they did back then," Skylar said.

"Your mother does," Rick turned to Cheryl. "Pretty as the day we got married. She still fits in her wedding dress."

"Stop it," Cheryl said.

"Do you still have your wedding dress, Mom?"

"Stop it, the both of you."

"I bet you looked real pretty, Mom."

The red-faced salesman finished his pitch, and four more commercials plus a halftime show came and went before anyone spoke again.

Cheryl used a light voice to break their silence. "You were with me. I took the call on our way back from the clinic."

Rick reached a hand over to his wife. She took it. Skylar became frozen in stone.

"You don't remember those days do you, Sky? You don't remember what you went through."

Skylar did not answer. She stared at the television as her blushing face hardened further.

"I remember," Cheryl continued. "Three times a week. I'd take you there after pre-school, and they'd stick that needle in your little arm. God, I hated that thing. That place. They'd call our name, and I'd lean over and tell you, 'You're next up, Sky.' I always told them to be careful because I was afraid they'd stick it straight through your arm. Your arm was so tiny I couldn't stand it."

"Why are you tellin' me this, Mom?" Skylar said. "I mean, I kinda remember."

"Because... you were so brave. You didn't cry one time in all those visits. All you wanted was a red lollipop at the end. I just couldn't get over how brave you were."

The second-half kickoff triggered Rick's sighs and spasms again, and the three wordlessly watched the home team go three and out.

"Just reminiscing, I guess," Cheryl said at one point.

As the score widened between the two teams and the game clock inched toward zero, the energy of the crowd and the announcers waned. So, too, did the energy wane in the room and the world outside the McNamara house. The dark veil of an evening in mid-winter, an evening so ordinary yet so unique, lulled them into an early lethargy, and Rick snored loudly halfway through the movie Cheryl and Skylar settled on after the game. No dinner was served. The three of them just took turns sneaking to the kitchen, cobbling together whatever seemed palatable, slipping back to their respective dens of coziness around the TV. An invisible energy drew them toward each other that night, and that which could have been said was not. Merely understood, sensed, and felt in ways words would have failed to convey.

Glued to the couch, sinking into the warmth, Cheryl achieved a state of physical and emotional equilibrium akin to meditation. The pace of her thought slowed, and while she did not tire, her attention ascended away from the movie, away from her personal affairs, away even from Rick who snuck up to bed without either of the women really noticing. It was as if Cheryl merely floated through time and space, observing but not acting, casting off the mantle of her burdens amid the hands of angels sprinkling fresh rows of snow outside.

She regained focus an indeterminate amount of time later, when for a brief moment, she felt the weight of the entire world resting on her lap. But the weight was not heavy in the manner it usually was to her. This time, it was firm but placid, universal but familiar, and although her eyes stared into the flashing imagery of the television, she saw something else more general, as back and forth she caressed strands of hair on a sleeping Skylar's head that had manifested in her lap. She tuned out the sound of the television and tuned in the sound of her daughter's deep breaths of sleep, and even though she stayed awake, her heart and her lungs slowed to sync with Skylar's. And back and forth, back and forth, she stroked her daughter's most perfect hair.

But the night, too, deepened, darkened, grew taller and longer, and after Skylar evaporated upstairs, Cheryl remained. Whatever was on TV was unrecognizable to her now, and the instinct of going to bed and snuggling next to Rick became oddly foreign. She kept breathing and staring ahead, and she settled into the comfort of her solitude. It was as if she was not at home but far away, at the top of a mountain or at the edge of the cliff, peering down into the sea.

She stayed this way, alone, until the time came.

And when it did, she rose, laced up her boots, put on two jackets, threw up her hood, and got into the patrol car.

And Skylar, tucked between layers of the night, rose from her slumber without alarm and took the hand reaching out to her. In a haste not of her own making, she dressed and scurried down the stairs. She slipped out the front door just minutes after her mother did, and she got into Ram's car, the car that had been waiting for her.

· · ·

Cheryl did not wipe away the snow as it peppered her windshield. The unit's lights illuminated flakes so weightless they floated like small spirits of the night or cosmic ashes hovering over the remains of a charred Earth. Something about it soothed her, and although her body coursed with more adrenaline than it did last night, the serenity she had achieved on the couch had dulled her fear and inhibitions. She drove down SR 639 as if drunk on the denial of the dangers lying in wait.

Her sole discomfort was the latent realization she would be going in alone, and for the first time since hatching her plan, she wondered if she might be better off coming back another night, another time, when she had real rest and backup. But more so as a woman of her word than anything else, she ambled on through the snow, determined to prove her dedication to Ellen Dreyer, even though her voicemail that afternoon was never returned.

By the time the neon-green rectangle reading "Wickham Road" flickered in her high beams, the snow had stopped falling. Cheryl took the turn slowly, and the unit rumbled over the snow-laden gravel road. She didn't look to her left while passing the entrance to Hank's Horse Farm, but the long exhale she released signaled a phantom piece of her consciousness still tasted its stain. The dashboard clock read 03:43.

She pulled over in front of an unlit Dreyer house. On the passenger seat, an array of metal equipment gleamed in the yellow glow of the unit's overhead light: her flashlight, her service weapon in its holster, three extra magazines of ammunition. One by one, she gathered them and fastened them to her belt, and finally with great effort, she opened the door and stepped out.

If the cold was biting during the day, it was razor-sharp at night. Although no wind blew through the meadow, she dreaded the thought as her nose and ears already began to lose their warmth. She fastened the ear flaps of her trapper hat under her chin, and after securing the contents of her belt, forced her fingers into already tight-fitting gloves made tighter by hand warmers.

"Okay," she said in synchronization with another deep breath.

The echo of her boots in the snow seemed to tear through the silence of the night, and with her hands in her pockets, she glanced at everything in her vicinity as she walked to the meadow.

A shadow stationed in the middle of the meadow stopped her dead in her tracks. She stared at it for a frigid moment, unsure if it was a tree she had forgotten about, or something sentient sizing her up.

"Hello?" she said.

The figure made fuzzy movements toward her. Cheryl kept her arms tight to mask the slow movement toward her gun.

"Bensalem Sheriff's Department. Is someone there?"

It came closer, and as her night vision shook off its rust, the figure's shadows softened, and its identity was revealed. She took her hand off her weapon.

Ellen Dreyer was the vision of an arctic vigilante. Her boots and snow pants blended such that they appeared a single garment, and the depth of their blackness was outdone only by the nylon vest strapped to her chest holding a dozen shotgun cartridges. The cylinders looked like weaponized hair curlers welded to her ribs. More loose cartridges rustled in a side saddle on her hip.

Cheryl saw all these elements, but she did not look at them. All she could focus on was the weapon in Ellen's hands, no longer her father's old wooden .22, but a black, pump action pistol grip shotgun with even more shells velcroed to its sides. Her back and shoulders looked loose but straight as she walked, and her untied hair billowed back like a dark cape around her head.

"Hi," Ellen said.

"Wow," Cheryl replied, more to the gun than to its wielder.

Ellen cleared her throat of cold, dry air. "Let's be honest. We have no idea what we're up against."

Cheryl looked up at Ellen. "We?"

A long beat passed between them, both of them gazing downward, as if sharing a private prayer to set aside the things that had brought them together at this time and place.

Ellen shuffled her stance. "I was thinking about Mark today. About Caleb. About what this thing—whatever the fuck it is— has done to my family."

"And to my town."

"Right."

"Right."

The two clicked on their flashlights, and Ellen led Cheryl away from what she predicted would be Mark's path. They waited.

"What do you expect to see?" Cheryl asked.

"I asked Aaron today. He says hello, by the way."

Cheryl faked a laugh.

"All he remembers seeing are two red eyes. It was dark, and we didn't get a chance to shine light on it."

"Safe to say, it's something quite strong though, right? If it takes something as big as a Sentinel to take it down?"

"I truly have no idea. Mark won't talk about it. He won't even let me go near it in his mind."

"I'm guessing it might be big. Might mean you aimin' that hand cannon up instead of straight ahead, unless you wanna hit a knee cap or somethin'."

"I won't be aiming for knee caps."

"What I don't understand is why nobody tried this already. Just to come out and shoot the damn thing."

"I have to assume they tried and it didn't work. I'm certainly not expecting to kill it."

"What then?"

"I don't know. Scare it? Distract it? Try at least to wound it if shit goes south?"

"If this is what killed Hank Teakle, I don't know if we'll have too many opportunities to—"

Ellen turned her head toward clumps of snow filtering down from the pines. "We have him. He'll protect us."

Appearing almost as if it were one of the trees itself, the Sentinel emerged from the shadows of the forest, its shoulders dusted in snow, its three yellow eyes glowing like guide lamps.

Ellen raised her voice over the incessant swarming of flies. "Let's trail him. You want me to go first?"

"Let me. I'll hold the light so you can keep two hands on that thing."

Ellen nodded and stashed her flashlight away.

"What's with the flies, by the way?" Cheryl said.

"I don't know. I think he tried to tell me the suit is dirty but I don't know for sure. He can be hard to understand."

"Are you talkin' to him now?"

"No, I'm talking to you."

"Right, of course. Sorry."

Darts of wind attempted to breach Cheryl's wall of chattering teeth and spill down into her lungs, but she shook them away with a shiver and fell in line roughly twenty feet behind the Sentinel. The taste and smell of wet metal flooded her senses. She glanced back at Ellen, shotgun in her hands—one on the grip, the other on the barrel. Her eyebrows were pitched in a tent of concern over her face as she gazed up at Mark. No words were spoken between the two as they trailed in the Sentinel's wake, and they walked for a long time.

Although the snow had stopped falling and it wasn't very deep, worms of it still crawled over the edges of Cheryl's boots, settling in her socks and dampening her feet. Each step was a precarious one. The Sentinel seemed to follow no trail while traversing snow-covered patches of ground both hard and soft, and footing was only sure once their feet stopped sinking. They bushwhacked through twisted foliage and vines hardened by the cold, using their hands to clear brush the Sentinel effortlessly evaded.

No creature of the forest regarded them, for those that lived here knew the invisible path of the Sentinel, and they freely surrendered these pre-twilight moments to the one who protected them. Cheryl and Ellen got colder. The flies kept buzzing. The Sentinel kept walking.

A branch snapped to their left. The two women spun toward the sound, and Ellen raised her gun. Another snap, and then a whisper from the same location.

Cheryl pointed her light and her gun at a sickly looking maple obscuring only parts of two people. "Whoever that is, come out of there. This is the Bensalem Sheriff's Department. We see you."

They stepped out, a young man and a young woman, glove-covered hands raised.

Whatever cold Cheryl felt in that moment instantly boiled into a scalding-hot rage. "Skylar! Goddammit! What in God's name are you doin' here!"

"We came to help you! What you're doing is dangerous! We've been reading the Grimoire, and we know about this thing."

"Go home! Right now!"

"We know about the Sentinel and the Nothus Noctis. We know about Sheriff Quinlan. We know why it's here and what it wants. We know everything!"

"Ram, you take her home right this instant. I might expect this from her, but not from you."

"Okay. Yes, ma'am. Come on, Sky, let's just go," he said.

Skylar shooed away Ram's hand. "No! Mom! We know where the Nothus Noctis came from, and we want to help you stop it. We can help you stop it!"

Finally, Cheryl lowered her gun. But she did not lower her light. She held it on the whites of their eyes, two deer stuck in her headlight. "Where did it come from?"

Ellen's voice buzzed like a gnat in her ear. "Cheryl, we need to move. We're losing him. He's not gonna wait for us."

It was Skylar who took Ram's arm now as she paced toward her mother in the snow. "A ritual hundreds of years ago. It all goes back to the Order of the Old Roses and the founding of Bensalem. It's all connected. They tried to summon something that would protect them, but they summoned a devil instead. It's been here ever since, killing people."

Cheryl looked at Ellen. Ellen jerked her head toward the back of the Sentinel, fading from their vision and their path.

"We'll talk about this at home. Go home. You're in so much trouble."

"Wait," Ellen said. "Are you armed?"

"No," Ram replied.

Ellen sighed and turned to Cheryl. "I hate to say it, but they're probably safer with us and the Sentinel than they are alone."

"We just followed you guys, so we don't know the way back." Ram stepped forward. "But Skylar's right. We have some knowledge of this thing and we know how dangerous it is. We know what it can do. We'll stay back, but we'll stay close. Right, Sky?"

Skylar nodded.

Ellen strafed back a few steps before turning to catch up to the Sentinel.

Cheryl cursed and hung her head. "Fucking dammit, you two! You stay behind Ellen. Do not get in front of her. And stay close. If you can't reach out and touch her, you're too far away. Is that understood?"

They both nodded.

"And don't you dare look at it, you hear me?"

Cheryl jogged past them to regain her position at the

vanguard. This time, though, she kept more distance from the Sentinel. They trekked as the starlight faded and the silence heightened, and even though the size of their party had doubled, each felt the sheer desolation and sorrow of this place bleeding down into their marrow. Speech, or the making of any undue noise, was unthinkable.

They stepped around trunks of pine trees thicker and taller than any living on the outskirts, almost from an alien planet. Random, diagonal scars had been cut into them. Bark had hardened around the scars that had been there for a long time, while exposures of white, fleshy wood indicated those made more recently. The volume of these tree scars seemed to increase as the party traveled further. Some of the trunks even bent in places where the scars were deepest.

They then came to a glade, where dying moonlight cast the snow in a bluish hue, and the soft rim of the sky appeared for the first time in an eternity. Beyond the glade, Cheryl gawked at what appeared to be some kind of structure. It looked like a massive tent made of sticks, a wild and feral-looking thing, like thorny and brambled ribs guarding a foul-beating heart. Seeing it there, realizing how much farther and longer they'd traveled than she anticipated, strings of regret pulled at her, not for the first time that night.

And then, everything stopped.

The Sentinel stopped. Cheryl stopped and threw a fist in the air, halting Ellen and the teenagers. Even the clouds seemed to cease their shifting through the open dome of the glade.

A guttural rumbling rose up about them, and when Cheryl turned around, two burning red lamps hung high behind her daughter's shoulder.

"Skylar!" Cheryl yelled.

Skylar did not turn around but winced in pain and clamped her hands over her ears. Ram grabbed her mid-fall but faltered when he glanced up at a massive and hellish creature, something half-man, half-deer towering over them, seemingly draining the gravity out of the air, pulling the world toward it, sucking their souls out of them through its long, bony snout. A heaving chest drew breath below a cervine head crowned in antlers. Long ropes of drool, or something like it, hung from its jaw as it walked on hooked and crooked legs toward Skylar. One of the drool ropes swung and crashed into Ram's face, but he didn't seem to notice, as his only focus was his girlfriend wailing in invisible pain.

The Nothus drew back a great hand, illuminating yard-stick-sized fingers in the pale glow of the night, and it clawed down at the teenagers with terrifying velocity. Ram screamed.

The Sentinel, furthest from the Nothus since it came upon them from the rear, pivoted and took monster-sized strides to-ward its adversary, but it did not outpace an absolutely frenzied Cheryl McNamara. She threw down her flashlight and emptied her entire clip at the apex of those two red eyes. A screech from hell itself and a cry of "Get down!" blended into vague echoes in her head. She dove in front of the teenagers and loaded another clip while a deafening blast exploded behind her. Ellen took two steps to her left. She fired the shotgun again, and again, and again, her shots having little impact on the Nothus—one resulting in a brief recoil of its shoulder, the rest either off-target or simply absorbed.

The Nothus screeched and swatted again, and its fingers rained down on Cheryl with such force they knocked the wind out of her lungs and the strength out of her body. She dropped her gun. Her head reeled. Screams and gunshots clouded her ears and her mind.

The two red eyes of the Nothus appeared as portals now, tunnels to her nightmares, a room of her soul she had not yet explored, and at once, everything around her began to fade. A desperate hand grabbed her shoulder, tried to pull her back, but fell away when the Nothus wrapped its hand around her waist and hoisted her high into the air. Her body erupted in pain when the Nothus speared four fingers through her abdomen, slicing her organs, severing her spine, pulling out fountains of blood on the release. Every muscle in Cheryl's body shut down.

And from up high, hanging by a thread of life, Cheryl was in the waiting room with Skylar. Skylar who was so brave.

The room was blue and bright under buzzing fluorescents. Happy cartoons and colorful animals splashed the walls with a kind of plastic joy. She beheld the child beside her.

Skylar wore a white skirt and green T-shirt. She swung her legs back and forth in the waiting room chair with a smile on her face, and her bald head reflected the world Cheryl loved and despised at the same time. A nurse walked in and looked at them. Cheryl smiled at her daughter, put a hand to her cheek. It was the softest thing she'd even known, and she whispered, "You're next up, Sky."

The Nothus slammed her body into the cold, hard earth, and Cheryl, her eyes still burning steel-gray embers, heard more than felt the bones in her body break. It was there that life drained out of her.

Skylar went apoplectic. She belted a scream that scraped the heavens, and she clawed at Ram's arms clasped tightly around her. He pulled her away, pulled her down, begged her not to get close because it was her the Nothus had its sights on, and then the Sentinel ran in and tackled it into a corner of darkness.

Screams from humans, cries from beasts, blasts from shot-gun shells filled the glade with carnage and chaos. The two titans swung and clawed and slammed in the shadows while Ram clung to a still-berserk Skylar. Ellen jogged over to them and joined Ram in pleas of retreat. It took both of them to drag Skylar away, crying and screaming, into the twilight.

DAY 6

When, in the pre-dawn hours, ice wedged in the joints of the mountain nearest Bensalem thawed under an emergent sun, and fresh snowmelt weakened the bedding plane, layers of ancient sediment failed, and an old slice of rock fell away.

Six large boulders hurtled down range and splintered into thousands of fragments upon impact with the base. They followed unseen roads into surrounding forests and fields, to new homes where they would spend the next billion years collecting moss, weather, and lore.

And in what would become a lasting curiosity in Bensalem, a white quartz deposit previously shielded in craggy limestone skin was exposed upon the mountain's new face, and it would shine after rain and gleam something heavenly when the sun sat high in the eastern sky.

. . .

The first mortal man to gaze upon the new face of the mountain was Derek Brady, sheriff in function if not in title, when it glinted in his rearview mirror on southbound SR 639. He had taken Ellen's call on his personal phone, and his head swam in a half-asleep stew of confusion and disbelief as he stumbled into his truck and turned over a reluctant engine.

Cheryl, dead? At the hands of some horrendous monster out there in the woods? Surely, this was some kind of a cruel joke or a nightmare. Surely, Cheryl's talk of monsters called bastards, of cults and witches, wasn't true? There had to be a logical explanation.

Lines of bright yellow light seeped through the seams of a quilt of corrugated clouds, and as the sun grew stronger, hotter, the clouds rolled away like waves on the ocean. More snow melted, and it bled down hills and rocks above the tree line like tears, turning the lowlands into a slurry of cold, wet, brown liquid.

Ellen and Ram were both pale and empty as they leaned on the fence surrounding the Dreyer house. Skylar sat cross-legged in the snow, in the slush, silent and gazing at the plain.

"The hell's goin' on?" Brady said, stepping out of the vehicle.

Ellen's face and neck were flush with blood. Warm white clouds billowed out from her mouth with every breath. "It's like I said on the phone. Cheryl's dead. We... we had to leave her in the woods."

"Because of this monster?"

Ellen nodded. "Yes. I know it sounds crazy. I know you... think I'm crazy, or thought I was crazy... but all three of us were there."

Brady turned to Ram. "What happened?"

"It's true," Ram said. His eyes were locked on Skylar.

Brady crouched to meet Skylar's gaze. There was a deadness

in her eyes he had never seen before, as if she looked right through him at some other, more pertinent thing. Mascara-stained tracks of tears had frozen to her face, connecting blackened eye sockets to purple lips. He extended a hand. "Jesus. Skylar? Hey."

She did not reply.

"We have to go get her," Ellen said.

"Hold on." Brady stood. "Let me deal with this first." He reached for the radio on his belt. "606 to dispatch," he said.

"Go ahead," Monica's staticky voice replied.

"Need, uh, need crime tech and EMT out here, stat. Dreyer place on Wickham Road."

"Copy. Everything okay?"

"No. Hurry it up." He sighed and put the radio away.

Reaching his arms around Skylar, almost hugging her, Brady pulled the girl to a standing position. Her legs wobbled.

"Ramsey? Can you take her home, please?"

"Uh, y—yeah."

"Don't you wanna question her?" Ellen said.

"Not like this, I don't. I'll get everything I need from you now and talk to her when she's had some rest. You were with her the whole time, right? She's practically an ice cube."

"Yeah. We were all together."

"Okay, Ramsey, take her home. I don't know if I'd tell Rick yet, okay? I'll be by in a couple hours, and after I assess the situation, I'll come talk to him."

Ram's face was long and weary. He plodded toward Skylar, took her hand—a brittle porcelain thing just barely poking through the sleeve of her hoodie—and led her to his car on the side of the road.

Only after the car was out of sight did Brady face Ellen again. "Okay, Ellen, what the hell is going on here?"

Her gaze faltered, as if ashamed. "How much do you know?"

"How much do I know about what?"

"About... this place. The things that dwell in that forest."

"Don't know much for certain, if I'm honest. Heard a lot of talk, though. You should know by now, I'm more of a see-it-to-believe-it kind of police officer."

She looked back up at him. "All right, then. Let's go."

Hands in her pockets, head bowed, she trudged into the forest. He followed.

. . .

In the minutes and hours that followed, Skylar McNamara endured a whiplash of emotions—pain, anger, confusion, fatigue—but her prevailing state was one of disbelief. She felt the loss of her mother in her body but not her mind. That she was gone was an impossibility, a mistake, a glitch in the matrix that could be undone if she maybe closed her eyes for a moment. The nightmare would be over, and she'd be back with her mother on the couch, in the car, in the clinic waiting for chemo—where, for some reason, she had found herself in dreams distressingly often. Worrying about nothing more than math tests and social circles.

But by mid-afternoon, and after a barrage of procedural questioning, all strength had drained out of her. She now lay on her bedroom floor with her cellphone to one ear, the muffled voices of Derek Brady and her father reverberating in the other.

"We have to find it," she said. "It's the only way to stop it. We have to find it."

"We will. We will find it," Ram said. "Let's get some rest first. I'm exhausted. I think if I have to explain what happened one more time—"

"There wasn't anything in there you found earlier? Not some kind of ritual or spell or some weakness it has?"

"I'm telling you, if there was something in the Grimoire sections I read, I would have found it. I've been through the entire thing almost three times now. I've spent so much time with it, I'm starting to memorize passages."

"There has to be something. There can't be nothing. There has to be something in the rest of the book."

"I mean, there doesn't have to be anything. There doesn't—"

"It has to be at the station. That's the only logical place. Right?"

"I have no idea, Sky. Why don't you ask Brady if he'll get it?"

"No. No, I don't want to involve anyone else right now. I don't trust anyone and we can't take risks. If we tip him off, he's liable to give it to someone else before he gives it to us."

"Yeah, I guess so."

"Ellen is the only one I trust now."

"Why don't we have her get it from him?"

"No, we have to get it ourselves."

The front door slammed shut, and her brother's voice blended with the other two.

"Fuck. Lenny's home," Skylar said. "I have to go. I'm going to the station."

"Wait. Sk—"

She hung up the phone.

Every part of her ached as she pushed herself up from the ground. Skylar threw her messenger bag together and dressed to leave the house but paused when she went to open the door. She put her ear to the door to try and make out the conversation among the three men downstairs. Lenny was crying, that much was clear, but actual words were unintelligible.

She opened the door, cinched her bag, and plodded down the stairs. The men stopped their conversation as she walked through them, and her fingers were around the front door handle when a voice stopped her.

"Hey. Where are you going?"

It took her a moment to find the strength to turn around. When she did, she received the bloodshot daggers she knew Lenny was shooting at her, and in looking at the other two, discovered Lenny's eyes weren't the only ones questioning her. It was as if all three asked the question, and it even occurred to her she wasn't precisely sure which one of them had asked it. She deflected their stares with short, sideways glances.

"I'm going out."

Lenny turned toward her. "Going out where?"

Skylar furrowed her brow and pursed her lips. "I just need some space."

Lenny spun toward Rick. "You're just gonna let her leave?"

But Rick was still looking at Skylar. "Okay, honey. We love you. Come home soon."

Lenny scoffed. "What? Dad! Sky, you were with her! What happened to Mom? What the hell happened?"

"Lenny, please," Rick said, putting a hand out.

Lenny's normally well-manicured appearance was beaten and tousled. The shirt under his sweater was half untucked, and his unwashed hair stuck out on the sides. All the angry young man's might had been channeled to his blaring red face, where every muscle squeezed as he teetered on the verge of a breakdown, clearly not his first of the day.

She shot one more glance at each of them before shuffling out the door in silence.

"Skylar!" Lenny yelled. Fists balled. Chest heaving. Eyes crying.

A warm wind billowed the ends of her hoodie as she marched toward her car. Her face was one of stone.

. . .

Skylar's busted car speakers didn't come close to providing the volume she sought. The grinding, lurching verse of an Alice In Chains song blared through them, guitars searing, drums firing. It was so loud and so deep, the bassline thumped her heart out of normal rhythm, and each note caused the speaker coverings to physically bulge in auditory agony. An invisible vice tightened around Skylar's neck and chest. She struggled to draw in oxygen, and she clenched the steering wheel with a death grip, but those actions did little to discharge the carnage inside her, as if her rage was an ocean trying to flow through a pinhole.

Some release came with the arrival of the chorus, when Layne Staley blasted a wall of sound that ripped right through her. She screamed in time with him.

There was such loneliness and distance in his voice, such fear, and for those few moments, she felt he of all people somehow understood her. He called to her through the gate of the dead, a bard singing hellish lamentations of the world he'd left behind. Maybe her mother was somewhere back there with him, wading around the swamps of limbo, trying to yell a message back to the land of the living.

Skylar screamed again and pounded her heels into the pedals. The car jerked, sped up, jerked again, and the wheels floated on the icy road. She saw the horizon change angles in her rearview mirror and her brain hit the panic button. Skylar slammed on the brakes with both boots, but it was too late. She was going too fast, and her car continued to spin.

A great thump sent Skylar directly upward, lifting her off the seat and bumping her head on the ceiling, but the car stayed level as it slid off the road, over the ditch, and into the grass off the shoulder.

There, shaken but not hurt, the car facing perpendicular to the road, Skylar just stopped. She turned off the radio, calmed her breath, and closed her eyes.

When she opened them, a man was approaching from the road. He wore a heavy parka and thick glasses. When he knocked on the window, she rolled it down.

"You okay, there?" he said.

"Yeah. Thanks. I'm fine. I think the car's fine."

"Are you Skylar McNamara?"

She paused and grazed her finger over the door lock button. "What?"

There was a hurried manner about the man. His words were fast and his motions jumpy. "I'm Roland Pierce." He shot out a hand through the window but Skylar didn't shake it. "I'm with the Order of the Old Roses. Do you have the Great Book?"

Her heart suddenly yearned for Ram. "The Great Book?"

"Yes. Grimoire Parentiqarum Rosarium. A sacred text written by the founders of Bensalem. It's a very important text for the Order, and I believe your m—" He paused a moment. "Listen, I know what the Nothus did to your mother. I'm terribly sorry."

Skylar started rolling up the window.

"Wait! Skylar, it's very important you listen to me if you have it. Envoys of the Nothus Noctis have been released and they seek the Great Book. They know it may hold the key to the reversal of the Nothus. They know the Sentinel is weak. They're waiting for it to die so the Nothus can roam free to kill as it pleases. Just like it did back then. You must tell me where the Great Book is so I can help you."

"How do you know who I am? Are you stalking me?"

He sighed. "If I'm being honest, I've been monitoring your mother. She was on the right path. I'm a High Deacon with the Order of the Old Roses. I was sent here by the Grand Elder."

"Right path?"

"Listen, I don't have time to explain." Something glimmered in his eyes.

"Neither do I." She rolled up the rest of the window.

"Wait! Please!"

But Roland's muted protests were heard only by Skylar's windshield. She turned the car back on, cranked the radio, gave it all the gas she could, and sputtered through the grass and back onto the road.

Roland, still standing in the field, shrunk in her mirror as she sped toward the station.

. . .

A clear, blue sky began to yellow as Skylar drove, and the sun faded from view even earlier than it had the day before. These were the rapidly diminishing days of mid-December. Each sunrise and sunset grew weaker, caving to the darkness on both sides of the day. Skylar, likewise, searched for light within herself and found none. The darkness of trauma had surrounded her, and it circled the fire in her heart like a buzzard over fresh roadkill.

The land was cold and vast, empty in a way that amplified her fatigue. Half white, half brown fields caked in shadow sandwiched the road, their velvety surfaces interrupted only by snow-capped hay bales glowing blue in the moonlight.

Patches of sycamores lined the turnoff to the station, shielding the concrete-block building from the sky and muting the warm light in its windows. Skylar hadn't visited the Bensalem Sheriff's Department in years, had no reason to, but it looked exactly as she remembered, down even to the jagged rectangles of peeling paint off the winter-riven trim and moss stains on a roof caving ever so slightly.

Her headlights penetrated the rear window of the lone police unit in the parking lot. The unit was the BSD standard brown and beige, and as Skylar brought her vehicle to a stop behind it, she mapped the various paths to her mother's desk based on who might be inside.

Brady was at her house, so it wasn't him.

Deputy Monica Nelson was a strong possibility and probably her best bet, based on their relationship. Monica, roughly ten years her senior, started as a babysitter to Skylar and evolved into something of a big sister as she grew into adolescence, serving as a sounding board for topics too awkward to bring to her mother. She'd be the easiest sell, as Skylar could probably just be honest about her reasons for searching her mother's desk in return for a few teary minutes of commiseration.

Uriah Mathias, a retired Air Force Staff Sergeant fresh off a tour in Iraq and just two months into the job, was a nice guy with whom she had little rapport. From their brief interactions and her mother's accounts, he was a left-brained rule follower who didn't deviate from norms. He'd be a challenge, as would Abner Davidson, the second-longest serving member of the force behind her mother, and Skylar's mind fritzed upon realizing he now held the record.

But as she rounded the corner toward the front steps, deliberations of conversation strategy quickly merged into a single lane of curiosity as a right-angled rim of white light shone bright across the top and long side of the door. She slowed her pace to consider why the door might be set like that, a few inches ajar on such a cold and solitary evening. In the summer, these woods teemed with noise from frogs and insects, little caretakers of the trees and not-so-silent observers of all covert deeds. But on these winter nights, the hardened ground and dead leaves provided them no haven, and the woody old police station stood alone on a cold island in the forest.

She landed heel before toe with each step to silence her approach, and she peered through the slivers of light bleeding around the edges of the door. A sound rose up around her, a rumbling she couldn't determine was real or imaginary. She put a cautious hand to the screen door and winced as its creaky hinges cackled in the night.

The sight nearly knocked her to the ground.

Deputy Monica Nelson lay in a billowing swath of blood on the floor.

Skylar clasped her hands over her nose and mouth and scurried to the body. Three gashes, each at least an inch deep, had been carved out of her neck, cutting out the flesh and exposing the ghostly cartilage of her windpipe. Blood both gushed and gurgled out of each gash, and only when Skylar recognized a pattern of bubbles spurting from the red madness did she realize the ribboned woman was still alive. A large bubble of blood blistered out from her neck and popped into a crimson rain.

Monica's eyes, beady and lethargic, locked onto Skylar's and then veered sharply toward the sheriff's office at the back of the station. Skylar shot her gaze toward it and then tracked the path of bloody hoofprints, massive and hideous stains, connecting the sheriff's door and Monica's body. When Skylar looked down again, the gurgling had stopped, and now, smooth streams of blood waterfalled over the curve of Monica's neck. The blood spilled out into three streams, eddied around a single point on the floor, and flowed forth as a river that steadily widened the dark pool she lay in, a pool now brushing against the edge of Skylar's denim-clad knees.

Another torrent of rage and confusion, what seemed like the millionth that day, boiled her lungs and esophagus. Rocking back and forth on her bloodstained knees next to Monica's corpse, Skylar kept both hands glued over her mouth as she stifled a handful of sobs. Only weak and excruciating groans of mourning escaped her.

Two clanks from the sheriff's office sucked her attention away. She froze, knees still on ground, hands still over her mouth, as she searched for more signs of activity over the humming fluorescent lights. Their incessant buzz seemed to grow louder as she took painstaking steps beside the hoofprints toward the office. The door was open, but the wall it resided on was angled away from her such that she could see nothing inside. She'd have to get right up to the threshold to uncover the identity of the interloper, the owner of these massive and hellish hooves, the cruel deliverer of Monica's demise.

Her head began to pound the way it did when the Nothus approached the party last night. She remembered the sharp pain that tried to take her down, as if the demon had specifically targeted her with its mental attack. To what end, she did not dare speculate.

She padded closer to the open office door, closer, closer, and the sound of an odd breathing pattern, like taking deep breaths through tightly pursed lips, grew more prominent with each step. Her heart felt three times its size as it pounded through her entire torso, the tension so palpable within her, she even grimaced as individual valves fluttered open and closed, blood surging past them. She took one hand from her mouth and lodged her fingers just behind the trim of the door, leaning on them to peek her head inside.

Behind the desk, a figure in a red robe with its back to her sifted through the contents of a cardboard box. Its upper body anatomy was completely obscured by the hood and robe. The back of the head holding the hood was massive from behind. Its bottom half was hidden by the desk. It stood taller than a normal person, maybe seven feet tall hunched over. Its gross breathing was louder and clearer now as it seemed to move slowly and calmly through the box.

Several such boxes littered the ground and the desk. All of them Skylar recognized from her family's home office. The box she thought last contained the Grimoire sat in the corner just inside the door, a corner much closer to Skylar than it was to the robed intruder. A barricade of clear packing tape covered the opening and stretched over its sides.

The thing seemed to emit another sound now, something much softer, a wet clicking or drool dropping that could only be heard when Skylar concentrated on it.

Looking at the figure and then back to the box, Skylar estimated four steps needed to reach it. But once that was accomplished, she'd have to silently lift it, having no knowledge of its weight, bring it back to her car, open it, and grab the Grimoire—if it was even still in there.

She pulled her head back out of the office and leaned against the wall right next to the door, only mouthing the word, *Shit*.

Monica's gun was still lodged in its holster, granted now on the opposite side of the station, and an old hunting rifle leaned in the corner by Abner's desk. She collected the rifle, turned off the safety, and retook her position by the door. Skylar peeked in again, and a cold jolt of lighting shocked her when she couldn't see the creature anywhere. It was just gone, but the Grimoire, as if placed there purposely, was open on the center of an otherwise empty sheriff's desk, also exactly where the blooded hoofprints ended.

Skylar swallowed a lump of dread and walked with the rifle toward the book. The fluorescent lights in here seemed to scream, even vibrate, with electricity above her. The book was open to a page containing a wall of Old English text and a pencil drawing of the Sentinel. As silently as she could, she closed the book and wedged it under her arm.

She turned around and nearly dropped both the book and the gun in shock.

It was standing in the doorway, occupying the room's only exit. Although the robe obscured most of its body, Skylar immediately recognized it as a smaller kind of Nothus. Its red hood was large enough to cover what looked like antlers, giving its head the shape of a hulking upside-down triangle that barely fit through the door. The snout was the most hideous thing she'd ever seen, bony and drooling, tongue hanging out one side, and its eyes were set like two dying coals under the hood's brim. The hooves were bloody but no longer left prints. A collection of long and knotted fingers hung from each of its sleeves.

The sounds it made, the breathing and the slurping, were back in full force now, and it slowly raised its terrible hands out as it walked toward her, quickly closing the distance. Twenty feet away from her, then fifteen, then ten, horrid sounds amplifying, eyes reddening, drool dropping.

Her arms shaking, Skylar cocked the gun and pulled the trigger, and a new panic flooded her when all that came out was a click.

"Oh fuck," she said. "Oh fuck!"

She flipped the gun in her hands, dropping the Grimoire, and she smacked the thing's snout with the butt. It opened its mouth and screeched to high hell, strings of saliva billowing from its jaws. It swiped a hand down, but its stop to screech had afforded Skylar just enough time to duck behind the desk, and its fingers, those massive wands of carnage, dented the wood when they hit the desk, sending splinters into the air.

"Hey!" shouted a male voice from the main office.

The creature then picked up the Grimoire, simply wrapping the fingers of one hand around the entire book, and moved out. Skylar scurried after it.

The man who had identified himself as Roland Pierce stood over Monica's body, her gun in his outstretched hand.

"Get out of here!" he said.

She pointed. "It has the Grimoire!"

"Move aside!"

She did, and Roland fired two shots at the hand holding the book. Those shots, unlike Ellen's from last night, ripped right through the beast and sent geysers of black blood blasting from the wounds. It dropped the book and screeched again.

Skylar made a run for it.

"No! Don't!" Roland said.

She sprinted through sentries of desks and threw over a chair in her path. The creature turned around and swiped down at the desk between it and the Grimoire, totally shattering it. She dove underneath it, flakes of wood and metal raining down on her, and she scooped up the Grimoire before rolling out of the path of another swipe. Skylar had almost cleared it when the third swipe snagged her hood, the force of which was so great it ripped through the cloth and yanked her back to the ground. Roland stepped forward and shot it three more times, and as Skylar scampered to her feet again, a new trickle of black blood sprinkled her back.

But the Grimoire was still in her hands, and now, she was past Roland. She stopped and turned around upon reaching the exit, only to be faced by a panic-stricken Roland barreling over Monica's body right behind her.

"Go! Go now!" he said.

He grabbed her by the arm, and they ran together to the parking lot, his car blocking hers.

"Get in," he said. "We have to talk."

Skylar didn't hesitate, and neither did Roland as his tires squealed in the haste of his reverse.

. . .

Skylar's head throbbed, and her heart ached in Roland's passenger seat. Vacillations between unrelenting fatigue and the raging fires of vengeance left her mind and body reeling. For brief moments, the only thing that felt real was the weight of the Grimoire in her lap.

"Where are we going?" she said weakly.

Roland's windshield wipers were whisking at full speed, but no rain or snow fell. All the sky held was a blue moon waxing gibbous across a dark sea of desolation. He was leaning so far forward his nose hovered barely an inch from white-knuckled hands strangling the wheel.

He looked over at her through foggy eyeglasses. "When was the last time you ate? You don't look well."

Skylar's mind searched for a trite reply but moved too slow to get words out. Her breath became deeper, her eyelids grew heavier, and the hum of fluorescent lights filled her ears as consciousness faded.

This time, she wasn't in the sheriff's office, but the waiting room of the chemo clinic. Everything was cold, colder than normal. The smell of antiseptic filled her nostrils. A handful of bald-headed children played with toys in a corner while parents sat in chairs lining the walls. Those not with their noses buried in magazines gazed longingly at their children, somehow from afar, as if processing the realization that this was the last time they'd ever see their most precious thing.

Skylar was glad her mother never looked at her that way. Her face was never blank or sad or droopy. It was always hard and focused, serious, ready to fight, and looking upon it made Skylar want to fight too. But yet, even with her mother's breath still on her skin and her last words still looping in her ears, it was a face Skylar was already beginning to forget—the distance between her eyes, the exact slope of her nose, the way one edge of her lips rose when she smiled. Was it the right or the left? The question itself shattered her.

Sensing her presence in the adjacent chair, Skylar tried to gaze over but was denied by an unseen force locking her head and eyes firmly on the closed door to the room with the needles, the door from which nurses would exit and children and parents would enter to share moments of pain.

Footsteps snapped through the hall behind the door, short and sharp but also deep, like high block heels or cowboy boots. As the footsteps grew louder, closer, they brought with them a very different sound, something smooth and full, a tidal wave building energy in another dimension. The door began to inch open, and Skylar recognized it as the rumbling she heard while cowering under the Nothus and entering the sheriff's office.

A deeper, rounder, scarier version of her mother's voice echoed from the door. "You're next up, Sky."

And the dangling brown hand slowly opening the door was attached to the red-robed hellion from the station. Its face was completely obscured by the shadow of the hood. It didn't move, just stood there, one hand holding open the door, the other hanging down, fingertips bent from their contact with the floor.

Something jostled her shoulder, and Skylar woke up.

"Hey," Roland said.

The neon lights of a late-night diner blared at her through the windshield. Roland threw the car in park and got out. Skylar rubbed her eyes and followed, still clutching the Grimoire.

They sat in a booth in the corner for ten minutes without saying a word to each other, only to the waitress who took their orders.

"Are we in Sperryville? Why did we come all the way out here?" Skylar finally said.

"To get away from that thing. There's more of them."

Skylar shifted her legs in a way that squeezed her cell phone uncomfortably in the front pocket of her jeans. She covertly pulled it out and set it beside her on the bench.

"What was it?"

"I'm not totally sure. It's some kind of derivative of the Nothus Noctis."

"How do you know there are more?"

Roland darted his eyes around the room before answering. "You know that clearing in the forest where it killed your mother? That's sacred ground. It's where the summoning ritual was performed just days ago, and it's under that dirt that the Nothus makes its home. They were created there in a ceremony the Order calls a Pariunt." He made air quotes with his fingers. "Spawning."

"Who summoned them?"

"I believe an old member of the Bensalem chapter. It may have even been the man who was the Sentinel before Mark Harcourt."

"How do I know you're not full of shit? How do I know you didn't summon them?"

He took a long sip of his coffee. "Because I tried to kill that thing back there. I put myself at risk to help you."

The food came—Roland's steak and eggs, Skylar's cheeseburger with onion rings. The waitress looked over them both uneasily as she set down the plates.

"What do you want?" Skylar said between bites.

"I want that book."

"Why?"

"The same reason you do. Our interests are aligned, Skylar. You want the Nothus gone, right?"

"Aren't you, like, the leader of the cult? Isn't this all your fault?"

Roland sighed and looked over to a family of five in the booth behind them. The parents sat on one side of the booth while all three children crammed into the other. All had soft smiles on their faces as they ate. None of them had taken off their coats.

"I'm happy to explain whatever you want. My official title is High Deacon of the Order of the Old Roses. I report directly to the Grand Elder. He is the leader of our Order, an Order that's been active all over the world for hundreds of years. We believe in many things. We do many things. Above all, we seek enlightenment."

"Enlightenment?"

"Complete and total esoteric wisdom." He gestured broadly

with his hands. "An understanding of the divine. Mastery of the natural world. None of these things are bad things, Skylar. We seek the things mankind has sought from its earliest days. In fact, it was quite mainstream in the 16th and 17th centuries. Back then, scholars, philosophers, and politicians examined the world through both religious and scientific lenses. They practiced alchemy and became responsible for many of our race's greatest scientific discoveries. They pioneered our exploration of the edges of the natural world—the world you and I can see and touch and interact with."

"They also burned women at the stake for having periods."

"I'll be the first to admit not all these men were perfect, but the vast majority of them were good and sought the betterment of mankind. They were responsible for many scientific discoveries and important advancements of faith." He took another sip and lowered his tone. "But sometimes in doing so, they discovered other things. Unnatural things. Evil and powerful things."

"The Nothus?"

"The Order of the Old Roses doesn't operate the way a normal religion does. We don't hold church services or ask for donations. Not from regular citizens, at least. We don't do any of that secular stuff. We can't. We can't even be known about beyond political and cultural circles we can't trust. Because what we do now is too sensitive. If people knew... well, what do you think would happen to the world if everyone knew about the Nothus? What would it do to society and religion? It's our job to guard the world from these terrible things."

"Is the Nothus one of those things? You must be doing a pretty shitty job."

"Do you know how it started? Have you been reading that book you have there?"

Skylar nodded.

"So, then you know about Judithe Peel? You know about the New King Salomon?"

Skylar stopped eating. "I know Judithe's story."

"If indeed you've read the Grimoire, you know what happened next. The Nothus killed hundreds of people in Bensalem before the first Sentinel was created. Among the dead was one of our Order's most important prophets and visionaries, the New King Salomon. He was a master of transformational alchemy. He tried many things to stop it but couldn't. He paid for it with his life."

"So then, how did they figure out the Sentinel thing would work?"

"His disciples were very adept. Too adept, some might say. After the Nothus decimated their people, the Bensalem chapter went down a path not sanctioned by the Order. Some call it the left-hand path. Have you heard of that?"

"I think so, actually. My boyfriend is really into that stuff. Magic and witchcraft."

"Well, I suggest he get out of it."

Skylar shrugged.

"You must understand. I came down here to put an end to the cycle of Sentinels. With Jane Harcourt's passing, we saw an opportunity to move past the old ways and achieve a more permanent solution. We want to reverse the ritual and destroy the Nothus."

"Is that how you do it? Reverse the ritual?"

"Well, we don't know exactly, but it's our best guess. But if there is a solution, it's there in that book of writings from the New King Salomon's original disciples. Where did you get it, anyway?"

"In my mom's stuff. I don't know where she got it."

He reached out a hand. "Don't you think you'd be better off letting me look at it?"

"Not really." Skylar rose from the booth. "You guys have let this thing just wreak havoc for hundreds of years, and now you want to fix it?"

"Skylar, we have too much to lose to quibble over this."

"We? Excuse me?" Her raised voice attracted the attention of other patrons. Roland's gaze sank to the floor while hers lasered through him. "Where were you last night when it was killing my mother? Huh? What about Monica? Who's next? Does your book tell you that?"

"Skylar, I'm sorry. I didn't—"

"I'm not giving it to you because I don't trust you."

"If you can't trust me, then who can you trust?"

Just then, the diner door swung open. Ram wore his typical all black—boots, pants, parka, beanie. "This is him?" he said.

"Yeah," Skylar responded.

"Not what I was expecting."

Skylar turned away from Roland and toward Ram. "Let's go."

"Wait!" Roland said as they departed.

Skylar turned around.

"They're gonna chase you. They're looking for that book too. They want to end the cycle of the Sentinels but in the worst possible way. They want the Nothus to run free. They want to do to you, to your boyfriend, to your father, to everyone in this town what they did to that police officer back there."

Ram and Skylar looked at each other.

Skylar shook her head.

"That book may be the only thing that can stop them. Their desire to obtain it is why I'm convinced it contains a solution."

She glared at him for a long moment and released an exhale through her nostrils. "I'll think about it."

Roland dug a card out of his pocket. She took it.

"Be careful, Skylar. Please."

. . .

SR 639 between Sperryville and Bensalem was straight, but no road ran straighter or truer than the hard line of Skylar's constitution. She took a hand off the wheel to pluck her cell phone from her pocket.

Rick had called twice and texted. *Where are u???*

She flipped it closed without responding. Her eyes danced across a luminescent dashboard.

"You're running low on gas," she said.

In the passenger seat, Ram crammed the second half of the Grimoire. Until Skylar's gas comment just now, they had driven in complete silence while he squinted at text, flipped pages and whole sections, and mouthed words to himself.

It was the first time Skylar could remember them in the car together without the ear-splitting bliss of heavy metal, usually a welcome third member of their conversations. She glanced at the unlit face of the radio and then back at the road.

"Anything?" she said.

"Eh, kinda," Ram said, squinting at the text.

"What?"

"My Latin is so rusty."

"Shut up. You're, like, the only person in the world who even knows it."

"That's not true. I was, like, the worst in my class."

"What does the book say?"

Ram pulled a flashlight from the glove box and shined its light on the pages. "Okay, well, I'm not through it all yet. The second half is set up a lot like the first, like a Bible with chapters and verses, but there are a lot more interruptions. Lots of drawings, diagrams, random lists of ingredients. Some of this stuff is mundane. Like, there are normal medicine recipes in here. Like, there's one for headaches. But then there are lists of ingredients and procedures for these rituals."

"That guy I was talking to at the diner mentioned one. I forget the name. Something about spawning. He said the thing that killed Monica wasn't the Nothus but a spawn that came from a ritual."

"Yeah, there's definitely a ton of rituals. I found the one they think Judithe used to summon the Nothus. That was actually in the first half of the book, but I didn't think it was relevant until now."

"It was an accident, right?"

"The text says she said it was an accident, but I don't get the feeling whoever wrote this believed her."

Skylar scoffed. "Typical."

"The name of that one was"—he flipped back several pages—"Sanitatum Silva, which basically means 'forest healing.'"

"Because she tried to summon a forest deity to protect them."

"Yeah, I think that's right. So, Judithe tried this Sanitatum Silva ritual but did something wrong, and instead of Herne the Hunter, out popped Nothus Noctis."

The two went silent as Skylar slowed the car and veered into a gas station on the side of the road. The bright overhead lights served as sharp contrast to the desolation of the road and of the land, so much so that it seemed almost out of place, a random injection of civilization into a nocturnal wasteland. Skylar hesitated before opening the door.

"Anything else?" she said.

"I'm not totally sure, but it looks like there were attempts to perform Sanitatum Silva in reverse that failed."

"Roland thought that might be the solution. To reverse the ritual."

"Here, I marked the section." He flipped forward a good two-thirds of the book to a page corner he had bent over. "Okay, this is all in Latin, so I'll try to paraphrase. Healing of the wood... healing reversal. Not correct nexum. Can't access something called... the core? A tainted bloodline. Something about familiarities... I think. Man, this doesn't make any sense. My Latin's not good enough." He looked at Skylar. "Hey, do you think Roland knows Latin?"

"Just try. What else does it say?"

"Attempt failed. Another reference to this *nexum* thing. Several other materials... I definitely can't translate those. Some kind of compound. A dead bird. Another season wasted. Edges of heaven. Nexum purity... something, something incomplete."

"What's *nexum*? A Latin word?"

"I thought it translated to, like, a connection or a conduit. A nexus, you know? But they use it in a weird way, like it's a physical thing or a person, even an energy or intention. This is definitely written in a style I'm not familiar with, and it gets stranger as the book goes on."

"What was that about a bloodline?"

"Well, I'm not sure exactly, but it did seem like every time this reversal ritual is attempted, the person who performed it died. I don't know if it was the ritual that killed them or the Nothus—I think the ritual—but it sounds like they stopped trying after the first Sentinel was created. Remember that passage we read about how happy they were when they discovered it stopped the Nothus? Remember they said they tried a bunch of alchemy and shit? I think this is what they meant."

Skylar undid her seatbelt and slunk to her side so she rested on the open Grimoire in Ram's lap. She stared straight ahead at the glove compartment. Ram put his hands on the back of her head and neck.

"I'm so sorry, Sky. I'm so sorry about all this."

She reached around for one of his hands and gripped it, squeezing his fingers between hers.

"You want any gum?" she said.

"Sure. You goin' in? I'll do the gas."

She nodded as she pushed herself up. He caught her before she was fully upright and kissed her on the lips. They embraced each other for a few fleeting moments—maybe ten seconds, maybe an hour—before she got out. Skylar pulled the remnants of her sliced hood over her head before they simply fell away. She sighed.

The convenience store attached to the gas station was no larger than a walk-in closet separated in two halves by plexiglass. The man on the other side of the glass—short, balding, wearing a vest with pearl snap buttons—paid her no mind. A plethora of brightly colored gums and candies grinned up at her from their shelves. She grabbed two packs of her favorite gum, glanced at the soft drinks, and strolled over to the glass.

"Buck fifty," the man said.

Skylar's attention was on the wads of bills and coins in her pocket, not on the rumbling slowly building in her head. Something small hit the glass, a pebble fired from the world's smallest slingshot, and when Skylar peered down at the counter in front of the man, she saw a pearl snap button spinning on its side.

Five long, thin, blood-coated rods were sticking through the man's chest. They pulled themselves gingerly out, sucking and squelching as they massaged the still-beating tissue inside him. His face was aghast, forlorn eyes glaring at Skylar. Two coughs sprayed the plexiglass in huge splats of blood, and his head slumped as red streams spilled from his lips and ran down his chin.

And when the jagged circle of blood on the glass had thinned and started racing in hundreds of lines toward the ground, the man collapsed in a crumpled heap. Standing there behind him, a red-robed Nothus spawn, holding fast its bony and bloody hand, now gazed at Skylar through the crimson-stained screen. Its eyes, as if set on a dimmer under its hood, morphed from nothingness to scorching red hot.

"Oh fuck!" Ram bellowed from the gas pumps outside.

Skylar booked it out of the store.

The pump was still in Ram's hand when another spawn emerged from behind the stall. It raised both hands in the air and slammed them down in a fury, missing Ram, missing the car, but slicing clean through the fuel line attached to the pump. It took a half step back as the flailing pipe drenched the area in rancid petroleum but swiped again, knocking Ram to the ground.

"Ram!" Skylar yelled.

Ram rolled underneath the car and was drenched in gas when he emerged on Skylar's side. He threw off his hat and parka.

"Fuck. Fuck!" he said.

Skylar jerked open the passenger door and began rifling through the glove box, but not before making sure the Grimoire was still sitting on the seat.

The frame of the car smashed across Skylar's back, pinning her down with a grunt and turning the interior of the car into a snow globe of flying bits of tempered glass. The spawn smashed the car again from the driver's side, cracking her back again and sending more glass flying. She clawed through the glove box while her legs hung out the door. The spawn screeched and smashed the car again.

Ram ran around the back of the car, picked up the still-spewing fuel line, and doused the spawn in gasoline.

Skylar slipped out of the wreckage and tossed a matchbook end over end toward him. "Hey!" she shouted.

Ram dropped the fuel line and caught the matchbook.

Skylar, Grimore in her arms, hell raked across her face, ran with a limp past him.

Ram plucked a match and used it to turn the entire book into a flaming card between his fingers.

"Fuck you," he said, flicking the flaming book at the spawn. He sprinted back to the road, crashing into Skylar's embrace and falling to his knees.

Gripping each other, both teenagers turned to watch a screeching spawn fumble around the car, completely engulfed in wild and raging orange flames. Only the very tips of its fingers could be seen flailing through the fire.

Seconds later, the earth shook when the car's gas tank exploded, lifting the vehicle several inches off the ground and sending a column of fire into the sky.

"Jesus Christ." Skylar said.

"Did you get—"

The force of another explosion, this one bigger than the last, knocked them both down again. The gas pump itself had exploded, and now the entire station was a holocaust of fire and burning metal.

"Yeah," Skylar said, picking up the Grimoire in the grass beside her. "I got it. We have it." She took a step but faltered.

Ram caught her and strung her arm across his shoulders.

"You all right?" he said.

"I'm fine. Let's go."

Neither of them stopped to check wounds. They just limped together on the shoulder of the road, propping each other up and holding on tight.

. . .

His master's orders rattled around in what was left of his brain, in what was left of him.

Silence the heretics. Clear the way.

Until the last heretic fell, until the last tool at their disposal was destroyed.

The New King Salomon's path was set. The way markers were in place.

No stranger to new bodies, the chafing didn't bother him. Unlike his first physical transformation, these gifts the New King Salomon had bestowed upon him were visceral and real, thorough in their making. The New King had taken the mortal coil of a man and imbued every cell, manipulated every pore, and commandeered every blood vessel to form a perfect crusader of death.

Sixty years ago, when the Elders coated him in that crudely slapped-together suit of black mud, his body stayed human while growing inside it. The thick armor suffocated his lungs, making every breath a chore that needed to be focused on to complete without pain. Movement caused his skin to rub against the coarse material, and his untreated wounds would bleed and fester for days and weeks at a time. Even his bodily waste had nowhere to go, making the smell from the inside utterly unbearable. Forty years free of it, that stench still lingered in his nostrils—a horrid puree of feces, metal, and rot. The pain and discomfort of that suit was a constant every single day of his underground life.

Silence the heretics.

But this time, his true form had changed. There was no going back, and now that he was past the initial pain, no part of him wanted to.

The transformation started in his lower body. Maurice cried out to his master, his god, when both of his knees broke spontaneously and twisted back so far that his legs now bent the opposite way. He moaned and mashed his molars when the bones in his feet were compacted into rock-hard hooves and the skin surrounding them simply fell away. Fruitlessly, he clutched his chest in excruciating agony as each one of his ribs expanded in both width and length, stretching his flesh and his tendons beyond their bounds, lighting countless searing fires inside him. The aching in his face was unbearable when his jaw, already maimed and broken, along with his nose, hardened and merged, and they extended, and extended, and extended, such that he could no longer see the ground directly below his new snout. The searing pain in his skull, when his eyes turned into hulking red balls too big for their sockets, was so intense he nearly pulled them out just to make it end, and a billion razor-sharp needles pierced what was left of his skin from the inside, amplifying his total agony, as thick, animalistic hairs threaded themselves through strained pores.

Patience. Soon, you will eat at the blessed table. But not yet...

It felt as though ten ruthless giants played tug of war with each of his fingers, stretching the bone, shucking the skin, popping the joints over and over again. At first, his new hands were so heavy he struggled to lift them, but with the pain also came strength, an unbelievable strength, and once it had subsided, he lusted to crush life with them. Worst of all these pains, though, were the antlers. Born from nothing but knots on his skull, they broke the skin of his scalp like knives, sending waterfalls of blood gushing down his beastly head and face, and they grew and splintered in what felt like a thousand directions. By this time, though, he had no voice to cry out and no mind to form words with, so all he could do was launchl formless screams in the void.

Yet for all the physical pain this transformation caused him, it inversely eased the one source of suffering he could not alleviate through all his trials and tribulations both above ground and below it—his pain of self. With each break, each growth, each snap, and each tear, the maze of his mind was stripped down into a single corridor of thought leading directly to his master. Gone were all memories of his time underground. Gone was the pain and trauma the world of the living had put him through. Gone was any semblance of identity or soul. Maurice Bacon even forgot his own name. He no longer needed it.

All he needed was his master, his lord, his New King Salomon. For his was the kingdom, the power, the glory, and with the Nothus and its envoys at his disposal, the achievement of New Atlantis was at hand.

At first, it didn't make sense, that the beast he had been taught to fear and been asked to fight every night for twenty years was not the enemy, but the vehicle.

Come, the New King Salomon whispered. *Follow, and descend.*

And heeding his master's new instructions, traveling deep into the forest, stepping through the door, and gazing upon the Chamber's splendor, all was revealed.

Silence the heretics. Clear the way.

And so, they did.

Just hours ago, one of the envoys did well to locate the book and slay the young policewoman but failed in securing it. Two more red-cloaked reapers marauding across the snowy plain followed the scent of their brethren's blood that had fallen on the girl's clothing.

The girl... The girl...

And right now, two more patrolled the perimeter of a great house on a hill, looking for ways in but not finding any. They could hear the German Shepherd growling at them through the front door, and they could see through the walls the three heretics sleeping inside—a burning young woman, her mother, and the boy who almost became the next Sentinel.

But there would be no more Sentinels.

Clear the way.

He, along with the rest of them, was behind the motel again, pacing in circles and chanting in low tones, smelling the stench of the heretic on the other side of the wall. Tonight, they would strike him.

But a sharp light rose suddenly from the far side of the building, and the envoys stopped in their tracks and turned toward it. A scream emanated from the source of the light. Although his entire world was now viewed through rose-colored orbs, the vague memory of purple cloaked the old woman standing there, frozen in terror. She screamed again, her words completely unintelligible.

The rest of the envoys remained still as he, clad still in his brown cleric's robe, strode toward her. The woman did not move. She just stood there, holding her light and screaming.

With the strength and fury of the New King Salomon, he drove one hand into her but missed the mark, his fingers penetrating the side of her neck and her shoulder instead of her chest. He was still getting used to his body. His second strike was accurate, and his entire hand speared clean through her stomach.

With all ten fingers now impaling the old woman, he lifted her into the air, oblivious to her moaning. Eruptions of blood poured down his fingers. With one quick movement, he twisted the entire upper half of his wretched body and threw her against the side of the wall. Some of his fingers slipped back out through the holes they had created in her, and others tore clean through the edges of her flesh. A smattering of pops and snaps erupted from the woman when she hit the wall, and then again when she hit the ground. Both tibia and fibula of her left leg jutted out from their casing of skin and pants. Her shattered ribs swam in a stew of hemorrhaging organs, and her left arm, already halfway ripped off by impalement, hung lifelessly on the ground, connected to its host by only a few desparate sinews.

A bubbling mix of words and blood seeped out of her mouth. Towering over her, he stomped a hoof into her face, shattering bones and sending sprays of blood and bits of bone into the air. Loose fragments of her brain and flesh dripped off his hoof before he stomped again, and again, and again. And again. And again. And again, until the woman's head was gone and its countless liquids and pieces lay in a pool of fresh rot behind the motel she managed.

On the other side of the motel, the screech of peeling tires ripped through the oncoming dawn.

. . .

Derek Brady hadn't slept in over a day. The bags under his eyes sagged down sunken cheeks, and his head teetered back and forth with fatigue. He couldn't get the gruesome image of his boss's tattered body out of his head. Nor could he shake the cold that had settled in his bones from the walk out there. He believed Skylar, Ram, and Ellen—that wasn't the issue. What creature or person could have possibly done that to her, and why, spun his tired brain in circles. After examining the wounds with the EMTs and crime tech team, the only thing that made sense was a force the three witnesses had described.

But a force like that didn't make any sense. It didn't when his sat him down in her new office and told him what Duke had said, and it didn't make sense now. How could something like that exist without him knowing about it? How could it exist at all?

The clock on his dashboard read 05:45, and the temperature gauge next to it read 23 F°.

The CB radio tossed a loud burst of static through the cab, followed by the panicked voice of Sperryville's dispatcher.

"A.P.B. Squad 14 to all squads. Repeat. Squad 14 to all squads. Structure fire and major petroleum leak at a gas station, Starbound Gas, that's S-T-A-R-B-O-U-N-D Gas, just south of Exit 37 on SR 639. Active fire, gas leak in the road, and the FD's on their way. It doesn't sound good. No sense of injuries yet. We can't get close enough. Unsure of the cause. Repeat, this is an active fire and gas leak. All available units, please respond. All available units, please respond. Over."

He pulled over and through his passenger side window gazed at the plume of smoke faintly visible against the navy panorama of night.

"Holy fuck," he said.

Brady picked up his cell phone, but before he could open it, it started ringing. "Uriah Mathias" flashed across the screen.

"Hey, Uriah, what—"

"Sir! You've got to get down here! Right now!"

"What? What's wrong?"

"Monica's dead! She's lying in a pool of her own blood right here in the office."

Brady blinked twice and swallowed, unable to respond.

"Sir, did you hear me?"

"Y—yeah. I heard you. Suicide?"

"I don't know. Her neck is all slashed up. I don't think so. I've called crime tech. They're on their way."

He knew the answer to his next question but asked it anyway. "Are you fuckin' kidding me?"

"Oh God. I wish I was. You better come down here."

"I'm on my—"

Brady dropped the phone. The skin on the back of his neck ran cold with pins and needles, and his eyes bulged at what he saw in his headlights.

Crossing the road in front of him and slipping into the forest were half a dozen cloven-hooved nightmares. They looked half man, half deer, all monster. All but one wore a red robe torn in places where hideous appendages and antlers poked through the cloth. The one in the front, the apparent leader, wore brown, and a dark and shiny liquid dripped from fingers as long as Derek Brady's arm.

Each step they took further broke his construct of reality, and as he sat, staring dumbfounded at them, a typhoon of dread drenched both his mind and his body.

Uriah's hurried and heightened voice echoed meekly through the cell phone by his shaking feet.

DAY 7

Every muscle in Skylar's body was sore. She couldn't feel her face or anything below her knees. Her head lolled in front of her, gazing wearily at their four black-booted feet trudging through the rocky grass on the side of the road. She had pulled her fingers back through the sleeves of her hoodie, but that did little to warm them. They ached with the stiff chill of winter while clutching the edges of the Grimoire, and she shivered, knowing the lingering feeling in them would soon be gone too.

She glanced briefly at Ram's face. Glistening lines of snot ran from his nose, and his lips were blue. His sights were set on the horizon, but the vacancy in his eyes led her to believe he wasn't looking at anything. Black soot and ash from the explosion patched the rest of his face, and his clothes still reeked of gasoline. The stench barely covered her own body odor.

Frozen sweat coated her skin, and her back, where the spawn had slammed the door frame down on her, throbbed in a dull pain, making it feel like her vertebrae might fall out of her spine at any second. She knew there was blood on her—black blood from the spawn at the police station, red blood from the man at the gas station—but she chose only to look down.

The pale globe of a dawn moon beckoned them forward, swimming in a blue sky layered over orange rims of sunrise. Most of the snow had melted yesterday, and while the night was cold enough to freeze the two road-bound vagabonds, its relative warmth had turned the plain into a sloshing marshland.

The grinding crescendo of tires on pavement built behind them. They did not turn around, nor did they react when the car's passenger, a massive woman whose corpulence completely obscured the driver, rolled down the window.

"Hey!" she said. "Hey, you kids all right?"

They kept walking, shoulder to shoulder, balled fists in pockets, eyes nearly frozen shut.

"Can y'all hear me?" she said, a bit louder.

They stopped, and with as little movement as possible, turned toward her.

The woman's jaw dropped. "Are—are you sure y'all are all right?"

Skylar's response was a phlegm-coated choke. "Yeah. We're fine."

With jagged lines of shock and confusion tattooed across the woman's face, she rolled up the window in horrified silence. The car drove on, and they stood and watched it for a moment before resuming their trek.

Skylar's cell phone rang, but neither of them had the strength or motivation to answer it. In fact, her first reaction to its tinny chime was one of apprehension, assuming it was her mother calling to berate her for not coming home last night. In that moment, and for the first time ever, Skylar wished for that call.

Two dull yellow lights, like the reflection in a cat's eyes, appeared on the asphalt void up ahead. They grew in size and shape, and the chrome grille of an SUV formed around them.

"Finally," Skylar said.

The SUV veered through the opposite side of the road and parked on the shoulder in front of them. Ellen Dreyer, clad in jeans and a down vest, opened the door.

"Jesus." She ran to Skylar and wrapped her arms around her. "Are you okay?"

Skylar wilted in her arms, but Ellen held her up. She heaved and cried for a brief moment, the warm trails of her tears brushing life into her cheeks again.

"Let's get you guys cleaned up. Are you hurt at all?" she said, looking over them.

"I'm fine," Ram said. "Skylar was in my car when one of those things smashed it. How's your back, Sky?"

"It's sore, but I'm fine," Skylar said.

"Can I take a look at it for you?" Ellen placed a delicate hand on Skylar's back as she escorted them into the SUV.

"I need to go home. My family needs me."

They followed Ellen's guided direction and warily slumped into her back seat. Instantly, the warmth of the cab began to loosen the stiffness calcifying Skylar's knees and ankles.

"Let me see your back?" Ram said.

Skylar leaned forward in her seat next to him.

With a gentle hand, Ram lifted the back of Skylar's hoodie up to her shoulder blades.

"Oh Sky," he said.

A thick, throbbing purple bruise ran the width of her back. The car frame had cracked her so hard that tiny bubbles of blood had formed where the mangled clasp of her bra strap pierced her skin.

Ram kissed her back twice before lowering her shirt back down. "There's a huge bruise. We should ice it. Does it hurt?"

Skylar closed her eyes and laid her head on Ram's shoulder. Ram sighed before wrapping an arm around her and pulling her in close.

"What happened to you guys back there?" Ellen said.

Ram shook his head. "There were two of them at the gas station. One burned in the fire. I don't think we saw what happened to the other one."

"Two what?"

"These... things. Things that looked like the Nothus. Spawns, apparently."

"Spawns?"

"Yeah. We don't know where they came from but we know they're after us. They're after the Grimoire and anyone trying to end the cycle." He took the book from Skylar's limp arms and began thumbing through it.

"What do you mean by anyone?" Ellen said.

"I don't know. We heard it all secondhand. There's a senior member of the Order of the Old Roses in town trying to stop it. He's the one who saved Skylar at the station. Did you hear about the officer there?"

A quiet moment passed. "Yeah," Ellen said. "Skylar told me over the phone."

Ram squinted and ran his index finger along lines of text.

"We have to end it," Ellen said.

Ram looked up. "End what?"

"The cycle. Mark is weak."

"Mark? The Sentinel?"

"Yeah," she said softly. "I think he only has days left. If that. I'm so worried about him."

Ram went back to reading.

Skylar's mind swam through rivers of dream. She drifted through the police station, the chemo clinic, and that murky wasteland of color she felt was a memory not her own, as if implanted or embedded deep within her centuries ago, waiting to be awoken at the right moment. Skylar tried to look closer at the shapes and colors, but they evaded her. The same series of blurry events unfolded. Green and yellow blobs—no, cones… trees, perhaps?—sat behind the shape of a young woman kneeling over an altar. Was she blond? And what were those stars she fiddled with? Pieces of something magnificent and bright?

The shrill tone of a cell phone jolted her back to waking life.

"Hey," Ellen said. She held the phone to her ear for a few seconds before taking it away and putting it on speaker.

Derek Brady's voice filled the car.

"Five or six of 'em, at least! These fuckin' hoofprints were out in the snow at the old motel! And they're all over the goddamned station! And—"

"Derek." Ellen said.

"They looked just like the ones in the woods—"

"Derek! Slow down!"

"The ligature marks on Monica's neck—"

"Derek! Derek! I have them here! They're with me."

"I can't… oh. Skylar? Ram? You guys okay?"

Skylar leaned forward. "We're okay. There were two more at the gas station fire. That's how that happened."

"Good God. How many of 'em are there?"

"We don't know," Skylar replied.

"Well, we might have killed one," Ram said. "We lit it on fire. It didn't chase after us, so—"

"These things are wreakin' fuckin' havoc," Brady said. "How

do we stop 'em? How do we stop this?"

Ellen glanced back at Ram and shook her head, a longing look in her eyes. "Did you learn anything?"

"Not yet," Ram said. "Well, maybe. I've got the Grimoire and I'm trying to get through the parts I haven't read. It seems like we can kill, or at least hurt, the spawns. Assuming they're kind of the same thing, they won't be able to do anything when it's light out. We know the Nothus' movement is restricted to darkness."

"Derek, where did you say they went?" Ellen asked.

"Into the forest. They just crossed right in front of me, like a herd of deer or somethin'. Except they were definitely not deer."

"Was it still dark?"

"Barely. But yeah, it was still dark."

"The thing we need to stop is the Nothus," Ram said. "I think this all stops once it's gone."

"How do we do that?"

"All we've been able to gather so far is that it was summoned through some kind of ritual, and that it might take repeating some version of that ritual to reverse it."

"What kinda ritual? Like a seance?"

"No, something more serious. Something the Order would have performed when they first got here to protect themselves. According to the Grimoire, it happened by accident when someone tried to summon an old deity they believed in back in England. These people believed all kinds of occult shit. But the ritual got messed up somehow, and instead, they summoned a demon. Or at least, that's what the text claims."

"Well," Brady said, "how the hell do we... I don't know... unsummon it? What do we need to do?"

All went silent.

"I know someone who can help," Skylar said, but she did not speak again.

For the rest of the ride home, Skylar withdrew into herself as layers of the world peeled away. Trees and mountains whisking through the windows lost their form and meaning, blending into a beige-gray slurry of anonymity. Ellen's car felt less to her like a vehicle driving down an earthly asphalt road and more like an interstellar travel pod hurtling into an abyss. She felt all at once directionless, timeless, and detached from reality, a sensation derived not by choice, but in yielding to a mysterious kernel of responsibility lodged somewhere in her memory. The only way to get closer to it, to find it, was to focus and to be alone. Not even Ellen and Ram, possibly the only two people alive who might understand, could help her now, and even the steel fortress she sat in held for her no quarter.

. . .

An angry young man greeted Skylar when she opened the front door. Lenny McNamara sat with his head in his hands on the living room couch.

"Where the hell have you been?" he said without moving.

His words were coarse and frail but sharp enough to nearly knock the wind out of her. She glared at him until he lifted his head, revealing a puffy red face and a mop of unwashed hair.

"I was out," was all she could muster.

He scoffed. "Out? Where?"

"You wouldn't understand. I'm trying to fix it. "

"Fix what?"

Skylar started toward the stairs.

"Hey! Where do you think you're going?" he said.

She glanced through the array of family photos trundling

up the staircase wall. The entire family unit was present in all of them, each taken exactly a year apart on her mother's birthday, because every year that's what she asked for. In the early pictures, Lenny either cradled Skylar or loomed over her with a brotherly smile. But as the years passed, the two children separated, eventually flanking their parents, with Skylar inching ever closer to Lenny's height.

"I fucking watched her die, okay?" Skylar said.

"Yeah, and what the fuck? What were you doing up there to begin with? What happened?"

"You wouldn't understand, Lenny. Trust me."

"Some monster? Seriously? People are saying Mom got killed by some monster out in the woods. And you were there, and you don't know how to explain it?"

"It's more complicated than that."

"How complicated can it be? Just explain it to me."

Skylar took her hand off the railing and sat on the steps. "It's more than just a monster. It's this thing that's been living out of the woods for hundreds of years. We don't really know where it came from or why it's here, but we're trying to figure that out. I am trying to figure that out. Really. I'm trying to fix it by avenging Mom."

"What were you guys doing out there in the first place?"

"We were trying to stop it. Mom was trying to stop it."

Lenny clapped his hands to his head and grabbed handfuls of hair, as if to pull it right out of his skull. Skylar's eyes tracked him as he crouched and stared at the ground. "That is completely fucking crazy. Listen to yourself. This is crazy talk, Skylar. How am I supposed to believe that?" He looked back up at her.

Skylar didn't have an answer. She just shook her head slowly, her eyes wide and her mouth hanging open.

"Sky"—he stood and took a step toward her—"I... I don't understand this at all."

Something fired in Skylar's heart as she beheld her brother's confusion. He stood at the bottom of the stairs with his shoulders hunched and his palms up. The rawness of his grief and the salty smell of his tears cast him in a haze of darkness. His eyes begged to be reached out to. Held. Loved.

Skylar threw her arms around him. He reciprocated and sobbed into her shoulder. She squeezed him tight, as hard as she could, and kept balance for the both of them. When finally he pulled away, his entire face was beet red and swollen.

"Where have you been, Sky?" he whispered. "We need you here. You're covered in... what is that?"

"I—I know. I'm sorry."

"I'm so confused."

"I know."

"Mom would want you here. Why weren't you here? Dad and I need you."

"I've... I don't know, Lenny. I don't know. I need to go."

"What? What do you mean you need to go?"

"I need to shower and change and get going. Ram and I are working on a way to fix it. We're working with the police."

"You're working with the police? How? You keep saying 'fix it.' There's nothing to fix."

"Yes. There is. The thing that killed Mom is still out there, and it needs to be fixed. It's hard to explain. I just feel really strongly about this. I can't even fully explain it to Ram. I don't know how to process it, but... but I just feel like that's where I need to be. That's what I need to be doing."

Lenny shook his head. "I just don't get you. I don't understand this. Have you cried at all? Are you even sad?"

"What the fuck? Of course, I'm sad!"

"Then why aren't you crying?"

"I don't know! I'm exhausted! Jesus, Lenny, why do you think I'm doing this? For fun? Stop judging me."

"Mom would want you here. She would want us all together."

A split-second image of the waiting room flashed through Skylar's mind. The colorful walls. The bald children. The Nothus spawn opening the door.

"I know, but... but she would also want me to keep fighting. Us. She would want us to keep fighting. She was out there because she wanted to stop it."

Her words bounced off Lenny's blank stare as if it were a brick wall.

"Lenny, I love you. I'm sorry I'm not here. I am grieving. Trust me. I'm just... I'm just doing it differently than you. I'm not doing this for me. I'm doing it for Mom. I feel like we're close to something and we have to see it through."

"Who's *we*?"

"Me and Ram. Ellen Dreyer. Derek Brady. There's also this guy who..." Skylar shook her head. "It doesn't matter. We're meeting at the police station to figure out a plan."

For the first time since coming home, enough silence passed for her to notice the sounds of the house. The hissing of the radiators. The ticking of the old clock on the mantel.

"Can I help?" he said.

"Help Dad. He needs you. You can help us by just... just help Dad."

Lenny took a deep breath and rubbed his eyes. He hung his head.

Skylar hugged him again. "Everything's gonna be okay."

He sighed. "No, it's not."

When she released him, she tip-toed up the rest of the stairs, careful not to wake a snoring Rick. Her cellphone had been dead for some time now, so she plugged it in and let it charge while she showered off the filth and the pain of the last twenty-four hours. She stood in the shower for longer than normal, leaning both hands against the wall and letting the spray massage her scalp.

Why was she obsessing over this? Was she really being a bad sister, a bad daughter? How utterly insane had this situation become? A dozen "spawns," as Roland called them, running around town and killing people?

Was Ellen serious about the Sentinel having just a few days left? How could she know that? What would happen then? Did the Grimoire really have a solution in it? What if it didn't?

Is any of this even real?

"God, this is so fucked," she whispered to herself.

. . .

Ram picked up Skylar in his father's truck, and they met Brady at the station. A pink, oval-shaped stain remained on the linoleum where Monica's body had been. Crime tech had just left, Brady said, and added that he cleaned up the hoofprints and the sheriff's office on his own. He was sitting glassy-eyed at his desk and didn't move when the teenagers walked in. Skylar surmised that he looked ten years older than he did yesterday morning. He sat at his boxy little desk in the corner, not in the sheriff's office or even the slightly larger one her mother had occupied as deputy.

Ellen joined them a little after noon. Skylar had to look at the clock on the wall to know what time it was because, outside, the cold and colorless world had not changed in hours. Ellen looked similar to how she did the night they encountered the Nothus, rugged and armed to the teeth.

"Nice gun," Brady said. "Amber'd never let me have somethin' like that."

"You can have it when the Nothus is dead," Ellen replied.

Ram didn't participate in the conversation. He sat with a curved back and a furrowed brow over the Grimoire, flipping pages and scribbling in a pad.

All looked up when Roland Pierce walked in. Skylar stood and walked over to him.

"This is Roland Pierce. He's with the Order of the Old Roses."

"Roland Pierce?" Ellen said.

He nodded at her.

"The same Roland Pierce who came to my house and lied about being a police detective?"

"Oh. You must be Ellen Dreyer?"

Ellen turned to Brady. "This is that asshole I told you about. Remember? Remember a fake cop came over and shook down Aaron for information?"

"Is that true?" Brady said to him.

Ellen turned back to Roland. "And your car was out there the night he was abducted. Wasn't it?"

Roland pulled his hands from his coat pockets and held them out in protest. "Okay, Dr. Dreyer, I can assure you I had absolutely nothing to do with your son's dis—"

"Caleb," Ellen cut in. "His name is Caleb."

"Caleb. Sorry. Caleb's disappearance. I had absolutely nothing to do with it. In fact, I was sent here to stop it, just like I'm here now. I'm trying to stop this. I'm trying to help. I can help you."

Ellen swiveled back to Brady. "I don't trust—"

"He saved my life," Skylar said, walking toward Ellen. "He saved me when I came here to get the Grimoire. He shot one of those things, and he knew where they came from. Right, Roland?"

"That's right. They were summoned by someone who's working against us using a Pariunt ritual. It's all there in that book." He pointed to Ram, who was still holding the Grimoire.

"Wait, who summoned them?" Brady asked.

"I believe his name is Maurice Bacon."

Brady and Ellen exchanged miffed glances.

"He was one of the last members of the local chapter." He paused and looked directly at Ellen. "And he was also the previous Sentinel."

"Hold on. Tell me about this local chapter," Brady said. "Who's all in it?"

"Frankly, I don't think anyone is anymore. There were only a handful of people in it when the events of the summer unfolded. Jane and her other son. Ethel Thomasin. Maurice Bacon. Jane and her son are both dead."

"Ethel moved to Blacksburg last year. We bought the house from her," Ellen said.

"That's right," Roland said. "I tracked down the only other two members. One of them passed from old age in November, and the other wants nothing to do with it. A frail old woman now."

"And what about Sheriff Quinlan?" Brady said.

"He was never a member of the Order. Though, he certainly was aware of their presence and their dealings."

Brady sighed. "So, this Maurice Bacon character is"—he gesticulated with his hands—"tryin' to help these monsters kill people?"

"I agree. It's all very odd. My Grand Elder suspected the Nothus may be drawing power from outside sources. Seems that it somehow commandeered Maurice to its cause. Anyone's guess as to why, but as those who've seen it can attest, it has powerful abilities to invade minds and dreams. If Maurice was already in a weakened mental state, he may have made an easy target. Even the most resilient minds can falter."

"So, do you know how to get rid of it? That's why you're here, right?" Ellen said.

Roland shuffled toward Ram. "I don't know for sure, but it may be enacting a version of the ritual that brought it here. I'm hoping the answer is in that book there."

Ram stuck out a hand when Roland arrived at his side. "Hi, I'm Ram."

Roland shook it. "Do you have it there?"

"Uh, yeah, hold on a second." Ram flipped back to a page he had dog-eared toward the end of the book. "Sanitatum Silva?"

Roland smiled. "Yes! Yes, that's the one."

Ellen left Brady's side and took a place next to Roland. Both of them peered at the text over Ram's shoulders.

"There are parts of this I can't understand," Ram said. "Is this really what we need to do? Do we even have a way of doing it?"

With an excited smirk across his face, Roland pulled a chair around to Ram's desk. "I don't know. Let's see what we have."

Ellen looked back at Brady. They both shook their heads.

"I need to check in with my team," Brady said. "Can I leave and catch you guys in a couple of hours?"

The question was directed at Ram and Roland, but both of them were lost in the book. Ellen responded for them.

"Sure. Go ahead. We'll let you know the next step."

Brady put on his coat and glanced at Skylar. She sat on

the floor against the wall with her arms around her knees. "You okay?" he asked.

Skylar looked up at him. "I'm just tired."

"Why don't you get some rest while I'm out? Want to camp out in the office?"

"I think that's a good idea," Ellen said in a soft, motherly tone. "You've been through a lot and haven't slept in two days."

Skylar nodded. She pulled herself up with the aid of Ellen's outstretched hands and lumbered back to the office. Her mother's boxes were still on the desk and the floor. A few family photos had made it onto a side table, and Skylar took a long look at the one of the family on a camping vacation when she was little. Rick and Lenny grinned as they crouched over a fire, and Rick held a pot over the flame. Skylar stood behind Lenny, white-blond hair and overalls, smiling so wide her eyes appeared closed. Her mother sat on the opposite side of the fire, not looking at the camera, but at her family.

"Hey," Ellen said, leaning in the doorway with her hands in her pockets.

Skylar turned around. "Hey."

"You're doing real good, Skylar."

Skylar faked a smile and a chuckle.

"You know, your mother and I spoke a few days ago about all this. She was really committed to helping heal her town. I know it was a lot for her to handle, but she did it fearlessly. I... I really admired her. I still admire her."

Skylar put the photo back down on the table.

"I see a lot of her in you. I see the same fearlessness. Whatever we're about to do or not do, it takes an incredible amount of courage. I just wanted you to know I'm proud of you."

Skylar kept her eyes on the photos as tears welled in her eyes.

"And if you ever need someone. You know, besides Ram. Besides your dad."

Skylar winced, blinking away tears, and nodded. "Thanks."

They shared a long embrace to the background noise of Ram and Roland mumbling to each other and the buzzing of fluorescent lights.

"Thank you," Skylar said again.

When Ellen left the room, Skylar took her mother's Bensalem Sheriff's Department jacket hanging on the back of the desk chair, balled it up, and laid her head down to rest.

. . .

Before heading out, Ellen made her way over to Ram and Roland. "You guys learning anything?"

Roland looked up at her. "I believe so. It looks like our suspicion was correct. Ram and Skylar did an excellent job interpreting this."

"Hah, thanks," Ram said.

Roland placed his palm facedown on an open page of the Grimoire. "Long story short, this book was written by the founders of Bensalem, some of whom were original members of the Order of the Old Roses. They were very learned in the ways of occultism. Magick, alchemy, that kind of thing."

"What, like, spells?"

"In a way, yes. Most of what they did was based purely in science and nature, but as their practices became more advanced, their discoveries led them toward the realm of the spiritual. Eventually, they became so skilled that they communed regularly with spirits, both good and evil."

"And that's what this is?"

"Yes. The Grimoire states very clearly that the Nothus was summoned in error. Some variation of that summoning is what will likely expel it."

"It also looks like they tried to do it but couldn't," Ram said. "They didn't have the right materials or the right people—we aren't sure yet—but they stopped trying when they discovered how to create a Sentinel."

"An imperfect solution, but a viable one," Roland said.

Ellen sat on a chair in front of them. "You said this person, Maurice, also used to be the Sentinel. Does that mean there's life after being a Sentinel?"

"I would assume so, yes. But also like I said, he may have been in a compromised mental state. Or physical state. Who knows, really."

"Was that a summoning spell too?"

"No, the Sentinels are a product of transformational alchemy. Turning one thing into another thing entirely."

"And then turning it back?"

"Right."

"Can we... undo the current Sentinel?" Ellen asked.

Ram craned his neck to look at Ellen. A dull silence hung over them.

"His name is Mark," she said softly.

"I... suppose we could try," Roland offered.

"He's been in there for forty years. He's... extremely weak."

"How do you know?"

"I just do. I know. Can we get him out?"

Roland's gaze dropped to the floor to ponder the question. "You may not like what you find, Ellen. He might look or act unlike a human anymore. That's if he even survives the—"

"I'll take responsibility. Whatever happens, I'll take responsibility for him."

Roland turned to Ram. "I might need some help with the procedure."

"Of course," Ram said to Roland, and then, "We should at least try," to Ellen.

. . .

Deep in the mist of sleep, Skylar heard someone walk into the office and sit in the chair behind the desk.

She then found herself walking along a soft, dirt road. She wore thin black shoes, more like slippers, that did little to prevent the road's dampness from seeping into her skin. The hem of her dress fluttered with each step, and a stroke of mud began to stain its off-white edge. Green grass and even greener bursts of summer strong trees lined her peripheral vision, but she was unable to look up from the road. Someone or something else controlled her vision and her movement.

A dulcet conglomeration of sounds filled her ears: birds chirping, insects whirring, horseshoes clacking, tools banging, people shouting. She even made out what she thought was the sound of a lute, or some ancient string instrument, being plucked in song. Aromas of fresh cut hay, wood shavings, and healthy grass filled her nostrils.

Something was digging into the meager meat of her shoulders, a bag perhaps, and only upon feeling the weight on her back did she realize her hands were gripping coarse, leather straps up by her armpits. The road got thinner, greener, and the nature-made sounds were amplified as the human-made ones receded.

"Aye, Judithe," a woman's voice called out, and the eyes Skylar saw through finally looked up.

The woman wore a Puritan dress and white linen cap. She

carried a basket of clothing under her arm and stood on the other side of the road by a log cabin covered by thatched roof. Off to the right, several more houses were stationed behind it, and further on, a handful of horse-drawn carts and people milled around what appeared to be some kind of colonial town square. Palisades of oak and birch trees, regal and fresh, as if having just been born under the light of the stars, guarded the perimeter of the town. The road she was on led directly into their leafy embrace, away from the town. But high above the trees, familiar sights lay ahead: waves of the Blue Ridge Mountains, and the craggy face of Old Rag dipped in evening's glow.

A voice came out of her that was not her own. "Good morrow, Missus Conroe. How fare thee?"

"Give me an answer on the chickens has thy father? Only four left now with an offer on the half."

"Hasn't an answer, he yet. Shall I call on Thomas to fetch him?"

"Do, and if he remains in desire of the trade, find me at the infirmary. My littlest is in need of lookin' after."

"Aye."

The woman nodded. "What task have thee in mind with that?"

"I venture to the oaks to seek the hunter's blessing."

"Aye?"

"Aye, the New King Salomon himself bade me."

"Look at you, fancy! Takin' a liking to thee, he has."

Two men riding horseback toward town, toward the body Skylar inhabited, neared them on the road. The woman looked up and greeted them, but just as the riders were about to pass between the women, Missus Conroe turned around. Her now-white eyes widened as she said in devastating clarity, "You're next up, Sky!"

One of the riders laughed at something the other one said, filling the space with boisterous noise. Both horses, their coats a shimmering chestnut, took slow plods onward, obscuring the Missus Conroe from sight. When they had passed, she was gone. The woman had left no trace.

Her feet resumed their muddy march. She walked for a long time as daylight grew dimmer and the road under her shoes petered out into grass. She stopped when she reached the edge of the forest, pulled out an oil lamp, and lit it. It bathed the forest in a warm glow, illuminating thick trunks and wild foliage, greens, browns, and yellows sprouting in all directions. Little lives teemed in their evening glory, crickets and frogs roaring, sparrows warbling down the day. One hand gripped a gathering of her dress to keep it from catching on twigs while the other held out the lamp. The bag's straps dug further into her shoulders in the absence of fingers to buffer them.

Something grabbed her arm. "Boo!"

She shrieked and turned around. The lamp illuminated the beaming face of a teenage boy. "Fie Matthew!" she said. She whacked him in the arm with her other hand.

"Ow!"

"You'll have me dead before we start!"

He laughed, grabbed her face with both hands, and planted a kiss on her lips. She kissed him back.

"Do show me mercy, Matthew. You gave me such a fright!"

"Come, have you the materials?"

She slung the bag down at his feet.

"Chose well his nexum, did he," he said, and kissed her again. Then, he opened the bag and began pulling out the contents, beginning with several large black bricks. "Altar stones. Heavier than the New King's hand, they are!"

"My shoulders ache from it."

Next, he withdrew a long, white linen. "Altar cloth. Hast thou the recitation?"

"My memory carries it."

"Well remembered!" He dug deeper into the bag, as if to explore another chamber below the main one. "What be the offering?"

"Pulvis Solaris."

He pulled out a small leather pouch. "Aye, but which?" He turned the pouch upside down, and out came a pewter-colored rock that filled his entire palm. "Herne requires the red, dost he not? Is this not the black?"

"T'was what the New King gave me."

Matthew pulled two more pouches from the bag, and opening both, found two more pewter-colored rocks. The lamplight bathed them in an effervescent glow, giving their hard edges a shine that twinkled in the night. He looked up at her. "But the fire imbues him. Does it not?"

"Matthew, t'was what the New King bade me summon."

"Thou'rt sure on it?"

"I swear it!"

He shook his head and began assembling the altar stones in a tight line. She took the cloth and draped it over them. Cupping the three pewter rocks in his hands, he took a deep breath. "Art thou sure on—?"

"Dost thou speak against our New King Salomon? Hast he not led us unto this land? What lies in your hand t'was what he gave me."

"Aye," he said softly, placing them in a row on the altar. When he finished, he leaned over and kissed her a third time on the cheek, this time softer, this time colder.

"Get thee away, now," she said with a smile.

He rose and took up a place beside a nearby oak.

Skylar, or Judithe, or whoever or whatever lived in the vision of this young woman, knelt before the altar. She drew a knife from her dress and ran the blade across two of her fingertips, and then she dabbed each of the three rocks with her blood before closing her eyes.

"O dear hunter, I arrive to thee in awe of thy grace. I, a lamb of the New King Salomon, drink from bounties he hath provided, and tis by his righteous name I entreat thee. Come now unto us and protect us. Serve us, lord of the wood, and defend our chaste Bensalem, our New Atlantis, with spear and shield. Accept thee—"

Something rustled in the grass. She paused but did not open her eyes.

"Accept thee this offering of the blessed fire. Let it be thine light and thine power. Let it shine for thee under burning sun. Let it warm thee in winter's night. Let it burn that which would be beset—"

A rumbling began to build in the forest, softer and deeper than thunder, more of a sensation than a sound. A sensation Skylar knew.

"Show us strength. Show us thy might. We thank thee that thou hast—"

Another rustling, then a pattern of footsteps. She opened her eyes, and only then did she realize how heavy she was breathing and how hard her heart was pounding. She whipped her head around the pale lamplight, a faint circle that extended only a few feet in each direction. Anything lurking a stone's throw beyond it would have been invisible.

"Matthew?"

The footsteps continued. They did not get closer but seemed to circle her, slow and plodding, deliberate, aware of their safety in the darkness.

She rose and clutched her dress. "Matthew? Be it you, Matthew?"

The footsteps stopped but were replaced by a guttural clicking sound, as if one were gurgling sand instead of water or rubbing a heavy stick against a washboard. It was an utterly alien sound in such a place as this.

"Matthew! Come out now! I'll have—" She gasped at what stepped into the light.

It was Matthew, but he was completely naked. His limp feet dangled a foot off the ground, and his head was twisted completely to the side. His mouth and eyes were wrenched open, unspeaking, unseeing. Three dark cords were wrapped around his neck, and they twitched slightly, two fidgeting faintly and the third slithering back and forth over the others, tightening. When Matthew levitated another step forward, the thing holding him by the neck appeared.

Its massive antlers, reaching high above the height of any man, were first to touch the lamplight, followed by the tip of its snout and its blazing red eyes. Darkness obscured it below the neck, but she could see the cords strangling Matthew were its fingers.

The fragment of Skylar that was still independent of this nightmare wanted to crawl inside Judithe's brain and trigger whatever synapses were needed to get her to run, to hide, to do anything to save herself. She wanted to plead with her that, while there was certainly no hope for Matthew, there might be hope for her if she could just—

Matthew's mouth emitted a wretched voice, one that

seemed to come not from him but from all around the forest. It was subtle but harsh, like someone trying to whisper and yell at the same time.

Vestem exuite.

The shock of the words struck her like a bolt of lightning. She stood there paralyzed, whites of her eyes bulging, pulse racing. Matthew's altered voice croaked again.

Vestem exuite.

"I—I—I—forgive me, my lord. I speak not the ol—"

Remove thy clothing.

With trembling hands, heaving breath, and eyes blurred by tears, she removed her shoes, her stockings, her dress, her undergarments, and finally, her cap. Matthew did not move an inch while she undressed, and neither did the beast holding him, save for those twitching fingers around Matthew's throat.

Kneel before me.

With her eyes on Matthew's lips, unable to look at the beast, she knelt. She winced and whimpered, and her shoulders heaved in hyperventilation. Her cheeks were boiling hot and coated in tears. But in the midst of the hell before her, she caught the slightest rhythm of movement from Matthew's chest. She wanted to call out to him, but her tears and her terror suppressed the urge.

Something compelled her to gaze into the red eyes of the beast. They swirled in cyclical patterns, wisps of ultraviolet light flaring into the night. For the first time, she noticed that the three ceremonial rocks she'd dabbed in blood had melted into glistening pools of silver liquid. They shone like stars.

Bring to me thy King.

Its eyes reverted back to tight vermillion balls. The rumbling that had been building suddenly stopped, and the natural sounds of the wood returned, save for her heaves and sobs.

And the beast, along with the limp body of Matthew Aubrey, shifted back into the darkness and was gone.

When she rose, a brisk gust of wind stung her skin. In frantic movements, she swung the lamp around her. As if they had never been there at all, the metropolis of trees and plants in her vicinity were all gone. Western stars sparkled bright under the Milky Way through the new hole of sky above her, and the smooth patch of dirt her feet stood on sent a dull chill through her still-trembling body.

And then there, at the far end of the newfound glade in the heart of the forest, a neon-blue rectangle of light appeared and called her forward. With each cautious step she took, its edges grew brighter, and a faint buzzing sound around it grew in volume. A doorknob appeared, and faint voices could now be heard underneath the buzzing. With the doorknob in reach, the blue light cast her face in a chilly cyan glow. She put a shaking hand on the knob and twisted it.

It opened up to the waiting room. A group of bald-headed children already tilted toward her sat motionless, as did the parents reading magazines in chairs lining the walls. Every single face staring back at her was featureless—no eyes, no mouth, just a smooth ball of flesh. The only faces that were clear were those of a childhood Skylar and her mother sitting in the same two chairs they always sat in. They turned toward her.

Her mother opened her mouth and said, "You're nexum, Sky."

Everything stopped. The dream world evaporated.

Skylar heard a door slam and familiar voices from her waking world—maybe Ellen, maybe Brady. She felt herself drifting back toward them through some in-between space, but something pulled her by the ankles with great force and yanked her away.

Its grip was so acute she could feel it rubbing against the skin around her ankles and now her wrists. It tugged her down, hurtling her toward an unknown destination. Screams and jeers of strangers echoed around her as she plummeted. The pain in her wrists and ankles intensified, and then she saw them.

A sea of orange faces lit by firelight, familiar yet unfamiliar, were cast around her. Fumes from the fire warped them into wavering mirages, things distorted and unreal. In the front row, a woman needing the help of two men to stand sobbed violently into her hands. One of the men holding her whimpered softly and whispered to her. The other shook his head disapprovingly. A young boy and younger girl standing in front of them gaped at their burning sister in terrified awe.

The flames began to rise.

It started as a trace on the bottoms of her feet, as if someone was tickling them and wouldn't stop, even though she pleaded and couldn't move. When that seething, gnawing burn had no skin left to agitate, it wormed into her flesh and her bone. It ramped steadily from an odd discomfort to diabolically hot, and it began to spread. She screamed and wailed, twisted and contorted, spasming every muscle available to avoid the pain, but the ropes binding her feet and ankles were tied tight. Her screams released more than just breath. Through them, she tried to eject every feeling, every memory, every ounce of her soul. Maybe if she could scream them all out of her—

A man on a pulpit spoke to the crowd, but she could only understand fragments of his speech between her screams. "Commission has found thee guilty... Judithe Peel, daughter of William... King Salomon denied unto thee his forgiveness..."

The nauseating stench of burning flesh consumed her as she wailed. She felt gobs of calf muscle slip through her skin, and the bones in her feet radiated like molten-hot steel. The flames rose higher and nipped at her chin and torso. The fabric of the shift she wore began to fuse into her skin, and then both layers of feeble protection melted away together. Pieces of her continued to burn, to char, to fall away.

Dripping. Plopping.

Skin. Muscle. Intestine. Bone.

In time, her lungs no longer had the strength to scream and her muscles no longer had the strength to squirm. The pain burning her body away began to subside, and as her mind failed and her vision faded, she locked onto one face standing out in the crowd. The New King Solomon was not smiling, per se, under the brim of his three-cornered hat, but the edges of his lips were curled up in a way that flattened the thin mustache across his face, and his eyebrows arched upward on a furrowed brow. His eyes, usually gray and thin, were completely white.

And then they, along with everything else, went black.

. . .

"Skylar! Skylar!"

Skylar's eyes plunged open. Ellen was kneeling over her, her black hair draped around her head like a cape.

"Hey! Can you hear me?" Ellen said.

"What... what happened?"

"You were screaming. It's over now. You're with us."

Ram, Brady, and Roland all gazed down at her under the office's drop-panel ceiling.

"You okay, Sky?" Ram asked.

It took her several moments to catch her breath. "I saw it," she finally said.

"Saw what? The Nothus?" Brady said.

"I saw... the summoning. I saw it all through Judithe's eyes."

Ellen helped Skylar into a seated position.

"Judithe Peel?" Roland asked.

She turned to him. "What's the nexum?"

"The nexum?"

"Yeah." She glanced at Ram. "Isn't it mentioned in the summoning? An ingredient or something?"

With a quizzical look stitched across his face, Roland knelt beside Ellen. "The nexum is... well, it's hard to explain. I guess the easiest way to think of it is the person who performs the ritual."

"Isn't that what the elders got wrong when they tried to do this?"

"Yes. We just took a long look at the ritual as it's written in the Grimoire. The nexum seems to be what they couldn't figure out."

One by one, Skylar looked at all four faces before landing back on Roland's. "I think I'm the nexum."

"How can that be?" Ellen said.

"I don't know. I just... I saw it all just now. I saw Bensalem. I saw Judithe. No, I was Judithe. I saw everything all through her eyes."

"Fascinating," Roland whispered.

"She had the wrong ingredients. She was set up."

"Set up?" Brady said.

"The New King Salomon gave her the... what's the ingredient? The black stones?"

"They weren't red stones?" Roland asked.

"No. That's just it. She used black stones. She said that's what the New King gave her."

Ram was nodding in astonishment. "That would make

sense. That's exactly how a ritual like this would go wrong."

Brady took a step forward. "Wait, hold on. Can someone explain this in... like, real person speak?"

Skylar ignored the plea, keeping her eyes on Roland. "Can we repeat the ritual?"

"We can try. I was going to suggest we try to perform it," Roland said.

"I think it needs to be me."

"Skylar, no way—" Brady began.

"Just hear her out, Derek," Ellen interrupted.

Roland bit his lip in apparent consideration of Skylar's theory. "How old are you?"

"Seventeen."

"So was Judithe."

A long silence hung in the room as Skylar received their stares.

"That's what a nexum is," Roland continued. "Someone with the right traits, the right intention to execute a ritual. It's a Latin word that means a conduit or connection, but it began to take on its own meaning in ancient occult circles. A caster must connect with their ritual in order for it to be successful, and some rituals require very specific nexums. Most don't, but summonings certainly do. Summonings are very personal, where a mortal asks a deity to leave their realm and come to ours. Their answer can depend, literally, on who's asking."

"So, in this case, a seventeen year old girl with... no ritual experience?" Brady said.

"It's possible. Things like age, stature, and certainly expertise are factors." Roland turned to Ram. "But Ram, remember the second and third attempts? They were done with girls Judithe's age as well."

"Were they related by blood?" Skylar said.

Roland's quizzical look returned. "Well, the names weren't listed, but I would have to assume not based on the dates."

Skylar scampered to her feet and rushed into the main office. The others followed. She hovered over the Grimoire, rustling its pages and nearly tearing its brittle seams. She stopped when she found the sprawling family tree. "I remember seeing this page when I first found the book."

"The first families of Bensalem," Roland said.

She and Roland both ran their fingers along the lines of the tree, mouthing silently as they studied the names.

"Her father's name was William," Skylar said.

Roland stopped on a name on his side of the page. "Here. W. Peel. Born 1582."

"Yes. That's gotta be him." Skylar scooched around the desk so that their eyes traced down the same slope of the diagram.

Brady caught a glance from Ellen and shook his head.

Roland furrowed his brow. "The Peel name evaporates pretty quickly it seems, but William's granddaughter married a B. Cotton. Cotton... Cotton... Atwater... three more Atwaters..."

Suddenly, he stopped and twisted his head toward Skylar. "Oh my."

Skylar didn't turn to meet his gaze. She was transfixed on the name above his finger.

"G. McNamara," Roland said.

"That's my great grandfather."

"E. McNamara."

"That's my grandfather."

"R. McNamara. Born 1954?"

"That's—"

"Rick," Brady said softly.

The room went silent and all eyes fell upon her.

"Sky, your name's not in there, though," Ram said.

Roland turned to him. "The book hasn't been updated in decades. See how the handwriting varies through the centuries?"

Skylar closed her mouth but kept her eyes on her father's name, written in sloppy black ink at the bottom of this eons-old page. She slowly backed away. Ellen caught her by the shoulders and led her into a chair.

"Skylar, you're a direct descendant of the Peels. I think you're right. I think you're our nexum," Roland said.

The three men stood in a row behind the desk, staring at her almost as if she were a foreign thing, like she had either been informed she won the lottery or had received a death sentence. Ellen remained behind her and tightened her grip, and she looked the men back like a lioness protecting her cub.

Skylar shifted her gaze to a photo of the unit at a community softball game a few years ago. Duke stood in the back row, wearing plain clothes and a fatherly smile. Brady knelt in the front next to Monica, both in red T-shirts and both holding her mother, laying across their arms and beaming.

Skylar finally spoke, her voice soft and low, as if testing itself. "What do I have to do?"

Roland picked up a chair and placed it directly in front of her. He sat, leaning his elbows on his knees. Something in his face softened.

"I'd be right next to you the whole time. I'll tell you exactly what to do. It's essentially what Judithe did. We just need the ingredients."

"I saw she had altar stones and a cloth."

"Those can be anything, really. Just a flat, clean surface."

"What about the black rocks? I watched them melt while

she was reciting something. Oh God, do I have to recite something?"

"You will, but I'll write it up for you and you can just read it. The stones? That might be a bit harder. Judithe used Black Pulvis Solaris. It's a combination of purified sulfur and black antimony. I have no idea where we might get such things."

"I do," Ellen said. "Skylar, your mother mentioned some kind of a laboratory in the back of Jane's old store. She said there were all kinds of chemicals and old books and things like that."

"Mentioned somethin' similar to me too. If that stuff's anywhere, it's gotta be there," Brady said. "But wait, why do we need these things? What the hell is black antimony?"

"Think of it this way," Roland said. "When these deities come to our world, they have to play by our world's rules. These summonings almost always involve an offering, a tangible thing that gives them power, or money, or whatever it is they desire. What Skylar said about the Pulvis Solaris mix-up makes sense. Benevolent spirits like Herne the Hunter often want what's called the Powder of the Sun, or Red Pulvis Solaris, but if Judithe Peel used Black Pulvis Solaris, especially if intending to use Red, well, that's something different entirely. The ritual can still be performed, but the result is—"

"The Night Bastard. The Nothus Noctis," Ram said.

"Precisely. A bastardized version. Something twisted."

"Where should we do it?" Skylar said.

"Did you see where Judithe was in your dream?"

"The glade. There was some kind of door there. She walked through it."

"The glade it is, then. You may also find a door. The Grimoire mentions something called the Black Door of the Bastard. I don't know what it looks like."

"How soon can we do it?"

"Well, as soon as we can get some Black Pulvis Solaris. I think that's all we would need."

"It's gettin' dark," Brady said. "I'll ride you over to Jane's store if you're ready."

"Thank you. I am."

"I want to go too," Ram said. "Is that okay?"

Roland put a hand on his shoulder. "Yes. I'd certainly appreciate the help."

"So, what? Everyone meet back here if the trip to the lab is successful?" Ellen asked.

"Well, you certainly don't have to get involved if you don't want. I know you've been through quite enough already."

Ellen shook her head. "We can't risk getting attacked by those things again. They'll surely come after us. You said you wounded one with a handgun, right?"

"Yeah. It certainly seemed that way."

"Count me in, too, then," Brady piped up from the opposite side of the room, where he had one arm already through his coat. "Ready, Roland?"

Roland stood and walked toward Brady, Ram a few steps behind him.

"Wait," Ellen said, only now taking her hands off Skylar's shoulders and crouching in front of her. "Are you sure about this?"

Skylar took a long time to answer, and the room showed no lack of patience with her pause. She took a deep breath and closed her eyes before speaking softly. "I heard Judithe screaming. I smelled her flesh burning. I felt every ounce of her pain. In a way, I... I feel like I died with her. Ever since I first laid eyes on that book, I've felt tied to this in a way I can't explain. If there's even a chance this could work, I want to try it. It feels like it's... on me."

Ellen took Skylar's hand. "It'll be on all of us. We'll all be out there with you. We'll defend you. We'll cheer you on. Whatever it takes." She turned around. "Right?"

"Right," Roland and Brady said in unison.

Ram smiled slightly and nodded. "Fuck yeah, we will."

"Okay," Skylar whispered.

In synchronized footsteps, Roland and Ram followed Brady out the door. But before Ram left, he turned around and blew a kiss to Skylar. She smiled, and then she waited until she knew their car was gone.

"Hey," Skylar said to interrupt Ellen gathering her things.

"What's up?"

"Have you heard of the New King Salomon?"

Ellen put her bag down and sat in the chair across from Skylar. "Vaguely. It's some kind of cult figure, right?"

"I don't know who he is exactly, but I saw him too. His eyes are all white. He was smiling at me when I was burning—when Judithe was burning. Judithe was convinced he gave her those specific materials."

Ellen's face screwed into a puzzled glare. "What are you saying?"

"I mean, I think whoever this was, if he's real or not, he's the one that was behind it. He set Judithe up to fail and let her die. He must have wanted the Nothus to come out."

"But didn't it kill his people?"

"Yes. It killed hundreds of them."

"Did it kill him too?"

"The Grimoire... said that it did. Yes."

Ellen sighed and leaned back in the chair. "Well, maybe he got what was coming to him."

"I don't know. I know I've said a lot of crazy shit lately, but I just... I don't know."

"Do you think Roland would know?"

"I kinda don't think he does. Either that, or he's hiding it from us."

"He did deceive me once before."

"I know. That's why I wanted to tell you."

An old radiator popped in the corner of the big room, and Ellen and Skylar looked at each other for a long time as the night grew deeper.

"I'll keep a close eye on him," Ellen said.

Skylar nodded.

. . .

Ram's text hit Skylar's phone a little over an hour after she arrived home.

We found it! Group's meeting back at the station at 2am. Love you. <3

She was sitting at the kitchen table with Rick and Lenny, plates of half-eaten meatloaf and roasted vegetables in front of them. The counters were lined with tin-foil-covered casserole dishes and glass containers of food dropped off by grieving friends and neighbors. Lenny and Rick did most of the talking. Rick asked that they not speak about the upcoming funeral, so they didn't, nor did they discuss the death of Monica Nelson or the other calamities festering in Bensalem.

They finished their meals and went through old photo albums on the living room couch together while the temperature outside plummeted below freezing. Even in her heated home, Skylar could feel the chill in her bones. Ellen had organized a telephone tree if anyone encountered Nothus spawns, and Skylar kept flipping up her cell phone to make sure she hadn't missed any calls. She hadn't, and for some reason, that worried her. Skylar tried but failed on many occasions that evening to stay in the moment, scaffolding smiles, feigning laughter, but ever since Ram's text, the ritual was all she could think about. She knew Lenny could tell her mind was elsewhere, but he didn't say anything until just before bed.

He stopped halfway up the stairs and half-turned toward Skylar reclining on the couch. "So, how's your, uh, mission going?"

She kept her eyes on the ceiling. "It's going okay, I guess. We're gonna try and take care of it tonight."

"Tonight?"

"Yeah. We have everything we need, and it needs to happen fast."

"What will you do?"

"We're going to perform a version of the ritual that brought it here in the first place." She looked at him. "I know it sounds ridiculous."

"A little... yeah."

"Ellen Dreyer and Derek are coming too."

"Wow. Quite a crew, huh?"

Skylar shrugged but was unsure if Lenny could see her do so.

"You guys need any more help?" he asked.

"I don't think so at this point."

"You sure?"

"Yeah. God forbid, if something happens to me. You need to be here for Dad."

"Don't talk like that. Please."

"Well... maybe just keep your cell phone on? We're gonna be out in the woods by Ellen's place."

"Of course. I will." He took two steps back down the stairs.

"I'm sorry about earlier."

"It's really fine. I know you didn't mean it. I didn't mean it either."

"I know." His head slumped. He kept his hand on the handrail. "This is just really hard."

"I know. It is really hard."

"Goodnight, Sky."

"Goodnight."

"I love you. Please be safe."

"I will. I promise. I love you too."

He climbed the rest of the stairs. Skylar closed her eyes while listening to him get ready for bed since his room was right above her. Once the creaking of the floorboards dissipated into the night, Skylar gathered her things and drove to Ram's.

They said very little to each other, just watched old movies in the dark. Skylar curled up against him and slept, his hand stroking the back of her head. He roused her when it was time to go, and Skylar took a deep breath before rising and getting into the car.

Even less was said at the station. Skylar and Ram were the first to meet Brady there, who hadn't left since returning from the lab. The teens looked like polar refugees as they sat half-asleep in boxy desk chairs, with their coats on. Brady was the opposite, pen in hand, churning through paperwork. He kept sighing and shaking his head but rose when Ellen arrived. She brought with her a thermos of coffee, and she and Brady shared a cup by his desk.

All looked up when Roland opened the door five minutes after 2:00 a.m.

"Sorry, I'm late," he said, scurrying out of the cold and struggling to manage the duffel slung over his shoulder. He dropped the bag on the ground and took a knee over it. "Man, this thing's heavy. Let me just double check we've got everything here. Okay, flashlights. Here, everybody, come take a flashlight." He laid them out in front of the bag. "Got the Grimoire. Black Pulvis, let's see... one, two, three. Okay. Good there. Thank you, Cleric Harcourt. And this pillowcase from the motel will work as a cloth. Oh. Altar. Is there a sort of small, flat object here we can use as an altar?"

"How small we talkin'?" Brady said.

"A couple feet by maybe a foot?"

Brady stood with a groan and shuffled to the sheriff's office. He started whacking at something. When he returned, he held in his hands a shield-shaped board that once housed Duke's deer antlers. "How's this?"

Roland chuckled. "Looks great." He reached into his pocket and handed Skylar a piece of paper. "Here's the recitation. You don't have to memorize it. You can just read it off the paper. So, make sure you've got good light. Sound good?"

"Sounds good," Skylar said.

Roland picked up the Grimoire and faced Brady. "Do you have a safe here?"

"Sure do."

"I think the spawns are most directly seeking this book. They know we have it but they don't know we have the knowledge we need from it. If we hide it here and keep it locked away, it just might throw them off. In fact, I'm nearly positive."

"It's been dark for hours. How come we haven't seen 'em yet tonight?"

"I don't know. I truly don't. But I don't want to give them another reason to look for us when we're out there. If they're seeking the book, they should have no reason to come after us."

Brady nodded and took it under his arm. "Well, that's nice, I guess, but won't we just be invitin' 'em here? What if they tear this place up?"

Roland clasped a hand to Brady's shoulder. "Then you'll have my Order's apologies and a very large sum of their money. We'll make sure whatever damage is incurred is repaired. You have my word on that. But this station is a perfect place to draw them—it's isolated, and it can protect the Grimoire. Just make sure no one is here."

"Yeah, no shit. I'm gonna hold you to that promise."

"In case we do need protection out there, do you and Ellen have what you need?"

"Yes," Ellen replied. "We're ready."

"What about you, Ram? Ready?" Roland asked.

Ram was gazing at his feet, as if lost in the maze of his shoelaces.

"Ram?" Roland repeated.

"Sorry... what?"

"Are you ready, Ram?"

Ram looked at Skylar. "I'm ready if you're ready."

The group watched her as she read through the recitation, but it was Ellen's gaze she met when she finished. "I'm ready. Let's do it."

. . .

Skylar felt the hands of anxiety wringing her insides, still burning from her night vision of Judithe, as she and Ram dumped out of Ellen's back seat. Wickham Road was a post-apocalyptic tundra at this hour, barren of light and any connectedness to humanity.

A jagged blast of wind battered the three of them. Ram closed his eyes and bristled in the cold. Ellen made a sound resembling a shiver and shot a glance to her lightless house high up on the hill behind them. Skylar gazed up at a frozen full moon, a round ice cube set against stars burning eternities away. She considered, for a moment, their unfathomable lifetimes, and she wondered if something as hellish as the Nothus lived in their orbit.

Brady's patrol car pulled up seconds later. He and Roland stepped out from each side, the latter clutching the duffel in his arms like an overgrown baby. Ellen opened the trunk of her car. Brady met her there, gawking at the shotgun again.

"Mossberg 500," Ellen said, strapping her vest over her coat. "I have two dozen shells on my vest and eight more on my hip. Think that'll be enough?"

Brady took out his handgun, released the magazine, and examined it under the dome light. "Got three more of these if it ain't."

Next to Roland, Ram swung the duffle's strap over his shoulder in the same breath he volunteered to carry it.

Roland peeked at his wristwatch and adjusted his glasses. "Ten minutes to three. Everybody ready?"

Another screaming gale pelted the party as they clicked on their flashlights. Skylar stretched the beanie on her head to cover the very tips of her ear lobes. Ellen's hair billowed in the wind.

Single file behind Roland, the party ventured forth into the forest's frigid blackness, all silent as they did so. Each of them, down to a person, achieved a sort of synchronization with the others, timing their footsteps and even their breath patterns as if conjoined by some remote purpose. And although each of them had walked a version of this path before the wilderness here was barbaric enough to untether even the most adept of wanderers. This forest was, and always had been, an untamed pilgrim realm that drove doubt into the hearts of men and delighted in the knowing of things its mortal occupants did not. They pressed on, on amongst stands of immense trees and moss-speckled boulders exchanging tales since times unknowable, on into bitter and ancient winds bleeding through them.

The moonlight faded as the trees thickened, their dead branches so numerous they painted over every speck of light the sky produced until a canopy folded around the party and became Heaven itself. Further on, sound faded, like it had in prior treks, as safe zones in the forest marked by animals fell into the nameless distance behind them. Bent and bruised tree trunks, as well as what felt like a deliberate drop in temperature, signaled their proximity to the glade.

A hellish screech echoed out in the trees to the left. As if they were a herd of deer peering into their doom, all five heads swiveled and stared in its direction. None spoke. None moved.

Not a screech this time, but a rapid series of guttural clicks behind them triggered 180 degree spins, and as their flashlights grazed a grove of lily-white birch trees, Skylar's landed on a set of long, decrepit fingers gripping the trunk nearest to her. She gasped, and the fingers slithered off and shrank back into the darkness.

"What was that?" Ellen said.

"It was one of them," Skylar responded.

Brady, arms raised and gun straight on, looked ready to pounce.

"I thought you said they wouldn't come for us!" Ellen said.

"Well, I—I don't know. Maybe it wasn't one," Roland said.

"Oh Jesus. I knew we couldn't trust you. Did you sell us out? You and your cult?"

"Dr. Dreyer, please. I don't think they're here. There might be—"

"Oh fuck!" Brady screamed, as a whisk of brown and red mass rocketed out from the trees and speared Roland to the ground.

Ellen and Brady barked incoherent commands and circled around to either side of the spawn, now mounted over Roland. Ram wrapped his arms around Skylar.

Brady found an angle he liked and put three rounds into the spawn's back, triggering a heinous cry.

"Get down!" Ellen screamed. She spun her shotgun over Ram's shoulder and fired at a second spawn just milliseconds before it tried to launch a hand right through Skylar's torso. The blast not only stopped the beast in its tracks but caused it to falter. Black blood gushed from its chest. Ellen reloaded and fired again, this time only grazing its neck, as the second spawn once more swiped for Skylar.

The first spawn somehow rose and dove at Skylar from the opposite side, but two more bullets from Brady's pistol were enough to knock it off course. Ram pulled Skylar to the ground and covered her with as much of his body as he could allocate.

While Ellen was in the middle of another reload, Brady put a bullet straight through the skull of the second spawn. It croaked something out of a smoking and bleeding chest and fell back, lifeless.

"Roland!" Skylar screamed.

Ram didn't release her.

The first spawn was still standing and squared up on Brady. One of his shots had ripped through its eye socket, and now, black blood flowed like a waterfall down its snout and onto the cold ground. Brady, fuming, ripped a primal scream and emptied the rest of his clip into the reeling spawn while Ellen, with a boot on the other one's neck, fired a point-blank round straight into its skull. The spray from impact sent a volcano of black, inky liquid into her face, and she squirmed and cursed as it smacked her.

Skylar wriggled from Ram's grasp and crawled to Roland.

His eyes were fixed on the treetops as short, white clouds of breath escaped his lips. He held both hands firmly over his left thigh, blood oozing from his inadequate fingers.

"Oh my God!" Skylar said.

Ellen sprang down to his side. "Somebody give me a piece of clothing!"

Ram threw her his hoodie.

Roland moaned in agony when Ellen pressed on the wound, three perfectly round holes, to get a closer look. A new wave of blood poured out of him.

"We have to get him out of here," she said, cinching the arms of Ram's hoodie above the wound.

"Is he gonna be okay?" Ram asked.

"I don't think it hit the carotid but he's losing a ton of blood. I don't know."

"How are we gonna get him out of here? Should we abort the—" Brady said.

"Lenny?" Skylar said into her cell phone. "We do need you. We need you right now. Can you come out here? Somebody's hurt. Please call an ambulance too. We just need to get him out of here. Yeah. We're in the forest off of Wickham Road. Yes. Yes, come quick. I have to go. Are you on your way? Okay. Thank you, Lenny. I love you. I'll see you soon. We're getting the fuck out of here." She looked up at Ram. "I can't do this. I can't go through with this. No way. I can't—"

"Skylar," Roland whispered. "You can. You can."

"I have no idea what I'm doing. You were going to show me how to do this."

"Judithe...Judithe showed you. I didn't show you."

"But what if something goes wrong? How do I know if—"

"If you're truly the nexum, you'll know...and you are the nexum."

Ellen slid her knee under his head and clasped his face with her hands. "Roland, look at me. Are you sure?"

"There's nothing I can do anyway. I'm not the nexum."

Ellen glared into Skylar's eyes, searching her resolve. "What do you think?"

Skylar sighed. "I—I don't know."

Ram crouched behind her. "I'll do whatever you wanna do. What do you wanna do?"

"Oh shit," Brady said, gazing back into the forest. "They're comin'." He loaded a new magazine.

Ellen removed her knee from under Roland's head and slipped her hands under his armpits. "Ram, we need to move him. Help me carry him into the glade. We're better off in open space where we can see them coming."

Roland groaned again when Ellen lifted him. Ram, still with the duffel draped over his shoulder, ducked under one of Roland's arms while Ellen stood under the other.

"It's this way," Skylar said, and she led them onward into the forest, deeper, closer to the glade. Hers was the only light guiding them.

Brady paced slowly backwards and muttered curses under his breath. He fired his gun.

Like an open stage upon which the eyes of the world watched, the glade welcomed them. They laid Roland in the center, and Ellen knelt to re-tie the makeshift tourniquet, flashlight clenched in her teeth. Brady hadn't joined them yet. He was still in the forest, and Skylar gazed back in that direction with a face stitched in worry.

He emerged moments later, huffing and puffing to the point of near collapse, one hand holding down his hat, the other waving his gun. "Ellen!" he bellowed. "Get ready!"

Ram, both hands gripping the strap of the duffel, plodded over to Skylar. "You wanna do this?"

She turned to him. "It can't happen here."

"What?"

"This doesn't feel right. We need to be...I don't know... Closer."

"Closer?"

Brady reached them and gripped Skylar's arm. "Whatever you're gonna do, you need to do it quick!"

"Fuck," Skylar said. She bit her lip and scanned the perimeter of the glade, where curdled cries rose and black shadows shifted in the trees. She stopped her scanning when her eyes landed on a gap between two sturdy pines, a hypnotic abyss somehow darker than the rest of the land. Even when she shone her light directly on it, only blackness reflected back at her.

She began walking toward the black, and then she jogged. Ram, duffel in hand, followed.

· · ·

Skylar looked back only for a moment. Brady cursed, Ellen rose, and Roland, propped weakly on his elbows, reeled as three spawns charged toward them. They galloped on all fours, screeches piercing the night and red robes billowing in their wake. Discharges from the guns illuminated the glade in fleeting flashes of hope, but as she turned away from them and approached the shadow, and only hope in that instant was that she'd one day see them again.

The commotion in the glade was such that she hadn't noticed the telltale sign of the Nothus and its spawns evolve from a dull rumble into a more nuanced roar.

"Do you hear that?" she said.

With the Black Door coming into view, the rumbling grew not only in volume but in layers. Where once it had been a single booming echo existing all around them, here it thinned into many tones, both high and low, both shrill and tranquil, both sharp and soft. They were voices, hundreds of them, talking over each other and seemingly not to any particular target, as if they were spirits dwelling deep in the darkness of the portal. Skylar couldn't make out their words, but for the briefest of moments, a cold hand touched her heart when she heard what sounded like her mother utter the word *Atlantis*.

She slowed her gait upon observing the sheer height of the door. It was a wooden, teepee-like monstrosity. Its wide base was supported by slabs of timber tapering into an apex adorned with untamed latticework of twigs and branches. Or were they antlers? From her vantage point on the ground and through the thin beam of a flashlight, she couldn't tell. All she thought for certain was that its twisted and deranged architecture must have been conceived by a mind trapped in an impenetrable maze of bedlam.

"It's solid," Ram said. His flashlight was pointed down at his right foot, well in front of the other and seemingly standing on a rocky surface under the threshold of the Black Door.

Skylar joined him and bounced her light in all directions, exposing what appeared to be a high-walled corridor of dark rock leading to an even darker destination. The voices were becoming clearer. Their words conveyed the frameworks of bizarre prayers, things uttered by some pagan and alien race, almost chanting.

Neither spoke as they ventured inside. Each step was slow and deliberate, and never a moment of rest was afforded to the flashlights, nor the wrists swiveling them, desperately searching for a sign of anything other than void. Skylar wondered if whatever surfaces her beam struck had ever seen light before. The slope of the floor began to grade downward, gradually at first but more severely when the path also began to twist such that the light of the forest became lost behind black, snaking walls. Ram's breath grew louder and shorter.

For the first time, she noticed her body temperature warming as she descended. She could tell it was a dry heat, one emanating from a place or thing burning at a fantastic temperature, and she gritted her teeth as she considered Judithe's charred and bound body hanging lifelessly to her stake. The voices were now so loud she would have had to yell to get Ram's attention, even though he was mere feet behind her. Their languages varied greatly. Only here and there could she pick out a phrase that even sounded Germanic, as most dialects were cruder, sharper. She dared not guess at their origins.

Ram touched her arm at the same moment the faintest of lights, a dull orange spectre, appeared further down the corridor. She turned back to him and nodded. They navigated several more twists and turns, as well as a widening of the corridor in which rows of stalactites formed draperies on an effervescent ceiling, and the orange light ahead cast a warm and flickering glow.

Something scuttled on the far side of the cave. Its sound was subtle under the voices, but the micro-vibrations Skylar felt through the rock told her it was a thing of great strength and capability. She and Ram both ducked simultaneously behind a stony articulation large enough to hide them. They crouched with their backs against the rock, and they stayed completely silent and still. Ram bear-hugged the duffel and sank his chin into its canvas. Skylar reached a tentative hand over to him and lashed her pinky around his.

. . .

"Two more on your six!" Brady shouted. He resumed shooting the spawn mere feet in front of him.

Ellen spun on the ball of one foot so fast that wisps of black blood coating her face and hair splattered onto the ground in front of her—in front of them—as if to draw a proverbial line in the dirt that would spell their doom should they choose to cross it.

The first one did, and Ellen fulfilled their covenant by ripping a shot that tore a chunk of putrid flesh out of its neck and sent splinters of snout bone hurtling in all directions. One piece spun back and opened a surface-level gash on her cheek, and now she bore two types of blood on her face. The scratch did not deter her, as she was already halfway to reloading when the second attacked her head on. The barrel clicked shut a split second before the spawn drove her to the ground, and although she was quick to fire, its tackle redirected her shot over its shoulder. Lying on her back, gazing up at the mangled, dripping, screeching cervine head crowned in antlers, she jammed the barrel of her gun into its snout with a grunt and rolled just far enough to evade its scraping claws.

As if it were struck by lightning, it seized when three bullets from Brady's pistol ripped through its back and shoulder. Ellen unleashed a hellish yell, smacked it in the snout, and wriggled into a seated position where she popped a shell out of her vest and began to reload. It knocked the gun out of her hands, and in a move driven by pure instinct, she gripped its robe, pulled it down onto her chest, lodged her feet under its waist, and launched her legs backward. It tried to hold on as it vaulted over her, but its fingers were too long to grip anything at this close distance. She rolled onto all fours and crawled back to the gun, but before re-loading, caught a glimpse of three more closing on Brady.

Ellen paused from shooting spawns to shoot daggers of rage at Roland.

"I swear! I don't understand!" he said. "They must've known! They must've known!"

The one she had thrown off was back on its feet, screeching, limping, and dragging the arm Brady had nearly shot off. Ellen, chest heaving and heart surging, raised her gun, took aim, and put a four-inch-wide hole through the top of its head.

Ellen had lost count, but that felt like somewhere around six or seven. She looked around at the Nothus spawn bodies littering the glade. Puddles and streams of black blood had turned its leafy dirt into an oil slick.

Brady earned a half-second of freedom between putting down his last spawn and squaring to fire on the next one, and he used it to wince and grab a deep stab wound in his shoulder. Ellen could tell it was bleeding badly and rendered his left arm nearly useless. But Brady lost his focus, gawking at the trail of his own blood slithering down the sleeve of his Bensalem Sheriff's Department jacket, and the first spawn to reach him from the next company of three slammed him down to the ground with an open hand. The second and third spawns advanced the first, and both stabbed the ground at the same time, but Brady put two bullets through the hand of the one on his left and rolled under it to evade the one on his right. As he lay directly under it, bulbous drops of black blood plopped in his eyes and mouth, and he squirmed and spit as if being forced to endure some sadistic water torture.

Ellen snuck behind the one that had knocked Brady to the ground. Mmouth closed, eyes calm, blood colder than the night itself, she leveled an execution-style round through the back of its hood. It sailed through the sky in a diving motion that mimicked an attack but ceased all movement after clattering to the ground. Brady wrapped his bad arm around the ankle of the spawn he lay under to prevent it from moving while he lifted the gun behind him and emptied his clip into the other one still standing. Before Ellen could duck out of his line of fire, one of his bullets grazed the vinyl pouch on her hip, spilling her shotgun shells inside it.

Brady groaned as he swept the spawn over him to the ground, grabbing its other hoof with his other hand and yanking them together. He gained the top position and muttered a litany of curses while repeatedly driving the butt of his pistol into its skull. It jerked violently under him, and its antlers sliced not only the sleeve of his jacket, but also the arm inside it—his good arm. But Brady seemed oblivious. He kept cursing and smashing, and after nearly twenty blows, each one eliciting a louder curse and a frothier smash, he finally stopped when the spawn's skull cracked like an egg and his pistol-holding fist sank straight through.

"Behind you!" Roland shouted.

As Ellen turned around, the first of the two spawns she put down earlier, the one with a chunk of its neck and snout missing, stood again. Its eyes smoldered in a clouded rage, and it opened what was left of its snout to release an absolute waterfall of black blood through an empty cheek. She backed away to reload, but the spawn slapped the side of her face and her neck so hard its fingers cracked, and she screamed in pain, dropping the gun. It repeated the same attack, but a battered Ellen was able to twist enough so that its fingers whipped her side instead of her face. Lying in the dirt, all the muscles in her back and shoulders deactivated, and she tried but failed to propel herself up with her legs and hips. Brady yelled and fired his gun.

This spawn then did something different than the previous ones. As if on a crusade to exact personal revenge, it got down on all fours and used its great hands to flip her on her back and pin her to the ground with an immense strength. With its head inches from her face, it released a scream along with another torrent of black blood, drenching her already soaked head and chest. She coughed and gagged and squirmed and energy poured out of her body as fast as blood poured out of the spawn's.

When she felt it place a spider-like hand across her face, such that two of its fingers lay over her open lips, she tapped the most utterly primordial instinct within her and clamped her teeth around them. She gnashed the slimy skin away until her molars reached the bone. Yet the spawn did not move its fingers. Her senses began to fail as more black sludge careened down her open throat, and the hands holding her down felt less like a spawn's and more like the hands of fate.

Her mind entered a fog before remembering Caleb and Aaron. All three Dreyers were at a swing set by their old home in Charlotte, North Carolina. Aaron had just come home from work. He wore a white button down loosened at the neck. His hair was tousled and his face was young and smiling. He pushed Caleb in a swing against the backdrop of a creamy, pastel evening. Caleb's eyes beamed at his mother with joy, with hope, with the promise of—

Out of nowhere, the spawn killing Ellen Dreyer was smacked away by an even more powerful force.

"Oh my God!" Brady said.

"Unbelievable," Roland muttered.

Ellen came back from the brink. She wiped her face while hacking gobs of black blood and bits of spawn skin out of her throat, and she weakly craned her neck toward a set of indomitable screeches.

There, the Sentinel—Mark Harcourt—towered over the spawn and rained quaking blows down upon it. With each strike, the number of cracks and snaps of its bones multiplied, and the spawn's solid form devolved into something resembling liquid, not through any magical force but by sheer pulverization. By the time Ellen sat up, still blinking and coughing, all that was left was a tattered red cape and tufts of fur soaking in a black puddle.

. . .

Skylar and Ram remained perfectly still behind the rock. Pops of muffled gunfire from above ground out-rang the voices and the movement of the other occupant of the cave. As Skylar clenched her eyes shut and gritted her teeth, she let their thunder imbue her with the irrational hope that her friends were winning. In recent minutes, the occupant's footsteps, heavy plodding clacks on the rock floor, had moved gradually further away.

Ram poked her hard in the arm, and she gazed over his pointing finger. Draped in faint orange light, but mostly in shadow, the back of the Nothus itself could be seen stomping down the corridor that had led them here. Then, he pointed to the other end of the cave where lights burned like embers in the distance. Skylar nodded.

Once the Nothus had passed out of her vision, Skylar stood. She clicked her flashlight back on before setting off toward the light. As they walked hand in hand in silence, the corridor's ceiling lowered, its walls narrowed, and all of its surfaces, including the floor, morphed gradually from black stone to a glistening substance lighter and somehow softer.

Ram stopped at one point and Skylar turned to him. His eyes, set wide on a colorless face, were fixed on the lights up ahead, and his arms clutched the duffel to his chest like a huge teddy bear. Beads of sweat popped on his forehead and ran down cheeks draped with his long, untamed hair. Skylar squeezed his hand to get his attention. He looked not at her but at the slimy ground before nodding and continuing on. She held his hand tight.

The voices were so clear now. The further they traveled, the less they seemed to emanate ethereally, but rather directly from the lights at the end of the corridor. Clearer, too, were markings on the walls and ceiling Skylar had assumed were just fissures in the rock. Dark purple lines branched and broke across increasingly lighter and softer surfaces, and the corners of the corridor itself buffed into a rounder shape. Skylar stopped when she saw what looked like movement in the walls, a faint quivering or pulsing, the way she imagined a stomach might look from the inside. She nudged herself closer to Ram and pressed on.

She had to suppress her gag reflex when the contents of the chamber came into view. Each of the lights, revealed to be hundreds of glowing, elongated ovals resting on the ground, was connected by a vein or cord to a slimy, pulsing hub of organic matter growing out of the ceiling. The mass had no real shape. It was just a large lump that tapered into a single, thick, purple rope before splintering off into hundreds of veins that attached to the ovals.

Upon noticing the oval closest to her was semi-transparent, Skylar stepped toward it with trepidation, her mouth stitched in a disgusted frown. It gave off an incredible heat, and she gasped at what she saw inside. The perfectly intact and naked body of the old man who had taught her to ride horses, old Hank Teakle, lay suspended in a pool of dark, wretched liquid. Although his eyes and mouth were closed, his body seemingly devoid of life, Skylar could hear, as clear as day, his gruff voice reciting a prayer.

"And let us drink their wisdoms through the chalice of his hands, ordained in righteousness and—"

Skylar looked at the pod next to Hank's, containing a woman she didn't recognize speaking a foreign tongue. She scampered around them and looked at two more, then two more. There were hundreds of pods, all just sitting on the putrid ground like embryos being harvested for their resources. The pod of a boy about her age caught her eye closer to the middle of the room. She navigated through more pods before reaching it, and she recognized the tenant's face and voice in an instant.

"Eternal life to the children of his tabernacle—"

Skylar gasped. "Ram!" she whispered. "This is Matthew Aubrey! This is the boy from the dream!"

She turned around to see Ram walking toward a pod much larger than the others. She followed him to the center of the vast chamber, where a space had been cleared to give this pod prominence. The corpulent ceiling organ hung directly overhead.

Inside this larger pod was another man she had seen before. Although he was skeletal thin and his leathery skin had turned gray with rot, his upper lip still bore traces of his trademark thin mustache. The pod's membrane pulsed and gave off a dry heat. His voice was high and thin, chanting in Latin, but something about it captivated her in a way that made her both curious and very afraid.

"This is the New King Salomon," she said.

Ram slung the bag off his shoulder next to the pod.

But then, out of a murky haze in the far corner of the chamber, something stirred.

It was a thing all black, shaped perfectly like a man, crouched over one of the pods with its back to them. The figure straightened its legs and stood to the height of a normal man, but it kept its face hidden. Its obsidian skin, terrible in its splendor, shimmered in the light of a halo glowing around its bald head. Both Skylar and Ram stood entranced as it slowly turned around.

Its legs were muscular and straight. Its waist and chest were trim and upright. Its neck was relaxed and focused. Black horns, small like bulbs, sprouted from its head, and its fingers, spread wide on outstretched hands, were twice as long as a normal man's. And in the instant it opened its completely white eyes, the hundreds of cacophonous voices all went silent.

. . .

The Sentinel stood like a mist-clad deity against a wall of barren trees in the glade. The acidic taste of metal wrapped itself around Ellen's tongue, and the swarming of flies filled her ears.

With great effort, Roland pushed himself up to a seated position. He opened his mouth as if to speak, but nothing came out.

Brady, too, stared slack-jawed at this giant lording over the spawn's pulp.

The Sentinel's three yellow eyes were set on Ellen.

Gazing up at those eyes, Ellen walked slowly toward it—toward him. A smile formed on her bleeding and dripping face.

"Mark," she said. "Thank you, sweetie."

Brady shot her a confused glance. Roland kept his eyes on the Sentinel.

Although she wanted nothing more than to hug him, to hold him, to thank him with the love he so yearned for, something stopped her from getting too close. She knelt in the glade and put her gun down. "I'm so proud of you. Thank you, Mark," she whispered.

Brady approached her from behind. "Did you say... Mark?"

"Yes," Ellen said, still holding the Sentinel's gaze. "That's Mark Harcourt. That's the Sentinel."

As if whatever forces of nature holding the Sentinel together left him, it fell to its knees with a crash that shook the earth. Several chunks of rock broke off its body when its knees made heavy contact.

"Oh... no," she said.

"What's wrong?" Brady asked. "And why'd you call it 'sweetie'?"

"He's weak."

Roland whimpered from the other side of the glade.

"Shit," Brady said.

Behind them, a brown-cloaked spawn, one slightly larger than the rest, was holding Roland by the neck as a shield in front of its body. This spawn was calmer, more controlled than the others. There was something different in its vaporous eyes, a twinge of depth and nuance not seen in the others. It stood completely motionless in the dead center of the glade amongst the slain bodies of its compatriots.

Brady drew his gun. "Put him down!"

Ellen heard the Sentinel stir but flared her hands up in a signal to stop him. The Sentinel obeyed. Brady, arms outstretched and eye locked over the barrel of his gun, took slow steps forward.

"I said, put him down!"

Roland opened his mouth. A voice that wasn't his, something deeper and darker, came out.

"Puellam mihi dā."

"What?"

"Puellam mihi dā."

"You're gonna have to speak English, motherfucker. I can hit you from right here. Put him down right now!"

"Give me the girl."

"Only thing I'm givin' you is the count of three to release him or you'll catch a bullet between your horseshit ass red eyes. Look around you. Your fuckin' donkey ass lookin' buddies are all dead."

"Wait!" Ellen said. "How did you know where we were? How have you been finding us?"

Roland didn't move, but the spawn did, its heinous snout and gnarled antlers catching a moonbeam through the trees.

"The boy."

"The boy?" Ellen whispered.

She turned to Brady for his reaction, but he had none. The spawn's forehead was his only focus.

"One!" he shouted.

The spawn tightened its grip on Roland's neck.

"Two!"

Roland's body spasmed, the life seeping out of him.

Brady fired a single round. The spawn jerked backwards and the light from one of its raging red eyes went out, as if a switch had been flipped or a candle blown out. Black blood poured from the socket and splattered onto a still catatonic Roland.

Brady shot the spawn two more times in the head. It took Roland down to the ground with it, and Brady rushed over, still peering over the barrel. The spawn released a screech that filled the entire world while Brady pried its fingers from Roland's neck. Roland blinked and coughed and gagged as breath came back to him.

The spawn didn't get up. It didn't fight back. It just lay there, screeching, wailing, and maybe somewhere beneath the binding layers of mutation and heartache, crying.

Ellen strafed behind it and fired a shot that cratered its skull and launched ill-fated balloons of black blood in all directions.

The glade was still, and finally, Maurice Bacon's pain was over.

But just then, a screech infused with scathing volume and power split the night and ricocheted through the trees. The three of them turned toward the Sentinel, now standing again, with its eyes fixed on swaying tree branches and two red rings of light.

. . .

The obsidian-skinned entity flickered in the pulsing light of the pods. Skylar could not stop looking into its eyes. Never before had she encountered so much depth in objects so bland and simple, those little white orbs. She sensed they were portals to other planes and permutations of reality. In them, she felt the terrifying gravity of peoples and times so ancient that all vectors of their history had faded to ruin, save for right here, as residue in the psyche of this demon, now using those same eyes to stare at a seventeen-year-old girl from Bensalem, Virginia.

Of all things, she was awestruck by its calmness, its sheer tranquility. It exuded a perfectly relaxed and controlled energy in this foulest of places—a dome-shaped chamber in the middle of the earth in which corpses, or spirits, or somethings, of those slain by a monster over hundreds of years soaked in sacks of black blood and fed a heinous mass of cells clinging to the ceiling.

And then suddenly, Skylar's entire soul sank.

It was not the spirit of Judithe, nor the burning fire of her mother's soul, or even her own survival instinct that told her this demon was an agent of immeasurable evil. It was the look on Ram's face.

When she regarded him, her best friend and most trusted

ally, a pyre of burning doom was ignited inside her. It was a doom the likes of which she had never known, even when she watched the Nothus hack down her mother. For the doom that Ram reflected back at her now was her own.

"My King," he said to it, "I have fulfilled thy charge." He turned to Skylar, his grin so wide it seemed to rip his face. "I've been so eager to tell you."

Skylar gasped and began pacing slowly backward.

Ram reached out his hands. "Your destiny is calling. The blood of the nexum fills your veins. The light of New Atlantis burns bright in your heart. You will be held in high regard among his children." He gestured broadly to the pods around them. "Come with me. Taste the bounty that the New King Salomon has provided us."

She watched in torrid shock as he walked toward the demon with his palms upright, his footsteps squelching on the wet and squishy ground.

Memories of light and laughter with Ram rifled through her mind. Until this moment, they had been so genuine. So real. The warm nights. The lazy afternoons. The car rides. The kisses. The butterflies. Everything, all of it, coagulating into a ball of acute emotion, and in a second, bursting. Melting. Now, she felt the coldness of those nights. She felt Ram's tongue slip down her throat like a serpent. She felt the butterflies in her stomach wither and die and turn into a poison staining her from the inside out.

Ram got down on his knees and began to chant. "His children will be seated at the table of his offering. Filii eius ad mensam oblationis eius consident. His children will populate the kingdom of New Atlantis. Filii eius regnum Atlantis Novae implebunt. His children will sip the blood of the heretics and will be enlightened. Filii eius sanguinem haereticorum sorbillabunt et illustrabuntur."

Ram stopped when he reached the demon. They locked eyes, and he knelt. It wrapped a long-fingered hand around the dome of his skull and now peered directly at Skylar. Ram shuddered, then convulsed. He convulsed again, cried out, moaned in pain. Ram clamped his hands to his head and screamed for it to stop. Skylar—shaking, crying—put her hands over her mouth to muffle her screams. A red stream of blood spilled out of his ear, its fat drops pinging the ground as they fell. He screamed again, this time wordlessly, only screeching louder and louder to release his pain.

His head shook violently, inhumanly, in the grips of this calamity's unflinching talons. That its hands stayed so still while Ram spasmed defied every observation of gravity and physics Skylar had ever witnessed. Blood dripping from his facial orifices whipped around his head in a red tornado. A sharp hissing sound, like water hitting the boiling coils of a stove, accompanied his wailing, and smoke began to waft from his ears along with more blood.

Blood. Blood. More blood. Blood that surged through the arms that had held Skylar tight. Blood that flowed through the sturdy shoulders she had leaned on. Blood that warmed the lips always smiling at her in the darkness. Blood that beat in the heart of the only one left she had ever loved. It was all pouring out of him.

When he screamed, she screamed.

Ram shook, and he seized, and he flailed. Then, he calmed, and he quieted, and he stopped, and the demon holding him let go, and his body crumpled to the ground.

Through tear-drenched eyes, Skylar stared at the headless, bloody heap of a man at the demon's feet. She clutched at her hoodie as her chest and shoulders rose and sank. Then, she took a step backwards, but her drained legs felt ready to collapse at any moment.

It did not open its mouth to speak. Instead, a dark and rasping drone echoed down from the walls and ceiling.

Be still, my child.

Skylar paced around to the back side of New King Salomon's pod, next to where Ram had dropped the bag. She kept her bleary eyes glued to the demon. Despite the vastness of the chamber and the awfulness of its inhabitant, Skylar saw and felt a world reduced to the singularity of her next action, her response to the horror that had just unfolded. It was so crystal clear that the weight of the realization itself implied it was a thing she had always known. It was as if the task of performing the ritual—right here, right now—had been programmed into her DNA and ran as subliminal code beneath the surface of her life. All she had seen, done, and lived through up to this point was in service of this moment.

Be still. All will be well.

Her hands shook as she unzipped the bag and began pulling out the duffel's contents, hawk-like eyes still locked on the demon. She padded her jean pocket to make sure the recitation was still there. It was.

"Who are you?" she said.

I am the New King Salomon.

"Then who's this?" she said, nodding to the gray-skinned corpse in the pod she hid behind. She didn't assume the demon was oblivious to her actions behind the pod, but held fast to a blind faith that led her hands through the initial steps of altar construction. First, the stones. The first was heavy, requiring both hands to lift.

A simple vessel. The form that harbored me above. But it was I who spoke through his tongue and saw through his eyes. He brought the first of my children here, to Bensalem, a land whole and chaste, the virgin of the world.

The second and third stones were somehow lighter. She placed them swiftly down and fished in the duffel for the trophy board.

"What do you want with these people?"

It began taking slow steps toward her, fingers like knives outstretched, halo burning around its horned head. It gestured broadly to the pods around it. *These are my children. They now populate my kingdom. A kingdom that waits for you, nexum.*

"Nexum? I know what you did to the last nexum. I saw you staring at her while she died, screaming for her life. You set her up. You watched her burn!"

Be not afraid. It is I who revealed these things to you. She was not meant for this world, nor are you. She bore unto this world my prince, and for this, she holds a seat of high regard at the table.

"Prince?"

The one you fear. The bastard son of the forest protector.

The pillowcase was hard to find, crumpled in the corner of the nearly empty duffel. As her hands worked, the demon kept walking toward her. Slowly.

A very great power lies in your blood, nexum. Your presence will be as a gift to our kingdom. It reached a hand out to her. *Will you follow us into the light?*

"I'm not falling for your shit. I don't care what you do to me. I have nothing to live for."

It was so close now that it peered over the pod at the altar. Something in the air changed. A quick whoosh of sound built in the chamber and suddenly stopped, all in an instant.

"Hey, princess, whatcha got there?"

Skylar's entire body went numb. It took her a long time to

find the courage to tilt her head, to peek over the edge of the pod, to put together the sight before her.

Her mother stood where the demon had. She was intact, naked and without blemish. Blond curls floated down to her shoulders the way they would on the best of hair days. The laugh lines across her eyes and the crooked smile she always had lit up her face. Even the age spots that had crept onto her skin in recent years were there in perfect photographic quality. It looked like her. It sounded like her. It even smelled like her.

"What is that, Sky?" it said.

Skylar's blood turned to ice water. Her heart thundered in her chest. Even slower than she had moved before, Skylar's hands inched into the duffel to grab the three jars of Black Pulvis Solaris.

"I wouldn't do that if I were you."

Skylar found one and set it by her knees. She found the second. Then, the third.

"Hey. Listen, sweetie, you better quit that. You really don't know what you're getting yourself into."

As Skylar began unscrewing the jar tops, she felt the scalding gaze of a shameful mother on her arms and shoulders.

"You don't want to be a bad girl now, do you? Remember what you did to your brother on Halloween?"

She stopped unscrewing. Her mind jumped back to a memory of sneaking into Lenny's room and stealing his entire stash of Halloween candy. A sea of bright and glittering plastic wrappers spread over the carpet by his bed, and Skylar ruled over the pile with eyes of wonder and fascination. Hands like claw machines, she raked as much as she could, as fast as she could, into her plastic lunchbox. Lenny returned to his room and cried to high hell, and when her mother found the lunchbox hidden in Skylar's closet, she let her have it.

Other, similar moments played in rapid succession in her mind—teachers yelling at her, classmates teasing her, junkie Justin pinning her against the lockers. She knelt there, cringing and petrified, in a bath of shame and embarrassment as they bombarded her. But even as she cowered behind the pod, she also felt her teenage self, the new but bold and confident young woman she'd grown into, tugging at heartstrings and imploring her to press on. For so long, that scared little girl had felt like home, but it also felt old and underutilized, like a childhood toy she'd outgrown. Her teenage self, her now self, felt like the future.

As she finished unscrewing the first jar and reached for the second, she realized the feeling on her arms and shoulders was real—they were getting hotter.

"Oh, Skylar, I'm so disappointed in you."

Her mind now jumped to Judithe, flesh so hot it melted and dripped off her blackening bones. That heat now wrapped itself around Skylar's arms, paralyzing their movement. Sweat popped broke out under her beanie and her jaws clenched. Moving her forearm just inches toward the third jar triggered a searing, unholy pain. But as sweat stung her eyes and as the burning, flaming, scorching pain persisted, so too did Skylar. She winced her eyes closed and groaned in agony as she unscrewed the third jar.

"Hey. Listen to me, you little cunt. Stop that right now."

On top of the burning sensation invading her body, those words sliced through her heart like a dagger. "You're not her!"

The demon impersonating her mother didn't move. Its fiery gaze grew hotter, its eyes burned brighter, and its voice grew louder. "Oh, I am, you fuckin' little bitch. I know that dirty slit of yours anywhere. I can fuckin' smell it. You think this hurts? You think Judithe burned? What she got was a fucking gift!"

Skylar pictured flakes of dead, quaking-hot skin peeling

off of her fingers as she slid them into the pocket holding the recitation. The coarse denim chafed, and she would have been convinced her hand was melting if she didn't watch it slip into her pocket with her own eyes.

Tears fell on the white paper marked with the logo of the Old Rag Motel. She gripped it weakly in fingers she could barely move as she read.

"Herne, most righteous of forest protectors, I come to you in great need of your blessing. It is I who came before you long ago, and through my misdeeds, did enter a daemon into my house that I now seek to rid—"

The fire spread further over her body. It seeped into her ribs and crawled up her neck, binding her jaw in molten pain. Even her tongue boiled inside her mouth.

"Take this offering of black antimony, and of sulfur, and return—"

"I never fucking loved you! I liked your brother better. You were such a shit daughter! I should have carved you out of my cunt myself! If you go through with this, I will haunt you until the day you die. I will run in the back of every dream. I will fuck your mind so hard and I will destroy you. I am hell!"

Skylar stopped reading and looked up at it. The form was still her mother's but the visage was gone. The eyes were brilliant white. The skin over its face and neck had thinned and was stretched over a much bonier face. The bottom half of its head was all teeth, long and thick.

A rip, a gush, and a thud on the far side of the chamber stole her attention away.

Lying half on the ground, half in a drained and deflated pod, Cheryl McNamara offered her daughter a frail smile. Her voice was strained and paper-thin, less than a whisper. "I... I love you so much."

"Mom!" Skylar blasted past her physical agony and strained to get to her feet.

Cheryl shook her head. "Don't. Finish... finish it... my brave girl... and I'll..."

Skylar's entire face caved in emotion. She wept at the sight of her mother, or at least some form of her.

"I'll see you... my perfect girl. I'll see you again," Cheryl said.

Skylar didn't look directly, but she could see, out of the corner of her eye, the demon had reverted back to its obsidian form. She sniffled, blinked tears from her eyes, and read while the fire on her skin raged on. "Take this offering of black antimony, and of sulfur, and return this daemon, this Nothus Noctis, from whence it came. Let it know never again the world it has entered."

In an instant, the pain was gone. She collapsed in utter exhaustion and physical shock.

Several more pods popped open, and their gangly veins detached from the organ on the ceiling, spilling fast-flowing black liquid.

When the vein connected to the vessel of the New King Salomon's pod detached, the membrane split, and his emaciated body spilled onto her. The stench was incredible, something worse and deeper than death, and Skylar flailed to throw him off of her as black liquid spewed.

More pops. More gushes. More severed veins and more black blood. More bodies trapped in pods—some for centuries—dumped out onto the fleshy floor of the chamber.

The New King Salomon, still standing calm and focused, twisted its head toward her.

Hell awaits you.

It raised both hands, and the organ on the ceiling popped into a sprawling firework of putrid liquid, coating the walls, the pods, the bodies, Skylar, a headless Ram, a lifeless Cheryl, even the New King Salomon.

Soaked entirely, Skyar scrambled to her feet and ran for the exit, but her legs were too weak, and she slipped and fell face-first into the quickly rising black liquid. On all fours, gasping for breath, she crawled for the corridor, shoving bodies, tattered pods, and torn veins littering her path. But the liquid rose fast, and when she finally gained her footing again, another wave of it crashed into her back and shoved her under.

Skylar no longer had the strength to fight it. Every ounce of her—physically, mentally, spiritually—was drained.

. . .

Roland was still thrashing in Brady's arms. He gasped for air, and his eyes, white-rimmed and burning with delirium, darted madly, as if they had for the first time seen light.

"I... I saw it," he choked out between breathless gasps.

"Saw what? What?" Brady said.

"Everything. I... I..."

"Hold on, buddy. Catch your breath." Brady waved Ellen over.

"You all right?" she said.

Roland, still heaving, looked up at her. "Skylar... you have to get Skylar."

"Where is she?"

"She's down there with it...She's doing the ritual... oh God. There's something terrible down there with her."

"What?"

Behind them, the Nothus had reached the glade. It screeched again as it brought a calamitous hand down on the Sentinel.

"You guys have to get her. I saw her down there with... with... I don't know what. But it's not the Nothus. It's something else."

Ellen's hair flew in the air as she spun toward the Sentinel. The Nothus had knocked it back down to its knees, and each vicious blow it absorbed, clanged through the glade like metallic thunder. Over and over, the Nothus slammed, and swatted, and stabbed, and screeched. Tiny bits of the Sentinel's armor exploded off its shell as the Nothus kept pummeling.

"But we have to help Mark!" Ellen said.

"I'll go get her," Brady said. "Where is she?"

Roland pointed to a pitch-black section of the forest draped in withered branches. "That way. There's a door."

"A door?"

"Yes. It's through that door."

From the other side of the glade, a new voice floated through the trees. "H—Hello?"

Out stepped a young man clad in an overcoat and holding a flashlight. The look on his face was a mix of exhaustion and shock.

"Lenny!" Brady said.

"Skylar called me." Lenny jogged toward the group. "I'm here for someone who's hurt."

Ellen began walking toward the Nothus. She loaded her shotgun.

"What the hell is going on out here?" Lenny asked.

"A little late to explain," Brady said. "This is the guy we need to move. Roland, this is Lenny McNamara, Skylar's brother. You can trust him."

Roland, now seated, looked up at them. "No... go get Skylar."

Brady put a hand up. "I'll get Skylar. Lenny'll stay with you."

"Wait," Lenny said. "Where's Skylar? Where's Ram?"

Roland winced, in what could have been pain or frustration

or both. "You're wasting time. Both of you, go! Now!"

Brady shook his head. "Come on," he said to Lenny. "Keep that light on and stay behind me."

Before following Brady into the trees, Lenny gawked at the Nothus and the Sentinel, two mythological titans battling towards mutual descruction on the opposite side of the glade. "Oh my fucking God."

"Lenny! Come on!" Brady urged.

Less than a second later, Ellen fired a shot that bounced off the Nothus' snout. Two of the Sentinel's fingers had broken off, and the armor on its forearms had thinned to half its original size.

"No!" Ellen shouted. She reloaded and shot the Nothus again, and again, the bullet bounced off.

"Ellen! Get away from it!" Roland yelled.

She ignored him and reloaded again. Her hands, shaking from rage, struggled to hold the barrel. She tried to load a cartridge but dropped it in her duress. "Fuck!"

The Sentinel's knees caved. It crashed backward and balled its increasingly brittle arms and legs. Two great strikes from the Nothus cracked and broke the Sentinel's right forearm, and the limb shattered into countless black shards when the bastard beast struck again.

Ellen switched and tightened her grip on the gun, and her pounding heart practically burst through her ribcage as she sprinted directly at the Nothus.

"Ellen! Don't!" Roland cried.

With a great heave, she swung the shotgun like a baseball bat into the Nothus' side. It didn't react at first, focused only on destroying its nemesis, but as Ellen kept swinging and hacking, it eventually let up its barrage on the Sentinel and simply looked her in the eyes.

As if a knife had been driven into her skull, Ellen's head exploded in pain. She fell to the ground, closed her eyes, and screamed. It wormed its way into her thoughts, her memories, her dreams, navigating her mind and her life inside her own mind. She could feel it moving around, touching things and moving them around. Roland's screams melted into blunted reverberations of sound bouncing through failing ear drums.

And then, as quickly as it had entered, the Nothus retreated from her mind, and all pain evaporated. Ellen opened her eyes.

The Nothus stumbled backwards, hands spinning in pre-dawn wind, and it released a cry so loud it blew Ellen's hair back. She desperately covered her ears as the cry sustained, longer and louder than any she had heard it release before. Small edges of bright white light began to emerge through the Nothus' fur, and then a great beam blasted through its open mouth. Its eyes, once immortal weapons of mental destruction, shot two more beams of light into the sky. Edges of light on its body became fissures, and as its death cry morphed from organic to something weaker and more distant, so very distant, the beams pouring through its eyes and mouth merged into a single column, consuming its entire snout.

The light was so blinding that Ellen lurched onto her stomach to shield her eyes. It consumed more and more of the Nothus until it became a single incandescent nebula of light and sound. It expanded further, and further, and further, until it nearly filled the entire glade, and then in one great sonic boom, the light exploded and was gone.

The forest was silent and calm. The Sentinel lowered its remaining limbs weakly to the ground. Ellen peeked her head up and looked around at the spawn bodies still littering the glade. She turned to Roland, eyes wide and beaming.

"She did it," he whispered.

Ellen crawled over to the Sentinel's side. She placed a timid hand on its bruised and brittle body. The shroud of flies typically swarming it buzzed above her head, and she had to squint to keep them out of her eyes. This close, the taste and smell of metal that invaded the senses of those who encountered it gripped her, and she tried to swallow down the foul taste to no avail.

The light from its three yellow eyes was fading, and the oncoming dawn glowed above them through the dome of the glade. The Sentinel shifted, twisting a few inches to meet her gaze. It made no sound or effort to get up, but what worried Ellen the most was that it made no attempt to communicate through her mind—the wavelength they had spent so much time talking through over the past three months.

For a thing of such size and power, its sudden helplessness and fragility struck Ellen in the gut, gnawing at her insides and twisting her stomach in knots. She wrapped her other hand around one of its last remaining fingers and gasped in horror when it snapped in her hands.

Roland, who had crawled over to them, gripped the armor on its chest. He hesitated for a moment before digging his fingertips into the material and pulling a handful of it away. He looked at Ellen, and she grabbed a handful, too.

Then, she grabbed another.

DAY 8

The first flakes of snow that morning fell in the mountains, where they always did, when the last, chilling vestiges of twilight gave way to a reluctant dawn. Clouds that marred the sky the previous evening remained tucked in their cosmic beds, and as the day awakened, they blended into a single, slate-colored veil looming in a misty repose. The mountains were all but gone, fading upward into nothingness, conversing with the heavens instead of the land. Beings that dwelt in that high and unknowable dimension might have summoned them that morning, as couriers of a message to a forest that had grown to forget tranquility and light.

But the town of Bensalem, largely unaware of the secret war it had long harbored, rose to a dawn of sorrow and confusion. Rick McNamara found sleep a few minutes after his daughter entered the Black Door, but before that had spent hours sobbing uncontrollably while clutching the most recent picture of his wife in clammy and shaking hands. The picture was six months old, and she wasn't doing anything remarkable, but there she was. Her hair. Her stance. Her hands. Her smile. Her heart was in that picture, and Rick wanted to rip his soul to shreds for just one more moment with her. One goodbye. One kiss. One snide remark. One "I love you." One glance.

One moment. Just one.

Maybe if he looked at that picture long enough—really concentrated on the blurry pixels of her face—it would sort of feel like her again. And if it did, maybe he could see her whenever he wanted, no—needed. And maybe, just maybe, if he could do that, he could find a way against all odds to stay with her forever. To stay with her in the picture, where she lived now and he did not.

But morning came. Rick put the picture down, and he decided against taking a razor to his wrist to test its sharpness when he saw the snow. He spoke to it.

"I love you too, bug," he whispered. "I miss you so."

. . .

Bensalem woke. The snow stopped, the clouds faded, and the mountains returned from their mist. By afternoon, a radiant sun lit the icy coats of trees into a landscape shimmering in ivory and crystal.

That light was the first thing Skylar saw when she opened her eyes.

The windows were blurry at first, unfocused grayscales surrounded by the dark curtains of her eyelids. She blinked several times to clear the haze and squinted at the day's brightness. It wasn't the android beeping of machines or the beige wallpaper that told her she was in a hospital, it was the IV needle stinging her arm.

Her first attempt to lift her limbs failed. When a sudden chill danced over her skin, she shivered, and the young man balled up in one of the two chairs in the corner stirred.

"Sky?" Lenny said.

She blinked at him. "Lenny?"

He scooched his chair to her bedside. "Hey," he whispered with a smile. "Yeah. It's me. How you feeling?"

"What happened?"

Lenny shook his head and stared at the deep sleep pooled in her eyes. It took a moment for the words on his tongue to come out. "You were right."

"About what?"

"Everything."

Skylar rolled her head across the pillow to gaze at the blinking stack of electronics beside her. "Everything hurts."

"Yeah, but you're gonna be okay. Just some hypothermia and dehydration. You've been out for about ten hours. You hungry at all?"

"Starving."

He chuckled. "That's probably a good sign. Let me go get you something to eat."

"Where's Dad?"

"He just left. I just got here. I took over for him."

"Was he worried? How is he?"

"Kind of a wreck, honestly."

"Poor Dad. I'll give him a call."

"I think a call from you would brighten his spirits a lot. But hey, what kind of food are you in the mood for? You want a big meal, like a meatball sub, or something?"

"Sure. Anything." He was halfway out the door when she called to him. "Lenny? What do you mean I was right about everything?"

Lenny was locked on something down the hall. His smile

widened as the squeaky axle of a wheelchair grew louder. He looked back at Skylar. "He'll explain."

Roland, clad in a hospital gown and wheeling the chair, rolled himself into Skylar's room.

Lenny patted him on the shoulder.

"Did you thank him, Skylar?" Roland said.

"What?" she asked.

"He saved your life."

Lenny chuckled again on his way out. "I'll leave you guys to it. One meatball sub, comin' up."

Roland grinned at Skylar as he guided the chair to her bedside. "How are you feeling?"

"Everything hurts," she said.

"You did it."

"I did?"

"Yes. The Nothus is gone. The ritual worked."

Skylar gazed out the window for a moment before turning back to him with a smile. "Are you serious?"

"Serious."

"How did you guys find me?"

"I suppose you could say it was a team effort. Remember how I thought Maurice Bacon summoned the spawns? Well, not only did he summon them, he actually became one. His mind and body fully mutated."

"What?"

"Maurice—the spawn, Maurice—snuck up on me in the glade, and he gripped me by the neck with his fingers. I thought he was going to choke the life out of me, but he somehow used my body as his mouthpiece. When he had me, when I was connected with him, I saw everything. I saw their present. I saw their past. Not just the spawns, but the Nothus itself. I heard them speaking to each other. I think they were able to see and hear and communicate telepathically. They have an incredible ability to attack the minds and dreams of humans."

"Jesus."

"I also saw you down in that cavern, but then, it all went blank when Ellen and Derek killed Maurice. Your brother had just arrived, so he and Derek went down and got you."

For the first time since waking, Skylar sat up. "They went down and got me?"

"Yes. They found you passed out in a pool of black liquid in that chamber. All of those pods with the Nothus' victims were feeding that massive organ, and that organ, whatever it was, somehow powered the Nothus and the spawns. Once that was destroyed and the veins were severed, the Nothus morphed into a ball of light and was gone."

She closed her eyes and sighed. "Did you see what happened to Ram?"

He nodded. "I'm so sorry. I had no idea. Truly."

"I can't fucking believe it."

He sighed.

She closed her eyes, spilling a tear down her cheek. "I thought he loved me. How could I have been such a fool?"

He shook his head. "Skylar, listen to me, when Maurice had me, and I saw that... thing, and I saw what it did to Ram..." He paused for a moment. "Only then did I realize the true level of evil we were up against. This whole time, we were working against something much more terrible and insidious than the Nothus Noctis. You came face to face with something much more clever and capable of fantastic evil."

"What was it?"

He sat back in his wheelchair and folded his hands. "I'm not sure exactly, but I have a guess. Are you familiar with the idea of a fallen angel?"

"I think so."

"Its human form and the halo would indicate traces of an angelic past, or some connection to them."

"It didn't have wings, though."

"Right, and its body was all black. So, certainly, it would have lost many of its angelic traits. Whether those traits were forcibly removed or willingly disrobed, so to speak, wasn't totally clear. But it seemed to want to emulate a king of Heaven, maybe a Heaven on its own terms." He inched his wheelchair closer to her. "What struck me was the contrast between its apparent obsession over gathering children for a kingdom, while also seeming incredibly... alone."

"What's the deal with the New King Salomon, then? That man in the big pod was who deceived Judithe and started this whole mess. I'm sure it was him. But then the angel claimed to be the New King Salomon. Which is it?"

Something shifted in Roland's eyes, as if retreating or bracing for a blow.

"Isn't he, like, the pillar of your faith?" Skylar said.

An echo of laughter seeped in from the halls. Skylar's stomach growled.

Roland rubbed his palms across the wheelchair's armrests. He sighed, and he spoke with his eyes closed, softly and slowly. "I'm not... I'm not entirely sure what to believe right now."

Skylar waited for his eyes to open before responding. In front of her, she saw not the wise and confident man she knew him to be. His face was vacant and lost, and he turned to gaze out the window instead of making eye contact.

"Well," she said, "if you don't know what to believe, what are you thinking?"

"I think you know what I'm thinking."

"That the Order's all bullshit?" She regretted the words as soon as she said them. "Sorry. I didn't mean it like that."

"No need to apologize. I believe..." He wheeled himself over to the window, where he scanned the corners of the vast picture of trees and snowy mountains outside. "I believe he at one point had very good intentions. I believe he led persecuted and misunderstood people from an old world to a new one in the name of spiritual freedom."

Both of them watched a murmuration of starlings ebb and flow through the air. Like a black hologram against a dusk-laden sky, they stretched, pulled, contracted, and expanded. They somehow moved both as many and as one.

Roland continued. "I believe life in the new world was hard. They settled in a land they knew nothing about. They didn't know its history or its secrets. And I believe they certainly didn't know that something was waiting for them. Where it came from, or what it wants, or why, I can only begin to speculate."

He turned his chair toward her again.

"But Skylar, I can tell you for certain... when that thing spoke, when it did what it did to Ram, when it... when it took your mother's form... it showed me that it was capable of ripping a human soul to shreds. I believe that when that man came here— the New King Salomon, if you want to call him that—the angel found something it had sought for a long time: an opportunity. It turned a bright vision into a terrible scheme. The Nothus was just part of the plan, the conduit needed to draw life from the real world, and the New King Salomon was just a means to summon it. I mean, just think about what that thing did to Ram! Think about what it did to you! It knew exactly how to get you to stop the ritual. It knew exactly what to say to hurt you, and it—"

"No."

Roland cocked his head, puzzled.

"It didn't get me to stop." Her voice was quiet but sliced through the room like a knife. "You know what I think? I think he was a weak man. He smiled while Judithe burned alive in front of her family. I don't care if it was really him or that angel smiling, pulling the strings inside him. If what you say is true, that the angel was here the whole time and just looking for a weak mind to conquer, I think it found one."

Skylar paused and let the hallway's muted cacophony invade their conversation. Even though the frosty lumps of hypothermia still ached inside her, she couldn't shake the sensation of flames on her skin. She glanced at her forearms, just to make sure they weren't on fire and, in doing so, wondered how long the memories would last.

She would never forget what she felt and saw down there. Skylar knew that. But as she grew older and began to cope with the rubble of her life, which memories would stand the test of time? Would the angel, with its horrible white eyes, haunt her like it promised? Would she see the Nothus and its spawns, screeching and swiping and drooling in the glade, every time a deer crossed the road in front of her? How would she remember Ram, the memory that in this moment she most craved to expel? Would she ever forgive him, or would the thought of his deception rake her heart until the day she died? She shivered.

"Hey. You feeling okay?" Roland said.

When Skylar bowed her head, the tears rolling down her cheeks plunged into the fabric of her hospital gown. She tried to lift her arms but failed. "Everything... everything hurts."

Roland wheeled back to her bedside, slow enough that the axel didn't squeak. "I know it does. I know. I know." He took her hand. "Some of those wounds will heal very quickly. Others will take time, but they will. Believe me. Even the deepest ones will."

Tears flooded her eyes and her fingernails dug into his skin. "Was that really her?" she whispered through more tears.

The longer Roland stared at her without an answer, the more her face melted over the sorrow boiling inside her.

"Was that her? Tell me!"

"I don't know, but I'll tell you this. If I know one woman who could somehow navigate all that cosmic bullshit down there, who could find a light in the dark—in that darkest of dark— because she knew her daughter needed her?"

Skylar seethed in her bed, teeth clenched, eyes pouring, all of it coming out of her now. Her grip was so tight it had broken the skin on Roland's palm but he didn't seem to notice.

He glanced over his shoulder at an entranced Lenny, standing in the doorway with a box of food in his hands, before turning back to her. "But whether it was her or not, I believe what she told you."

"What's that?" she said, wiping her eyes.

"That you'll see her again."

Skylar smiled.

. . .

Three floors down, in the north wing instead of the south, Caleb sat on Ellen's lap. A machine similar to the one plugged into Skylar, but beeping at half the speed, loomed over the husk of a barely conscious man.

Mark Harcourt was 45 years old but looked 100.

His skin was bone-pale, wafer-thin, and riddled with withered purple lines. Ellen had weighed his ghastly body at 87 pounds upon admittance, and she chided Caleb for staring at his bulbous knees and ankles, the only parts of his legs that looked alive. She had tried and failed a half dozen times to locate a vein healthy enough to insert the IV, and the cluster of his puncture wounds now saturated the entire elbow area into a black and blue cloud. Just another part of him that looked dead.

His chest, a rib-laced coffin of failing organs, rose and fell less than an inch without the ventilator she had just unstrapped from his withered lips. Wispy gray hairs, each sad and frail attempts at life, sprouted sporadically on his head. A great, black wound in the middle of his forehead marked where the manufactured third-eye had been. Roland had removed the rock—a pearlish silver thing, just like the tiny pebble Jane had placed in Caleb's head—and identified it as a mercury derivative as he discarded it. He remarked that he had no idea how it worked, only that he wished greatly to never see it again.

Yet all of these sights combined did not eclipse the horror of his stench, for as soon as the remainder of the Sentinel's suit had been removed, the mystery of its ever-present shroud of flies was revealed. Mark's body, from his chest to his knees, was coated in several caked-on layers of human waste. The smell of the suit had masked it to human noses, but it struck Roland like a sucker punch to the face when exposed. It was too much for him to bear, and he crawled away, vomiting.

As he did, the warning he had issued—"You might not like what you find"—reverberated in Ellen's head. Dialed into doctor mode, she held her nose and suppressed her gag reflex as she checked his pulse and his breathing. All trepidation and regret was washed away when she felt faint signs of life still beating inside him.

Now, nearly twelve sleepless hours later, Ellen's soul fluttered in anticipation as he finally opened his eyes. She held Caleb tight, and she whispered instructions to watch and stay quiet, to let Mark look and talk first. What she wanted to say but didn't, because Caleb wouldn't understand, was that this was about to be his first human interaction in over forty years, and his brain's decay might be as bad as his body's.

Mother and son watched him intently and from afar, the way one might gawk at a newborn through the glass, as he navigated his new, old world. The only pieces of him that moved were his neck and his eyes. Their movements were so slow and slight, clearly straining. After taking in most of the hospital room, the corner of his mouth raised a hair up toward a smile when his gaze landed on Caleb.

"Mark?" Ellen said.

He blinked, and when he opened his blue eyes again, they were on her.

"Hi, Mark. It's me, Ellen. Can you hear me?" She rose, placing Caleb on the chair that had been hers and crouched by his bedside. "Can you see me?"

A litany of pops from a barely functioning jaw accompanied the opening of his mouth. "Ye..."

Ellen sighed and grinned, and with a mother's gentleness, wrapped her hands around his. She had never held a skeleton's hand, but imagined this is what it felt like—hard, knobby bolts wrapped in clammy leather. "You've been through a lot, Mark. Your name is Mark Harcourt and you're here in a hospital. You're no longer the Sentinel. You've done your job. It's over. We're going to get you back to health so you can live out your—"

Water that had been in his eyes slid down his sunken cheeks.

"It's okay, baby," she said. "I'm here. I'm here."

He opened his mouth again, emitting something resembling

a choke, a flushing of forty years' worth of phlegm. "Hi..."

"Oh, Mark. I'm so glad you're here. I'm so glad you're back with us."

"I... called you... on the phone."

"My God. Yes, yes, you did. You did call me on the phone. That was you, wasn't it?"

He nodded softly. "I... to warn... you."

"I know. I know you did. I—I'm so sorry. Do you remember Aaron? My husband?"

"Yes... I visited... said to him in dreams. He closed... the gate."

"The gate?"

"The...gate."

"We thought the gate meant the light. Is that what you meant? Turn off the lights?"

"Open the gate. Light... lights... yes. I forget my words."

It was a notion Ellen had considered in recent months. Mark was Caleb's age—or younger—when he was put in the ground forty years ago. If she did somehow manage to rescue him, what would be left of his ability to speak and communicate? As far as she could tell, there had been no language between them, only senses and mental connections. She knew he could hear her but had no way of knowing what he interpreted, because everything he showed her came unsolicited. They were speaking, tuned to two different wavelengths, and all she could do was hope that he marginally understood.

"You're doing so good, Mark. You're doing so good."

"Open the gate... turn off... the lights."

"The lights are off now, baby. It's all over. The Nothus is gone. You're all done. There won't be any more Sentinels. It's all over now."

"Ba... ba... bad. Over."

Ellen pulled out a tissue and wiped her tears before wiping his.

"Thank you... Mommy." he said.

Her first instinct was to correct him. Would it have been the right thing to do? The smart thing to do? She moved back from the bed and beckoned Caleb over. "Mark, I want you to meet someone. This is Caleb. Do you remember Caleb? He's my son."

Ellen half expected Mark's entire face to crack from smiling when Caleb approached. A choke that could have been a fractured laugh spilled out from his gaping mouth. Ellen crouched behind a standing Caleb and rested her chin on his shoulder.

"My friend." Mark said.

"Hi, Mark."

"Hi..."

Ellen whispered to Caleb. "Can you thank him?"

"Thank you, Mark," he said.

"Thank you for what?" Ellen whispered.

"Thank you for being my friend in the ground."

Ellen's breath hitched when she looked at Mark again. "Mark," she said as tears spilled from her eyes, "I cannot tell you how grateful I am that you took care of Caleb when he was in the forest. He told me you talked to him and kept him safe. I...I was so scared, Mark. I thought I had lost him. I did lose him."

"Caleb... understands... my good friend..."

"Yes," Ellen said. "You will be good friends for a long time now. We're going to take care of you. We want you to come live with us when you're healthy. We want you to be a part of our family. We have a big house and a big fluffy dog. You'll sleep in a warm bed every night, and we'll have plenty of food and fun games to play. And nothing bad will happen to you ever again. Would you like that?"

Mark's eyes, losing steam, shifted to the ceiling, but his smile remained.

Caleb turned to his mother. "He says he wants to."

"Good," Ellen said, smiling.

"He says he wants to talk to me alone for a minute."

"Oh... of course." She took a deep breath as she rose. "Caleb, I'm gonna try and call Daddy. You stay here with Mark. I'll be at Dr. Mirsa's desk right across from the room, okay?"

Caleb nodded.

Before Ellen left the room, she took a long look at Mark, at Caleb. The pain of last summer would always stain her heart. If it wasn't in the front of her mind, it was in the back of it, and every waking and dreaming moment was an exercise in mitigating that pain.

She remembered the mother bird and touched her chest. Ellen remembered the promise she made to that bird, and feeling something near wholeness, smiled again at her boys before leaving.

. . .

The withering monotony of the pattern on Roland's hospital gown—clumps of navy dots stippling cornflower-blue cloth—scraped at his mind. It made him wonder if the designer's charge was to create something as bland as possible, and if so, why they weren't all just white. Why go through the trouble over a piece of cloth that people didn't even look at, only bled on and died in? Even the fucking ink seemed like a waste. Yet still he stared. He rubbed the cloth in his fingers and sighed as the pattern went on and on for what seemed like miles. Anything to distract him from what he knew he needed to do next.

In the silence of his hospital room, in the mire of his existential crisis, Roland made a great effort to not look at the cell phone on the table as he turned to look out the window. The last few days, it seemed, had been an everlasting state of cold. Freezing temperatures, blistering winds, and seething spawns of a bastard that came from a black door were things almost home to him now. That tonight would be spent in an actual bed with access to painkillers for the wound in his leg, devoid of physical threat, was a train of thought he had yet to embark upon.

Roland was alone, but his cell phone's presence on the table next to his bed was so powerful it felt like another person. Four times it had rung in the last few hours, and four times Roland had ignored it. Only one man had the number. Only one man had the truth.

A nurse came by and helped him get out of the wheelchair and back into bed. He asked her to turn the lights out but keep the blinds open, saying he wanted to fall asleep to the sunset. With the door closed and the nurse gone, the cell phone's presence was magnified. He had been given so much morphine that he couldn't feel most of the leg the spawn had impaled, but he did feel a cold trickle of blood running across his pelvis when he shifted over to his side.

He sighed and flopped back onto his back. He looked at the phone, a gray bar of metal cut vaguely out of shadows. A green light, the light of an incoming call, adorned its screen, casting the room in an alien glow, and its shrill ringtone cut through the silence. He ground his molars together as the phone rang on.

When it stopped, he looked out the window. Night would be here soon.

"Fuck it."

He picked up the phone and dialed the number that had just

called him—the number that had called him five times now—and the Grand Elder answered.

"Deacon!" he said. "Finally! Where have you been?"

"I'm in the hospital. I've sustained an injury."

"Do you have the book?"

"I do. It's safe."

"And what of the Nothus? What of the Sentinel?"

Roland could tell the Grand Elder was in his Manhattan office. Mahogany offered such splendid acoustics. "Didn't the New King Salomon show you?"

"What happened to the Nothus Noctis?"

"It's gone."

"It is?"

"The Nothus has been destroyed. Mark Harcourt has been recovered. He's two floors down in the same hospital I'm in right now. Bensalem is safe."

"Remarkable! Oh, bravo, Deacon. What's Mark's condition? And Maurice, did you find him? What's his condition?"

Roland put his other hand on the leg he couldn't feel. He shifted his weight to take even more pressure off of the wound. His tone, unlike the Grand Elder's, was subdued. "Maurice is dead. Mark is frail. Unconscious but alive, last I checked."

"Understood. Well, I can't thank you enough. What you've done for the Order, it's just tremendous. When can you be back in Manhattan?"

Roland closed his eyes. He went back to the place Maurice— the spawn and bedlamite—had taken him when those leathery ropes clutched his neck. Centuries of fire and pain flashed before him. Roland saw men suffer and die, struck down by a beast not of this world's making. He heard screaming and smelled blood, watched as the carnage of hell unfolded under the oppressive gaze of two stone white eyes.

"Deacon? Are you there?" the Grand Elder said.

"Sir, you didn't answer my question."

"What? What question?"

"Didn't the New King Salomon show you?"

"I lost touch with him, remember? I have been unable to see through him in quite some time."

"What did you see when you could?"

"Excuse me?"

"What did you see through him exactly? Did you see what I saw?"

The Grand Elder paused. He ratcheted his voice down to meet Roland's, calm and sullen. "I don't know what you're talking about."

"Because I saw many things. I saw a black door that led to an underground lair. I saw the Nothus' victims—hundreds of them—suspended in sacs of organic bile, connected and feeding the lifeforce of a sick entity. I saw Judithe Peel burning at the hands of the man we call the New King Salomon, and then of course, I saw the fallen angel that controlled him. Surely, you know the one I speak of?"

The Grand Elder didn't answer.

Roland was whispering now, compelled by the most basic of instincts to do so. "Our New King is no king at all, is he? Just a host for an angel that fell from God."

"Deacon—"

"I saw its eyes, white like pools of ivory. They washed over the Nothus and its victims. They bled through the forest and the streets of the town we call Bensalem, not just today but hundreds of years ago. I saw it all."

"Deacon—"

"It was here when they arrived, wasn't it? Those same white eyes burned in the sockets of the New King Salomon—"

"Deacon! Pl—"

"The one we exalt and lift up as the foundation of this Order—"

"Deacon! Please!"

"Is it true, Grand Elder? Is that the true form of our New King Salomon? Is the vision of New Atlantis a lie?"

For all of the Grand Elder's protesting for Roland to stop speaking, he took quite a long time to reply. "Listen, we shouldn't talk about this over the phone."

"I'm not coming back to Manhattan without answers."

The Grand Elder scoffed. "Oh, grow up. This is not at all what you think."

"What is it, then?"

He took another calculated pause before answering. "Careful, Deacon. Oh, you must be critically careful here."

"I have risked everything. My life, my career. Tell me what it is I have to lose now and I'll consider how careful I need to be!"

"You need to calm down. You're acting like an absolute child."

"Why didn't you tell me about it? Why didn't you let me see what you saw?"

"The ability I have to see through the New King's eyes is no gift. Do you think that's what it is? Do you think I haven't seen the things of which you speak? I have seen it all. I didn't tell you because I wanted to spare you."

"Spare me from the truth?"

"From the pain! Of course, I know about the angel!"

"Then who is our New King Salomon?"

"He is exactly who you think he is."

"Apparently not! Apparently he was a man who led a death cult into a slaughterhouse!"

"His name was Jacques Laurent Toussaint. That angel commandeered him as a boy, well before he came to the new world. It was written in one of our 17th century texts that he encountered the angel when he became lost in a cave in his native France. The bargain he struck to find his way out was to be the angel's vessel on earth. It gave him everything—persuasive power over men, knowledge that made him a savant in science and alchemy."

"Why have I never seen this text?"

He chuckled. "There is so much you have not seen. The position of Grand Elder is a lonely one, Deacon. This knowledge rests at my feet alone, just as it did my predecessors. Come now. Drive to New York and we'll keep talking. I don't like discussing this over the phone."

"I don't know."

"I have high hopes for you, Deacon. No, I didn't tell you in advance, but why do you think I trusted you with this mission? Why do you think I denied your request for assistance and insisted you do this by yourself?"

He did not respond.

"Deacon Pierce, whether you like it or not, you have now entered our innermost sanctum."

"Are you saying you condone the slaughter of innocent people? Is that what our faith is about?"

"I don't condone it. But how many have died for Christianity or Islam? Does the Pope lose sleep over his priests abusing children?"

Roland's head began to hurt. He put his other hand to his eyes and squeezed the bridge of his nose. "Then… why did you send me here to end it? If you don't care, then why bother?"

"Of course, I care! I told you why I sent you. I lost touch with the New King and sensed something was wrong. You confirmed that, didn't you? Maurice's recklessness risked exposing everything."

Clacks in the background of the call told Roland that the Grand Elder was pacing around his office. He could picture it—expensive suit, hands clasped behind his back, one eye always on the blinds.

"The truth is this. Whatever it is that sustained this Order in the 1600s is not what sustains it today. We don't need angels or Sentinels or even a New King. We have our science. We have our alchemy. We have our connections and our network around the world. Was Jesus real? Is Heaven real? We're not in the business of selling Heaven anymore. We're in the business of fixing the world's greatest problems and that's exactly what you accomplished. The death of the cleric and the emergence of Maurice presented us with the perfect conditions to fix something that was now only a problem."

"I don't know what happened to the angel."

"You don't?"

"No."

Just then, a blast of arctic wind clattered the stiff and seamless hospital windows. Tree lines swayed like brown waves on the ocean. Roland's skin prickled with a cold he feared he'd never forget.

"Well," said the Grand Elder. "I suppose we'd better hope there's no New Atlantis after all."

The wind petered out into stillness, and Roland hung up the phone.

. . .

Caleb sat back in his chair. He closed his eyes. So did Mark.

At one point, Caleb chuckled and, at another, whispered a single word, "Angel."

Outside, the sun diminished behind a frozen and sprawling mountainscape behind Bensalem. And as the day drew down, notch by notch, so too did the mechanical beeps from Mark Harcourt's heart monitor. The room became quieter and more serene, and also heavier, as if the gravity between Mark and Caleb was the axis upon which all the world spun. They kept their eyes closed, speaking in whatever way their alchemical afflictions allowed them, until the beeps melted into the sustained hum of arrest.

That one-note song carried away a boy who only ever wanted to be loved, and with him, the secrets of the last Sentinel.

Caleb opened his eyes, sat there for a moment, and then went to go get his mother.

Everything was black outside Mark Harcourt's window, save for microscopic twinklings of cabins far off in the distance. Even the moon and the stars refused to come out, tucked into their bed of clouds high above the horizon.

EPILOGUE

Bensalem woke to a white and gleaming open sky. Wind sliced the air like an ice-cold razor while the mountains leaned back and regarded still-frosted treetops blinking in morning light. The very foundations of houses littering the valley shivered in their permafrost casings, as if buried in tombs of cold, hard earth. Tombs so far removed from earthly consideration that to even be forgotten—at one time built and cared for but no longer—would have bestowed to them a solace not given to things never known at all.

Steel chains, unflinching in their own metallic frigidness, grinded as they lowered Cheryl's coffin into the ground, as they did for Ram's, and for Monica's, and for Mark's. There was no memorial for Maurice, because no one remembered him. A thing never known at all.

Those who survived, those who had seen, surveyed the rubble and embarked on a reconstruction not lacking in sorrow. Yet as they dug out from their long winter, there dwelt within them an unspoken closure, not generated from individual hearts but from the firmament of their collective unconscious. In memories and in dreams, they learned, or relearned, the permanence of loss as they looked on toward spring. They saw the historical body of Bensalem stripped down to its cartilage, both the good and the bad, as shapes and colors dancing along the edges of the horizon.

And it was on a sultry summer morning, nearly a year to the day since Caleb's abduction, that Skylar took the old dirt road out to the forest. She squinted and shielded her eyes from the sun with an outstretched hand as crickets and grasshoppers chimed in the wheat grass. The strap from her messenger bag dug into her shoulder.

A breeze swept through the meadow, stirring amber-soaked stalks and blue and white wildflowers into a euphoric dance meant only for her. Beyond the threshold of the pines, the ground had softened. Her hands were warm and steady, and she marched infused with the spiritual collateral of both those whom she had defeated and those she had lost.

Everything was a palette of green—stalks of dark pine, dangling blankets of rich kelly, yellowish clumps of moss fat on eons-old boulders. Birds, flashes of red and blue and brown, darted in all directions, and from them poured out songs both beautiful and proud.

In the months that had passed, Skylar had learned to both fear and cherish her solitude. It had a peculiar way of divining her toward balance, toward truth, especially in moments of immeasurable pain. The ones that hurt the most were those where she momentarily forgot that her mother and her boyfriend were dead. She'd think of a thing she'd want to tell them, only to realize she couldn't, as if there was nothing wrong with them, but it was her who had no mouth to speak. Grief would morph insidiously into guilt, and it would scald her as she pushed it down, down,

down. She had good days and she had bad days, but today was neither, merely the culmination of a task she had promised herself and her mother she would undertake as soon as she was strong enough.

Skylar trekked the overgrown path that had gone untraveled by any man or beast since it ended. She kept walking as the trunks around her began to scar and twist, and she was nearly overtaken by emotion upon realizing this place was no longer dark and silent. Light poured down through the boughs, and small creatures chirped and chittered in their new government of the area. She placed a hand on a piece of twisted bark and kept walking.

And the glade was there, but it was not. For above her, the gaping hole carved out of the trees still offered a sphere of sky, but below, the once scornful and barren ground had greened. She did not notice the tattered frame of an old metal folding chair being swallowed by fresh thicket. Noonday light rained down upon her as she squinted again and slowed her pace.

When she slung down her messenger bag, her back was caked in sweat. She knelt and pulled out the hand shovel. Light surrounded her as she dug, an angelic gardener reaping harvest. When she finished, she took a deep breath and placed the Grimoire in the hole she had made. And with bare hands, not with the shovel, she washed it away with dirt and patted it firm.

In a vestibule of oaks along the edge of the glade, something stirred.

Skylar rose.

With the gentleness of a newborn, a long-legged doe approached. Behind it, two fawns, eyes glassy and backs speckled white, peeked out from behind their mother's flank. Skylar's breath hitched as she stared into the doe's steel-gray eyes. A squirrel dashed along a leafy branch above them, and two warblers serenaded each other from opposite sides of the sphere of light. The fawns folded their legs, sat, and rested their heads.

The glade was silent for a moment while Skylar and the doe stared at each other.

It was her, but it wasn't her.

And then, as peacefully as they had arrived, the doe and her fawns fell back into the trees, silent and undisturbed.

A #1 Amazon bestselling author of horror and dark fiction, Drew Starling is a husband and dog dad who loves strong female leads, martial arts, and long walks in the woods with canine companions. He would like to think his plots are better than his prose, but strives to make his words sound both beautiful and terrifying at the same time. He listens to Beethoven, Megadeth, and Enya when he writes, and he'd be absolutely delighted if you'd consider joining his mailing list — which you can do at drewstarling.com. You'll receive two free short stories when you sign up! His only rule of writing: the dog never dies.

If you enjoyed NOTHUS, please consider leaving a review on Amazon or Goodreads! Reviews on these platforms are one of the best things you can do to support indie authors and publishers.

Also by Eerie River Publishing
Infested by C.M. Forest

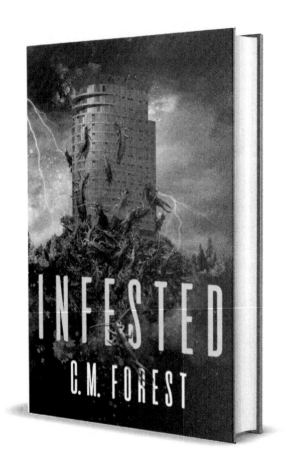

More from Eerie River

Eerie River Publishing, is a small independant publishing house that is devoted to releasing quality horror, dark fantasy and dark fiction novelas and anthologies.

To stay up to date with all our new releases and upcoming giveaways, follow us on Facebook, Twitter, Instagram and YouTube. Sign up for our monthly newsletter and receive a free ebook Darkness Reclaimed, as our thank you gift.

https://mailchi.mp/71e45b6d5880/welcomebook

Interested in becoming a Patreon member?
Patreon membership gives you exclusive sneak peeks at upcoming books, early chapter releases, covers art as well as free ebooks and discounts on paperbacks.

https://www.patreon.com/EerieRiverPub.